"Tell me what's wrong," Jack said bluntly.

Meg looked up at him, her eyes pleading with him—for what, he didn't know. *"Sha'awéé' náháleeh,"* she said in perfect Navajo, her voice barely a whisper.

He stared at her. The breath went out of him. "What did you say?"

"Sha'—"

"Speak English!" he said. How dare she tell him *this* in his own language! Did she think it would make it easier for him to hear?

"I'm pregnant, Jack," she said. "The father of the baby—he's—"

"No!" Jack held up his hands and backed away. "I was wrong—I don't want to hear this."

"Jack," she said when he reached the door.

In spite of his intense need to run, he looked at her. And she was so beautiful. Even now. With her sad eyes...

And somebody else's baby inside her.

RITA
—Award—
Winning
Author

Dear Reader,

The skies won't be the only place to find fireworks this month. Special Edition has six wonderful, heartwarming books for your July.

Babies are fun in the summer, and this July we're highlighting "the little ones." We begin with RITA-award-winning author Cheryl Reavis, and our THAT SPECIAL WOMAN! title for the month, *Meggie's Baby*. You last saw Meg Baron in Cheryl's book, *One of Our Own*. Now Meg returns to the home she left—pregnant and seeking the man she's never been able to stop loving. In *The Bachelor and the Baby Wish*, by Kate Freiman, a handsome bachelor tries to help his best friend achieve her fondest wish—to have a child. And the always wonderful Susan Mallery gives us a man, his secret baby and the woman he's falling for in *Full-Time Father*.

And rounding out the month we've got the ever-popular JONES GANG—don't miss *No Less Than a Lifetime* from bestselling author Christine Rimmer. Also, it's time for another of those SWEET HOPE WEDDINGS from Amy Frazier in *A Good Groom Is Hard To Find*, and Sierra Rydell brings us a sizzling reunion in *The Road Back Home*.

A whole summer of love and romance has just begun from Special Edition! I hope you enjoy each and every story to come!

Sincerely,

Tara Gavin, Senior Editor

Please address questions and book requests to:
Silhouette Reader Service
U.S.: 3010 Walden Ave., P.O. Box 1325, Buffalo, NY 14269
Canadian: P.O. Box 609, Fort Erie, Ont. L2A 5X3

CHERYL REAVIS

MEGGIE'S BABY

Published by Silhouette Books

America's Publisher of Contemporary Romance

To my brand-new beautiful grandboy—whose stork
flew neck and neck with the deadline of this book.

Special thanks to Robert Young of the University of
New Mexico in Albuquerque for his very gracious help
in translating English phrases into Navajo and to
Glenda in the linguistics department, who let me pester
him. Any mistakes are mine, not his.

 SILHOUETTE BOOKS

ISBN 0-373-24039-2

MEGGIE'S BABY

Books by Cheryl Reavis

Silhouette Special Edition

A Crime of the Heart #487
Patrick Gallagher's Widow #627
One of Our Own #901
Meggie's Baby #1039

*Family Blessings

CHERYL REAVIS,

award-winning short-story author and romance novelist who also writes under the name of Cinda Richards, describes herself as a "late bloomer" who played in her first piano recital at the tender age of thirty. "We had to line up by height—I was the third smallest kid," she says. "After that, there was no stopping me. I immediately gave myself permission to attempt my *other* heart's desire—to write." Her Silhouette Special Edition novel *A Crime of the Heart* reached millions of readers in *Good Housekeeping* magazine. Both *A Crime of the Heart* and *Patrick Gallagher's Widow* won the Romance Writers of America's coveted RITA Award for Best Contemporary Series Romance the year they were published. *One of Our Own* received the Career Achievement Award for Best Innovative Series Romance from *Romantic Times* magazine. A former public health nurse, Cheryl makes her home in North Carolina with her husband.

Cheryl's wonderful *FAMILY BLESSINGS* series continues with Lillian's romance—coming up in 1997 from Silhouette Special Edition!

UTAH

COLORADO

ARIZONA

NEW MEXICO

Shiprock

Chuska Mountains

Many Farms
Community College

Chinle

*Canyon de Chelly
National Monument*

Ganado

Window Rock

Hubbell Trading Post
(National Historic Site)

Gallup

N

*Petrified Forest
National Park*

Chapter One

Listen. Listen to the wind.

He remembered the admonition as if he were hearing the voice of his grandfather, the old man, long dead now, whose name he dared not speak. He shivered in the cold air. The sun was going down and the earth teetered on the edge of darkness.

"Daniel," he suddenly whispered. "Daniel Begaye. It's me—Jack."

Let the old man's *chindi* hear him, he thought. Let his ghost come. Let him know that all his efforts had been wasted and that his grandson hadn't believed the only relative who had ever taken the trouble to try to teach him.

The wind suddenly rose around him, driving the sand so hard that he had to turn his face away. He laughed softly to himself. If he had been the fanciful sort, he might have believed that Daniel Begaye—or whatever was left of him—was displeased by his disrespect.

But Jack wasn't fanciful. He was the consummate realist. He believed only what he could touch and taste and see, not what he heard in the wind. No evil, disgruntled ghosts and no playful boy gods could frighten him.

He stood for a moment longer, until he suddenly realized that he wasn't alone. He turned sharply, surprised by the man's presence regardless of the fact that it was the Navajo way not to intrude upon another person's thoughts. He recognized the tribal policeman immediately, and he stopped short of giving a resigned sigh. Jack had a long history of ups and downs with Lucas Singer, both as a young runaway and as a grown man who had presumed too much regarding one of Lucas's relatives.

Jack looked at him now in the semidarkness, unable to see his face clearly. Not that he needed to see it. Lucas Singer had always worn the same expression where Jackie Begaye was concerned—a smooth, unemotional mask he thought hid his reproof and his pity that yet another of The People had gone astray.

Jack waited for Lucas to speak, mindful of his grandfather's Navajo teachings, after all.

"I've brought you another customer," Lucas said. "I found him sitting along the road a couple of miles back. Damn near ran over him."

"You sure he's not sick?"

"I think he's drunk, but you're the one in charge here. Maybe you'd better look at him."

Jack walked with him toward the rectangular, cement-block building that was the mission's men's shelter, a bit surprised at the deference Lucas Singer was showing him. Lucas had been a tribal policeman for a long time. He knew the difference between drunk and sick as well as anyone, just as he knew that Jack's question had been a token attempt at stonewalling the establishment—a gesture he would always feel obliged to make. Jack could think of no apparent reason for Lucas to be here. His days of patrolling the reservation's back roads had long since passed. Now he worked in a supervisory capacity in the law-enforcement building in Window Rock. The mission shelter was far enough off the main road to discourage any of the clientele from hitching a ride to the nearest off-reservation bar, and it was hardly on the way to any of the police substations.

"Snow coming tonight," Lucas said as they walked across the rough ground.

"Who says so? Dolly or the TV weatherman?"

"Dolly," Lucas said.

Jack smiled. He had first met Lucas's mother when she had been a volunteer at the receiving home for abused and abandoned children in Window Rock and he had been a newly arrived inmate. She was as traditional as they came, and if the venerable Dolly Singer said snow would arrive tonight, he would definitely have to chop more wood.

"I see Dolly sometimes," he said to Lucas. "When I go into Window Rock for supplies. I still do exactly what she tells me to."

"You and me both," Lucas said.

Jack opened the shelter door. The wind snatched it out of his hand, slamming it against the handrail hard enough to crack one of the glass windowpanes. He let Lucas go in ahead of him, fighting to get the door closed, annoyed with himself at having inadvertently been the cause of an expense the mission could ill afford.

Inside, Lucas Singer's "customer" was protesting loudly at having his dirty clothes taken from him by one of the mission volunteers, an elderly man who looked much too frail to accomplish his intent. But looks were deceiving, and Winston Tsosie had had years of practice. The newcomer was stripped and put into a clean bed with minimal delay in spite of his objections.

"What do you think, Winston?" Jack asked, walking over to peer at the man, who was already snoring loudly on the cot.

"Don't smell no diabetes," Winston said. "Don't see no knots on his head or bruises anywhere. Damn beer drunk," he concluded, the gentle way he covered the man with a worn blanket belying his contemptuous tone.

Jack felt the man's pulse and smelled his breath, then checked the reaction of his pupils to light with the small flashlight he carried in his shirt pocket. He agreed with Winston's cursory assessment. Drunk. Not diabetic coma, not a head injury and not some kind of fever.

He straightened up to find Lucas watching.

"You miss the marines?" the policeman asked, and Jack laughed. And while Lucas didn't laugh with him, he did smile, apparently because both of them recognized that the question was ludicrous.

"You learned something from them," he suggested after a moment.

"I learned a lot from them—mostly that I don't like people telling me what to do."

"You knew that when you were ten years old, Jack."

Jack glanced at him, ignoring the allusion to his checkered past. "It was this old man's fault," he said, clasping Winston's shoulder. "All his code-talker stories. He made me want to be this big Navajo marine hero like him."

Winston shook his head, nonplussed by Jack's teasing. "You would have been a dead hero if you'd been in the Pacific with me. Them corpsmen like you—they didn't last long." He went on about his business, taking the man's dirty clothes to be washed and dried. The shelter's acquiring a second- or perhaps thirdhand washer and dryer had been a minor miracle, and Jack still marveled that the men could now leave the place better—in appearance at least—than when they arrived.

"You get paid anything for doing this kind of work?" Lucas asked him with his policeman's bluntness.

"I get what I need," Jack answered obscurely. He walked out of the sleeping area toward the small kitchen-office down the hall. "You want some coffee?" he asked over his shoulder, hoping Lucas would decline.

"That would be good," Lucas said, following along. "It's cold out tonight."

The reply was not what Jack had hoped, but at least it implied that Lucas didn't intend to be here long. He turned on the light in the small room, then poured some coffee into a cup and handed it over, with no indication that Lucas had any choice but black.

"Not bad," Lucas said, taking a sip. "You know you could probably make a fair salary working for one of the reservation clinics."

"Doing what? Making coffee?" Jack said obtusely.

Lucas clearly didn't appreciate his wit. "You can't be using half of what you learned in the marines here," he said. "Experienced medical people are hard to find on the rez. You could —"

"I could," Jack interrupted. "If I wanted to be tied down."

"You're not tied down here?"

"Not like I would be if I had to work eight to five and fill out government forms all day. I hate paperwork and I hate keeping the clock. I had enough of that in the military."

Lucas made a small sound of understanding and glanced around the room. The sparse, worn-out look of the place undoubtedly made it obvious to him that there were no imposed government regulations and no clock-watching here.

"So, Lucas," Jack said, deciding that he had observed Navajo social decorum long enough. "Are you going to get to the bottom line or not?"

Lucas took another sip of his coffee.

"Did somebody die?" Jack persisted.

Lucas drained his cup and set it in the sink. "No," he said. "Somebody came home."

Jack had already pursed his lips to ask who, but he abruptly changed his mind. There was only one person's homecoming that would bring Lucas Singer all the way out here. He poured himself a cup of coffee instead.

"So," he said again, forcing a nonchalance he didn't begin to feel. "How is Meg?"

"Maybe you could tell me," Lucas said.

Jack set the coffeepot down carefully, taking considerably more time than the task required. "No, I can't," he said carefully.

"Can't?"

"Now, look—"

"You want the bottom line, Jack? Here it is. Meggie's come home. She's got one semester of graduate school left and all of a sudden here she is. No announcement that she's coming. No explanation. No nothing. I want to know if you're the reason. There was a time when Meggie would have done anything for you—"

"Yeah, well, that time is long past."

"Is it?"

"You know it is."

"Are you in some kind of trouble? Did you call her at school and make her feel sorry for you?"

"No, I'm not in any kind of trouble and I didn't call her. If you want to know the reason she's come home, why don't you just ask her?"

"I have. Sloan and I both have, but she won't talk to me or her aunt. Something's the matter and I want to know what it is."

"Well, you're asking the wrong person. I don't know," Jack said, with a good deal more patience than he felt. He understood Lucas's agitation. When Lucas Singer married Sloan Baron, he had become Meggie's uncle. Uncles were important in Navajo culture, and even though Sloan and her family were white, Lucas had never for a moment shirked his responsibility to Meggie or her brother, Patrick, or to her half-Navajo brother, Will. Clearly, he still took the job seriously.

"I haven't talked to Meg but once since she left the rez," Jack said.

"She wrote to you."

"I never answered her letters."

"Why not?"

"What was the point, man?" he said, glancing in Lucas's direction, wondering when Lucas would remember that it was he, Jack Begaye, who had ended the relationship. He had left the reservation—joined the marines and left the country—just to make sure that it stayed ended.

"She always worried about you," Lucas said.

"Meggie always worried about everybody," he countered.

He changed his mind about the coffee and abruptly poured it down the sink. He could feel the tension in Lucas Singer, tension that he himself mirrored, though not for the same reason. Lucas thought he was lying, that he'd suddenly resurrected his great expectations where Meg was concerned and that he had somehow enticed her back here without her big graduate-school credentials. But Jack couldn't get past the fact that Meg had come home. And something was wrong, something bad enough to bring Lucas all the way out here.

Meggie.

"If you've started up with Meg again—if you've given her some kind of hard-luck story—I want to know about it," Lucas said.

"I told you, I haven't talked to her but once since she left the rez."

"And when was that?"

"I don't remember," Jack said.

It was a lie and they both knew it.

"Jack, I'm telling you—"

"And I'm telling you. I don't know anything about this!"

"If she talks to you—if she comes to you for *anything*—I want to know about it. Sloan and I will take care of whatever Meggie needs. Did you hear what I said?" Lucas yelled, because Jack abruptly turned and walked away.

"Yeah, yeah, I heard you," he said without looking back. "Don't let the door hit you in the butt on the way out.... What?" he said to Winston, who stood at the end of the hallway, obviously eavesdropping. "You get all that, or did you miss something?"

"The one missing something ain't me," Winston said mildly, shuffling along with him toward the main room. "You got trouble coming, boy. And you don't even see it."

"Mind your own business, Winston."

"Ain't got no business—too damn old. I got to mind yours. So what are you going to do? Are you going to stand up against this trouble when it gets here or are you going to run?" He didn't say *like you always do,* but he might as well have.

"There is no trouble, Winston. Even if there was, it's got nothing to do with me. Nothing."

"You know, wishing will get you a good corn crop, as long as you remember to dig the holes after the last frost and plant deep—"

"Winston, go do something, okay?"

The outer door slammed loudly as Lucas left the building.

"Lucas is right to come here," Winston said, looking in that direction. "You always was too wild for Meggie. Everybody knew that, even you. Only Meggie, she didn't know it."

"I don't want to talk about this!"

"Good idea, Jack. Talking ain't no good. Thinking is better. You go think how maybe you can fight this trouble and not leave Meggie crying again. You think what you can do for her so Lucas and her brothers don't kill you."

"Winston—"

"Everybody's sleeping. We got enough wood chopped. I can keep the stove going. Go on, boy. Maybe you can find your harmony while you're at it. You ain't had that in a long time."

The truth was that he had never had his harmony. Mother Earth and Father Sky. Being one with nature. Jack didn't believe the teachings of his own people. Meg Baron was the one who had believed. Meggie, the little white girl with blue eyes and flying red hair, was more Navajo than he had ever been.

Walk in Beauty, Meggie.

No. I'm not going to think about her.

But the memories came crashing in on him, one after another, flooding his mind with images. The first time he saw her at the children's receiving home in Window Rock. The first time he talked to her. The first time he kissed her—

No!

Oh, Meggie.

She had been nine when they met—"almost" she'd told him in her diligence to always tell the truth. He'd been "almost" twelve and made a point of *not* saying so. He had hated being forced to stay at the receiving home. It was a place for children, and Jack hadn't thought of himself as a child in a long while. Meggie had been sitting at one of the tables in the dayroom, playing with a little Navajo boy—her half brother, Jack took great pains to learn. He'd been intrigued by her presence there, by her laughter, by her red hair. He saw immediately that she talked to everyone—maybe she'd even talk to him, he thought. It took him days to get up the courage, to perfect just the right nonchalance to approach her. One afternoon he casually sat down at the table with her and her little half brother, Will. She told him about the trouble in her family with such candor and lack of self-pity that when she finally asked how *he* had come to be in the receiving home, he'd given up his deepest, darkest secret without a qualm.

"My old man hates me when he's drinking," he'd told her.

And she'd looked at him with quiet understanding, with an empathy that overwhelmed him. It had been all he could do not to cry.

"You're lucky," she said. "My father hated me all the time."

She had become his friend that afternoon. And, regardless of the way they'd parted years later, he still thought of her as that. He had been there when she'd worked through the pain of her father's death. He had been there when her family had lost custody of Will. At the worst times in Meggie Baron's life, when even *her* relentless optimism failed her, *he* had been there.

What's wrong now, Meg?

He abruptly found himself outside the building without a coat, and he didn't want go back inside to get it, in spite of the biting wind.

But the back door opened.

"Here!" Winston called. He tossed the forgotten jacket to him when Jack walked in his direction.

"Jack," Winston said when he turned to go. "*Níká adeesh-wol.*"

Jack stood for a moment, then nodded, in spite of his skepticism.

I'll help you.

How could this old man help him? he thought bitterly. Neither of them knew anything about Meg's situation, and perhaps he himself didn't want to know. Whatever the problem was, it had nothing to do with him. They had gone their separate ways. It had been too long.

He gave a soft sigh. All these things were true, but the old ache was still there. The one that came every time he thought of Meg Baron. The one he'd endured all this time without her.

"I'll be back," he said abruptly. For once he would take at least part of old Winston's advice. He would go and think, and he would deliberately let himself remember.

"You going to stay away from the whiskey and them bad women?" Winston asked.

"When have you seen me with either one...lately?" Jack added the last because of the soft sound of dispute Winston made. He didn't wait for an answer. He got into his old pickup truck and drove to the road that would take him to Window Rock, knowing exactly what he would do when he got there. The same thing he'd done a thousand times between the ages of sixteen and twenty. The same thing he'd done after the last time he'd talked face-to-face with Meg. He would drive slowly by the Singer house. He would see it dark and quiet, but he would still know that she was there.

And then, in spite of Winston and the shelter, in spite of his own good intentions and his need to find his long-lost harmony, he would drive into Gallup in search of oblivion.

I can't sleep.

Meg finally sat up on the side of the bed. It must be after midnight, she thought, but she made no attempt to see the clock. The house was quiet now. She couldn't hear any voices in the kitchen. Sloan and Lucas must have ended their furtive discussion about her and gone to bed. And Will had long since turned off his pounding, "teenage boy" music.

She smiled to herself. Will reminded her so much of Patrick at that age. Both the Baron brothers seemed to need a great deal of racket in order to reach manhood. They had to be bombarded with noise, while they themselves lapsed into silences practically no one could penetrate.

The smile gave way to a wavering sigh. She worried about Will. He was trying so hard to find his rightful place in the world. He had learned to be white and he had learned to be Navajo. The problem was whether or not he could integrate the two. And there was nothing she could do to help him. There was nothing anyone in the family could do, because none of them were in his predicament. Lucas could understand better, perhaps, than she and Sloan and Patrick. He managed to move successfully between the two cultures. But still, when everything was said and done, Lucas knew without a doubt to which ethnic group he belonged.

She moved to the window, taking the top blanket with her and wrapping it around her shoulders. There was no moon tonight, no stars. The wind rattled the cottonwood trees and moaned against the corners of the house.

Chindi noises, she thought. *Ghosts in the wind.*

The wind didn't sound like this in any other place she'd ever been. It was no wonder the Navajo believed the worst of it.

She could see the sandstone monoliths behind the house and the lights of Window Rock off to her right. Jack Begaye had found the ancient footholds to the top of the rocks. How many times had she and Jack climbed them before Sloan found out and put a stop to it? Meggie had had such good reasons for wanting to be up so high then, reasons that Jack had understood perfectly. God would be able see her from heaven—and so would her father.

She'd loved this place of rock and wind from the very first time she saw it. She had been nearly nine years old then and completely brokenhearted, because the wayward father who had abandoned her and her brother Patrick had suddenly died. He had been seriously injured in a car crash, and she and Sloan and Patrick had come all the way from North Carolina to see him—even though they hadn't known where he was until the telephone call came in the middle of the night. But he'd died. He left them no money, no explanations for his long absence or how he came to be on the Navajo reservation, no words of love or farewell. The only thing he left was his three-year-old, half-Navajo son, Will, whom none of them had known existed. She'd been so afraid then, in spite of Sloan's steadfastness, just as she was afraid now. She knew that Sloan and Lucas were worried about her, and she couldn't help it.

She shivered, more from fatigue than from the cold. How much time did she have? How much time to shore up her courage so that she could tell Sloan the truth? How much time before those people realized she had left, before they started making inquiries? How much time before they came here?

Meg knew what she needed to do in the meantime. She needed to be quiet, to just *be*. She would find her harmony and subsequently her strength, and then she would turn and face all of them and try to endure their disappointment. Sloan. Lucas. Patrick and Will.

Jack.

She gave another sigh. She had heard Jack's name in Lucas's conversation with Sloan this afternoon. But when he realized she was near, he'd abruptly changed the subject. And she hadn't asked him any questions. She didn't want Lucas to think that her coming home had anything to do with Jack Begaye. She supposed that he'd returned to the reservation after his time in the military—he and his new wife. He must be here with her, she thought. Why else would everyone be so careful not to mention him?

Patrick had told her just before Thanksgiving that Jack was getting married. It had been that piece of news that put her into such a state of despair, though it shouldn't have. She had learned about disappointment very early on. She had learned that people had their own agendas. Her absent father hadn't suddenly remembered her on her birthday or at Christmastime, and he hadn't gotten well and come home to live with her and Patrick—no matter how much she wanted it. And she had learned that Jack would go his own way regardless of how important she thought they were to each other.

Even so, she had to believe that disappointments didn't always prevail. There was Will; he was here. As a child, she had loved her new half brother immediately, and she had wanted so much for him to become a part of what was left of the Baron family. But they had lost him for a time. First to his real mother, who stole him out of the receiving home—not so much because she wanted him, but more as an act of defiance. That defiance put Will directly into harm's way. It was Jack who'd found him, and he and Patrick brought him back safely, only to have the Navajo court take him away again. She and Sloan and Patrick had had to give up their legal petitions and return to North Carolina without him. Meg's only real comfort during that terrible time had been Jack Begaye. He had written letters to her then, ones filled with news about Will, ones that gave her such a sense of this place that she had been more homesick for it than she had ever been for her North Carolina home.

But we aren't children anymore, she thought. He had his own life, and he'd made it more than clear that she had no place in it. She couldn't deny that she still wanted to see him. She needed to see him. She needed to know that he, at least, was happy with his choices.

She went back to bed, expecting to toss and turn again, but she fell asleep immediately and woke to a gray and snowy dawn. She dressed quickly in the half-light and went to stand outside in the cold air, facing the East and the new day the way her Navajo grandaunt, Dolly Singer, had taught her.

"The voice that beautifies the land..." she whispered in broken Navajo, trying hard to remember the words. "The voice above...the voice of the thunder...among the dark clouds.... The voice that beautifies the land...the voice that beautifies the land..."

She stopped suddenly, her eyes welling. She couldn't remember any more of it. Her harmony was gone, and *he* filled her mind.

"I'm so sorry," she whispered, wiping at her eyes with the back of her hand. "You understand, don't you? I know you can hear me. I promise you—I promise I won't let her win."

Chapter Two

In spite of the bad weather, Jack took the man Lucas Singer had delivered to the mission shelter into Window Rock to see a doctor. He told himself that the trip was a necessary precaution. It was also a chance, however slight, to see Meg. If he had business at the clinic where her aunt happened to be an *azee' neikahi,* and if that aunt happened to be there today, and if Meg happened to drop by for lunch, say, then the coincidence would simply be the metaphysical Coyote's meddling and certainly no fault of his.

Jack timed his arrival at the clinic shortly before noon, no easy task given his patient's opposition to being awakened and transported, Winston's penchant for minding somebody else's business and the bad weather. Convincing an obviously skeptical Winston that he hadn't behaved badly last night—no binges, no brawls, no accommodating women—hadn't been easy.

Jack found it hard to believe himself, but his need to lapse into his old "wildness" had somehow dissipated about the time he turned off Route 264 and onto Route 666. He had driven on toward Gallup a few miles, then had turned around and come back to the shelter, blaming his sudden lack of self-indulgence on the precipitous arrival of Dolly Singer's snow. And next time he wouldn't leave Winston dozing in front of the wood stove when he came in from a near fall off the wagon. He'd wake the old man up, show him the exact time, let him see for himself that, while Jack Begaye might be feeling sorry for himself, he was indeed alert and sober.

The clinic was crowded. Coughing, sick people—most of them children and the elderly—filled the chairs and either sat on the floor or stood around the walls. Jack saw Meg's aunt immediately. She was obviously harried. She needed help, and it surprised him that he felt inclined to give it.

"Sloan," he said, intercepting her on one of her flybys. "What can I do while I'm waiting?"

He watched the emotions flit across her face.

Surprise—What are you doing here, Jackie Begaye?

Worry—Have you seen Meg, Jackie Begaye?

And finally a resigned acceptance born of necessity. She abruptly smiled, a smile that reminded him more of Meggie than he would have liked.

"I need an interpreter/history-taker, Jack. A lot of the older ones don't speak English. Could you find out names and what's wrong? Oh, and how long they've been sick?"

"I can do that," he said, reaching for the clipboard and pencil she handed him.

"And if they're taking any medicine."

"That, too," he assured her.

"Thanks, Jack. You're not sick, are you?"

"No, I'm here with one of the men from the shelter—the one Lucas brought us last night." He said it as if she knew that Lucas had already been to see him, again watching her face. She did. The worry was back.

But she made no comment, abruptly leaving him to collect the names while she busied herself somewhere else. It was clear to him that she realized he might want to make some inquiry about Meg and that Sloan wasn't about to make it easy for him.

He worked steadily for an hour, eventually branching out to explain the treatments ordered, always mindful of who came in the front door, or more to the point, who didn't. He was not mindful, however, of who left, missing the man from the shelter only after he was long gone. Jack gave a resigned sigh and continued taking names and conditions. There was nothing he could do now for his missing charge until Lucas or some other tribal officer brought him to the shelter again. Jack had been devious enough to put himself in Meg's anticipated path; he would now be devious enough to stay in it—at least for a while.

"Where's your friend?" Sloan asked him eventually.

"Gone. I think he had pressing business elsewhere," he said, helping an elderly Navajo woman out of a chair.

"I'm surprised he's still alive," Sloan said, taking the woman's other arm.

"You know him?"

"Of course, I know him. That was Eddie Nez."

Jack gave her a quizzical look as they walked the woman down the hall to an empty examining room and gave her over to another nurse.

"I know a lot of Eddie Nezes."

"This is the one Margaret Madman lived with. The one who would have shot you and Patrick when the two of you went to steal Will away from her."

Jack frowned, a bit taken aback that he hadn't recognized the man. But he hadn't really seen his face, except when he'd been in a drunken stupor, and Eddie hadn't been much for conversation on the way into town. He had sat with his head bowed and his hair in his eyes, and Jack hadn't taken the trouble to press him for details about his clan and his family so he could sort through all the reservation's duplicate names to identify precisely who he might be.

"In that case, I'm surprised he's still alive, too," he said. "That was a long time ago. He was a worn-out alcoholic even then."

"It's a wonder you and Patrick weren't hurt trying to get Will out of there."

"I was hurt. Lucas had them double my community-service time with Dolly for running off from the receiving home again. That woman nearly worked me to death."

Sloan smiled, reminding him of Meg again, and the conversation lagged, even by Navajo standards.

"As you say," she said finally. "It was a long time ago."

"Jack! Jackie!" someone called, and they both turned. A girl whose name he didn't remember waved excitedly from a doorway down the hall. "When are you going dancing again? We miss you down at Benny Joe's!"

He nodded in her direction and turned his attention back to Sloan.

But she was already walking away and taking with her his chance to ask about Meg. The girl—Mary Ann, he suddenly remembered—was bearing down on him.

"Mary Ann," he said, smiling when she reached him. "I didn't know you worked here."

It was all the invitation she needed, and she bombarded him with conversation.

What's wrong with me? he thought in the midst of it. Mary Ann was lively enough, pretty enough for anyone's taste. She didn't care about going to school in another state or big graduate degrees. She liked the things he liked—hot chili and cold beer and dancing at Benny Joe's—with no strings attached. She liked him, and she was more than a little impressed by his status as an ex-marine.

But the more she talked, the lonelier he felt.

Meg, when am I going to get over you?

Never, apparently, and the nagging possibility that she was in trouble only made it worse for him. He managed to send Mary Ann on her way after a time, fobbing her off with a vague promise to come to Benny Joe's soon. The waiting area was all but empty, but he looked around it again and then outside in the parking lot to make sure that Eddie Nez hadn't returned.

Eddie Nez, the bootlegger. Jack was still surprised that he hadn't recognized him—and vice versa. As a boy he'd been scared to death of Eddie, even when he'd had to go see him on legitimate business—buying illegal whiskey for his old man.

The senior Begaye had been one more clever, careful sort—sending his oldest boy, Jack, to make the buy, letting *him* be the one to get caught. It had taken every bit of courage Jack could muster to make that bold attempt to steal Will Baron out of Eddie's trailer, even with Patrick Baron's help. But he'd done it, and for one reason only. For Meg. He hadn't been able to stand seeing her so worried about her little brother and so afraid.

He gave a short laugh. Jack Begaye—hero. Winston's war stories hadn't been the only reason he'd tried to become the big Navajo knight in shining armor.

It was snowing again when he left the clinic, a dry, blowing snow that didn't stay in one place long enough to block the roads but made it next to impossible to see them. He drove slowly back to the shelter, and when he walked in it was clear that Winston had been waiting for him, primarily because of the old man's overt determination to appear otherwise. He loved to make announcements—the four-hundred-pound-gorilla-jumping-right-into-the-middle-of-the-table kind—but they had to be done in the unhurried Navajo way.

"So what's happening, Winston?" Jack finally asked after Winston had swept the same spot in the dayroom at least three times. The television blared in the background, its picture fuzzy because of the weather.

"I'm sweeping," Winston said, quietly pointing out the obvious without interrupting his push-broom rhythm.

"You been sweeping the whole time I was gone?" Jack persisted, trying not to smile.

"No," he said, moving slightly to the left. "I been talking to Meggie."

Meg? Jack thought wildly, caught completely off guard. *Talking to Meg? Damn, that's a really big gorilla, Winston.*

"When? Where?" he asked, trying hard to keep his voice neutral.

"Here," Winston said. "While you were off with Eddie Nez."

Here, Jack thought. *She came here. In a snowstorm.*

"So what did she say? What did she want?"

"She wanted to know about your wife," he said, cutting loose gorilla number two.

"My wife?"

"Yes."

"What wife?"

"She didn't say," Winston advised him, still sweeping.

Jack stood for a moment, started to walk into the office-kitchen, then changed his mind.

"But you told her I didn't have a wife," he said.

"No."

"No? What do you mean, *no?*"

"You don't say much, Jack. I don't know if you got a wife or not."

"Winston, you know I don't have a wife. I don't have a woman. I don't even have a dog."

"I know you don't have a wife *here*—unless you keep her hid. But you were a marine. You went to San Diego. You went overseas. Women like marines. Women like to get married. Maybe she's in San Diego. Maybe she's overseas somewhere."

"I can *not* believe this!"

"It's the truth," Winston said mildly, sweeping nothing in the opposite direction.

"What made Meg think I had a wife, for God's sake?"

"She didn't say," Winston advised him again.

"Well—did she say anything else? Is she coming back?"

"Which question you want me to answer, Jack?"

"Both of them!"

"You got no harmony, Jack. You get too excited, yell too much."

"Winston!"

"The first answer I will give you is this. She didn't say if she *is* coming back. She didn't say if she is *not* coming back."

Jack waited impatiently for the second answer.

"The other thing is I think she's worried."

"Worried," Jack repeated. "About what?"

"I couldn't tell."

"Well, didn't you *ask?*"

"No," Winston said, clearly offended that Jack would even suggest such a breach in Navajo etiquette.

"You've known her since she was a little girl, Winston."

"That's why I don't ask."

"You sure as hell ask *me* anything you want to know."

"I got to ask you so I can tell you what to do," Winston said, his feelings obviously hurt now. "Somebody has to tell you what to do, Jack. You ain't got no relatives to do it."

"I thought you said you'd help me."

"I am helping, Jack."

"Oh, yeah. Have you got any more gorillas up your sleeve?"

"I don't know what that means, Jack."

"It means—never mind what it means. So you think she's worried."

"Yes."

"Why?"

"Why is she worried or why do I think she's worried?"

"Why do you think she's worried," he said, trying to be patient—or at least civil.

"Meggie's face shows her harmony." Winston shrugged. "If she's happy or sad or worried, it's on her face."

"Well, what could she be worried about? I know, I know," Jack said, holding up his hand. "She didn't say."

"I wasn't going to say that," Winston said. "I was going to say it's not our business."

Jack stood staring at the floor. Meg had been here. She thought he had a wife. She was worried. And it's not *our* business.

Who's business was it then?

"What?" he said, because Winston had made some comment.

"I said, could be we need some wood chopped."

"Yeah, okay," he said, sighing heavily. He turned around and went back outside, his mind still in turmoil. The snow had stopped, but not the wind. He had to walk hunched over to the woodpile bracing himself against the cold. And he had to force himself to concentrate on the chopping, swinging hard to translate his exasperation with Winston and his concern about Meg into flying wood chips. He worked steadily, not seeing the car drive into the parking area until it had already stopped.

He didn't recognize the vehicle, but he should have. A woman in a heavy coat and jeans got out and walked toward him in long, easy strides. He stopped chopping, realizing who she was about the time she said his name.

Meg. He couldn't see her hair, her hands. He could only see her eyes—her beautiful eyes—showing between the plaid knit cap and the red wool scarf.

Meg. Shivering in the cold.

The mere sight of her took his breath away.

She crossed the distance between them quickly, her eyes smiling, as if she belonged here, as if there had been no time and no distance and no harsh words between them.

"Finally!" she said, smiling still. She pulled the scarf down; he could see her mouth now.

"Hello, Meggie," he answered, every bit as nonchalant as he had been that first day in the receiving home. He gripped the ax handle hard for something to do with his hands.

"You're not an easy person to find, Jackie Begaye."

He didn't say anything. No remark came to mind that wasn't completely inane. He put the ax aside and bent over and began to pick up the wood.

"So," he said without looking at her. "What brings you back to the rez?" He would begin in generalities. Then he would get to the specifics.

"I live here, Jack. Remember?"

"Yeah, well, it's been kind of hard to tell that the past few years."

"You were gone, too."

"Yeah," he said. "I was gone."

He chanced a look into her eyes. Hers slid away. She abruptly leaned down to pick up the two pieces of wood at her feet.

What's the matter, Meggie? he thought.

He began to walk back toward the building. She trailed along with him, as she had a hundred times before in a hundred different places.

"Then why are you out here?" he asked quietly, the words coming on white clouds in the freezing air.

She stopped walking. "I just wanted to see you, to say hello. That shouldn't surprise you, should it? We were friends a long time."

"*Were* being the operative word here," he said unkindly.

She looked up at him. "That was your choice, not mine. I'm sorry. I've made a mistake, haven't I?" She abruptly handed him the wood she was carrying. "I'll go now. Nice to see you again, Jack."

"Meggie, wait," he said, dumping the wood onto the ground. Winston, and who knew how many curious others, stood watching from the dayroom window. "Wait!" Jack called, because she didn't stop.

She turned to look at him and gave a quiet sigh.

"I just . . . I need to know what you want, Meg. What you could possibly want . . . from me. Do you understand?"

"I understand, Jack. It's . . . I've been feeling . . . nostalgic lately, that's all. It's some kind of crazy mood I've been in or something. I was lonesome for my childhood, and you were a big part of that childhood. I just wanted to see you. I wanted to remember, to reminisce about things. Like the time we got arrested for horse stealing."

He smiled in spite of himself. "You thought we were going to get hanged."

"I was sure of it. And Lucas told us if we were going to start a life of crime, we'd better get different sidekicks. Everybody he asked remembered seeing us—the red-haired white girl and the Navajo boy."

"But not the horse," he reminded her, and they both laughed.

"See?" she said after a moment. "This is exactly what I needed."

Perhaps, he thought. *But what is it you want, Meg?*

He stared at her, in a way that was decidedly un-Navajo, trying to see if he agreed with Winston's opinion that she was worried.

"And I wanted to give you my congratulations," she said.

"For what?" he said, deciding to be unhelpful in spite of his protests to Winston.

"For your marriage, of course."

"What makes you think I'm married?"

"Aren't you?"

He didn't answer, still staring at her.

"Aren't you?" she said again.

"No. Who said I was?"

She frowned. "Patrick said you were getting married. I thought—"

"Patrick was wrong."

"He said you brought her here to visit."

"I brought a marine buddy here to visit. She wanted to see the rez. She was interested in shamans and native healers. She wanted to talk to some of the medicine men."

"Oh," she said, still frowning.

"You know how rumors get started here. Or don't you remember?"

"I remember, Jack. I remember everything."

They stood in silence for a moment.

"What about you?" he asked finally.

"Me?"

"Are you getting married?"

She gave a short laugh. "No."

"Any good prospects?"

"No," she said again. "Well, I guess I'd better go. Sloan will be expecting me. You know how she worries."

She turned and walked away. He waited until she was about to open the car door.

"Meg," he called. "Are . . . you all right?"

She smiled. The smile was forced and did little to reassure him. She held her arms wide. "Don't I look all right?"

"Yeah," he said. "You look fine."

"So do you. I want to know when you got to be such a hunk." She was teasing him now, but he wasn't fooled. "Well, goodbye, Jack," she called, giving him a little wave.

You look fine, Meggie, he thought, watching her start the car and slowly drive away.

But you aren't.

Chapter Three

I never should have gone.

The thought kept running through her mind, relentless in its truth. She hadn't wanted to "reminisce," as she had so tritely put it. She had wanted Jack Begaye's closeness and she had wanted his serenity. How some people would laugh at her notion that Jackie Begaye could be serene, much less that he could communicate it to someone else.

But he had always had that kind of comforting effect on her, even when he was one of the abandoned children at the receiving home. She had always felt safe when he was around—protected. She had really thought that seeing him today, being with him, even for a little while, would make her feel better. Instead it had left them both miserable. She had mistakenly expected the same kind of warmth and mutual admiration they'd had when they were children, and she'd been sadly disappointed.

Jack had changed. He didn't even look the same. He was a man now. Muscular. Strong. The ex-marine—the stranger who looked at her in a way Jackie Begaye never would have. For one brief moment she'd thought she'd recognized something of the old Jackie when she looked into his eyes, but it had quickly been replaced by a kind of troubled wariness she would have been hard-pressed to explain. It was as if he expected the very worst from her. But *he* was the one who had left the reservation—and her—when he knew how much she cared about him. He had to have known, and yet he had gone.

The last time she'd seen him—two years ago—had been so painful that it still hurt to think about it. Jack, home on leave. Jack, drinking too much and accosting her on the street in the middle of Window Rock, insisting loudly until the tribal police came that he wanted to show her and her big college friends the so-called "Indian problem" firsthand.

But she had known that he didn't mean any of it. She had seen his anger and his pain—and how much he resented her seeing it. It had always been that way with them—he had both loved and hated her for understanding. He had both loved and hated her for never making any exceptions for his bad childhood. She had always expected him to behave like the decent human being he was, and in spite of herself, she had always forgiven him when he hadn't.

He's not married, she thought, finally letting herself acknowledge the news that had startled her so. And why wasn't he? He must have met hundreds of women during his time away. Surely one of them would have meant something to him. She had been fully prepared to accept the fact of his *marriage,* not the fact that he was *free.*

She gave a sharp sigh. She was as lonely now as she'd been the day she'd left here. And she had to stop this. It didn't matter if Jack was married or not. It didn't matter that she still felt the same. And thinking about it did nothing to restore the harmony she needed.

The winter sky finally cleared, the snow clouds giving way to broad patches of a cold and brilliant blue. The roads weren't that bad, and she took the long way home, with the radio blaring the kind of music Will preferred, the kind that drove away all semblance of coherent thought with its hard-driving beat.

When she reached the Singer house, no one was home. She thought that Sloan and Lucas must be working late again. She had no idea where Will might be. As much as she loved them, she was glad to have a little time alone, a chance to examine why she still wanted to cry even knowing that Jack hadn't married, after all.

The house was so quiet. She stood just inside the kitchen door with her coat still on. The only sound she could hear was the faint buzz of the electric wall clock. The face of the clock was set in a red plastic teapot. She, Patrick and Will had given it to Sloan and Lucas as a wedding present years ago. It had been Meg's idea. She had thought all kitchens should have a red teapot wall clock.

She gave a quiet sigh and looked around her. This was home to her, and yet it was so hard for her to be here. The questions—both asked and unasked—were taking their toll. And given the circumstances, the situation was only going to get worse. Her mind shied away completely from the prospect of having to sit down with Sloan and Lucas and tell them why she'd come home.

She looked around sharply at the sound of a car, one that drove by slowly but didn't stop. A few minutes later it came back again. This time she could see the license plates. California.

Don't panic, she thought. *Maybe it's not them.*

But this wasn't the tourist season, and the car pulled carefully into the driveway.

But it was just a matter of time, she thought, in a panic after all. *I'm not ready. I'm not strong enough yet.*

She abruptly let the curtain fall back over the window and waited, standing where she could see out but hopefully couldn't be seen. After a long moment, she heard tires spinning as the car backed out of the driveway. It hesitated for a moment before going back in the direction it had come.

She breathed a heavy sigh of relief, but the relief was short-lived. She was too easy to find here. She was Lucas Singer's niece. One mild question in any of the businesses in Window

Rock and some bystander would cheerfully reveal her where-abouts.

She picked up the telephone and dialed the law-enforcement center. Someone answered immediately.

"Hi," Meg said brightly, still looking out the window. "This is Meg Baron—"

"Meg, welcome home! This is Mary Skeets. What can I do for you?"

"Mary, I'm glad it's you. I just need some information," she said, not in the least surprised that Mary Skeets knew she was back. "I wanted to go see Dolly Singer. Do you know if she's in Window Rock or at the homestead?"

"She's at the homestead, Meg," Mary answered, and if she wondered why Meg hadn't asked Lucas this question, it didn't show.

"Oh," Meg said. "Well, I think I'll go on up there. Would you tell Lucas that, if he's around?"

"He's here. Don't you want to talk to him?"

"No, I don't want to bother him. Just let him know where I've gone, okay?"

"Okay. The road up there's not bad, but I'm not sure you can get all the way into Dolly's place by car. Well, you know what it's like. You better take your emergency kit and wear your walking-in-the-snow clothes," Mary said. "And you better go right now if you're going to make it before dark. And tell Dolly one of the officers will come by and make sure she's got enough wood."

"Yes, I will," Meg said to all of Mary's suggestions. "Bye, Mary."

"Should I tell anybody else where you are if they ask?" Mary said before Meg could hang up, and Meg knew exactly which "anybody else" she meant. Clearly, the ever efficient grape-vine had not only reported that Meg Baron had come home but also that she'd been out to the mission's men's shelter to see Jack Begaye today.

"No, just Lucas or Sloan," she said. "They're my two wor-riers. Bye, Mary," she said again. "And thanks."

"You drive carefully," Mary answered, and Meg smiled. She had always liked Mary Skeets, the tribal-police dispatcher and amateur matchmaker.

Meg hung up the phone and moved quickly about the house to find some warm clothes and socks and underwear to take with her. It would be cold at Dolly's place. She raided the pantry as well, tossing whatever tidbits she thought Dolly might like—peanut butter, dried fruit, orange marmalade, a box of vanilla wafers and several small cans of condensed milk—into her backpack.

Then she left a somewhat obscure note as to her whereabouts in case Mary Skeets didn't give Lucas her message. Or in case Lucas didn't understand it. Mary was legendary for her ambiguous communiqués—not that Meg's own note was any better.

"I'm being ridiculous," she said out loud, but she made no attempt to make the note less cryptic.

And she was very careful to be sure there was no car with California license plates anywhere around before she opened the back door.

Jack waited three days before he went into Window Rock to buy groceries for the men's shelter. It took him that long to accept the reality of his situation. It was very simple really. He didn't want to see Meg Baron again—ever. And he wanted to see her with all his heart. Nothing had changed where she was concerned, and realizing that had actually given him a kind of peace. Winston still had a hunk of Japanese shrapnel in his hip. It bothered him all the time—some days worse than others. Jack's relationship with Meg Baron was very similar to that, and he, like Winston, was just going to have to learn to live with the hopelessness.

If I see her, I see her. If I don't, I don't, he thought philosophically when he reached the edge of town. *Either way, it's not the end of the world.*

"It just feels like it," he said under his breath.

He halted at a stoplight and immediately saw Will Baron in the truck directly opposite him. Jack was struck by two thoughts—first, that Will should be in school at this time of day, and second, that he should *not* be riding around with Eddie Nez. The cutting-school thing Jack could have easily dismissed as none of his business; he'd certainly taken his own share of self-declared vacations from the classroom. But an association with Eddie Nez was something else entirely. Surely Will knew who Eddie Nez was. And surely Will's mother, the notorious Margaret Madman, wasn't back in the picture. Jack hadn't heard anything about her whereabouts in years, but he had known her well enough to know that she wasn't above doing whatever it took to make Will Baron feel sorry for his long-lost Navajo mother.

Jack looked over his shoulder to verify the identity of the two people in the truck as it crossed the intersection, and he shook his head. Will was doing the driving, at least. There was some chance that *he* would be sober.

Damn it all! The last person Will Baron needed to be hanging around was Eddie Nez.

But there was nothing Jack could do about it. No matter how potentially hazardous the situation, he was the last person who should interfere. He'd already done his interfering when Will was three. Coyote, the Navajo's metaphysical mischief-maker, must be laughing his head off at the doings of the well-meaning Jack Begaye—stealing a little boy away from a big bad bootlegger just so that same boy could pick up where he left off when he was grown. That is, if Coyote wasn't too busy laughing his head off about Meg Baron coming to the mission shelter.

Jack bought the groceries, using Winston's carefully penciled list and throwing in some extras with money out of his own pocket. Life was short. Winston and the rest of the men needed an occasional bag of chocolate chip cookies and some Neapolitan ice cream to break the monotony.

When Jack returned to the shelter, Winston was waiting for him sitting in the sun by the back door.

"I think I got one of those things you asked me about," he said when Jack got out of the truck.

"What things?"

"The gorilla up my sleeve."

Jack frowned and handed him the lightest grocery bag.

"You want to hear about it?" Winston persisted.

"Do I have a choice?" Jack countered.

"No. It's pretty much too late now."

"So tell me."

"Patrick Baron is waiting to see you. He's inside."

Jack swore under his breath. He couldn't remember the last time he'd seen Meg's older brother, much less talked to him. The two of them may have stolen Will away from his mother and Eddie Nez—an admittedly dangerous albeit successful undertaking—but they'd never really been friends. His friend in the Baron-Singer family had been Meg. Patrick had made it clear years ago that Jackie Begaye would never be good enough for his sister. Unfortunately, Jack had had no choice but to agree with him.

"He ain't happy," Winston said helpfully.

"Well, I'm not happy, either," Jack assured him. "And I'm damned tired of being hassled for no reason."

"They got a reason," Winston said, taking another bag.

"Yeah, like what?"

"Meggie wants you—and you ain't much of a catch."

"Winston, where do you get this stuff?"

"She came out here just to see you, didn't she?"

"Seems like a lot of people have been coming out here just to see me."

"Yes, but she's the only one that don't want to kick your butt."

Jack laughed in spite of himself. "Well, you got me there, old man. Lead on. I might as well get this over with."

Patrick Baron waited in the office-kitchen, standing with his arms folded. He hadn't changed much, Jack thought when he saw him. Still overprotective and bossy. He worked as some kind of computer consultant at a bank in Flagstaff, which surprised Jack. Jack had always thought Patrick hated living on the rez in particular and in Arizona in general. Well, he *had* left the rez; he just hadn't gone far.

"Patrick," Jack said, offering his hand. Patrick didn't take it.

"This isn't a social visit, Begaye," he said.

"Then let me save you some time. Lucas has already been here. I don't know why Meg left school. And if I did, I wouldn't tell you—" He broke off because someone came into the shelter by the front door.

Winston stepped into the hall to see who it was. "Another gorilla," he advised Jack under his breath as Will Baron walked in.

"Where were you?" Patrick asked him without prelude.

I know the answer to that one, Jack thought.

"I had some things to do," Will said.

"What things?"

"Things!" Will looked around the room at everything except Jack. "I said I'd be here. I'm here. So did you tell him?"

"Tell me what?" Jack asked, tired of being a spectator.

"We want you to stay away from Meg," Will said, finally glancing in his direction.

"Does Meg know you're here?"

Neither of the Barons answered him.

"That's what I thought," Jack said. "Look, boys. We're all a little too old for this. I told you and I told Lucas. I don't know why Meg came home. We don't talk. We don't write letters. We don't—"

"You're missing the point here, Jack," Patrick said.

"What point is that, Patrick?" Jack said with equal sarcasm.

Winston began to purposefully put away the groceries, his position of interested referee clearly established.

"We don't care about any of that," Patrick said. "We want you to stay away from Meg *now*. You got it?"

"I got it," Jack said pleasantly. "No problem. You don't want me to see Meg, I won't see her. Unless, of course, *she* wants to see *me*. In which case you can both go to hell."

"I'm not kidding, Begaye!" Patrick said, grabbing him by his shirt front.

"Neither am I," Jack said, his temper still in check. "Now let me give *you* a little advice. You don't want to put your hands on me like that, Patrick, because, thanks to Uncle Sam, I know at least ten ways to break both of your arms. I care enough about Meggie not to want to do that, but don't push your luck."

They glared at each other until Patrick suddenly released him, probably because, Jack realized, several of the shelter residents had gathered in the hallway to watch.

"I think we understand each other," Patrick said, and Jack gave a short laugh at this height of overstatement. Patrick Baron didn't understand a damn thing—and neither did he. All he knew—all they both knew—was that something had happened to Meg, something she wouldn't share with either of them.

"You just remember what I said," Patrick said, stepping around him. "Let's go, Will."

"Will," Jack said as the boy was about to follow Patrick out the door. He waited until Patrick was out of earshot. "What were you doing with Eddie Nez today?"

"That's none of your business," Will said, his protective-brother persona still intact. But he was clearly taken by surprise.

"Lucas know you and Eddie are bosom buddies?"

"I told you it's none of your business!"

"You watch yourself, you hear?"

"You're the one who needs to watch, Jack. Patrick and me—we're not going to let you hurt Meg like you did before."

"I didn't hurt Meg."

"The hell you didn't! You went off and left her, man, and you didn't say anything. You didn't even tell her you were going—did you think she could read your mind? She just looked around one morning and you were gone—not that she wasn't used to that kind of crap. It's the same way our old man left her and Patrick. He just packed up and the hell with them. Thanks to him, Meg expects everybody to do that sooner or later, but for some reason she never expected it from *you*. You didn't even write to her, you sonofa... Something is *wrong*, man.

That's why she's come home. She needs somebody to help her—and that somebody ain't you. You don't care about Meggie. You just want to get in Patrick's face. You want to show Lucas you don't have to listen to nothing he says anymore. Now you leave her the hell alone!''

Chapter Four

Maybe I did. Maybe I did think she could read my mind.

But it was for damn sure he hadn't been able to read hers. It had never occurred to him, not once, that she'd see him as a carbon copy of her old man.

But I didn't abandon you, Meggie. Honest to God, I didn't.

No. He'd just packed up and left and to hell with her. Jack closed his eyes, trying to shut out the memory of Meg Baron when she was nine. Meg Baron when she was nineteen.

I would have hurt you more if I'd stayed. Don't you know that?

He had wanted her so badly. He'd been strong enough to leave, but not strong enough to stay here.

"What?" he said abruptly, because Winston made some comment behind him.

"I said she's staying with Dolly Singer. Up toward Fort Defiance."

Jack gave a heavy sigh and said nothing.

"Meggie," Winston added.

"I know who you meant, Winston."

"You going up there?"

"No."

"Probably for the best," Winston said after a moment. "Lucas and Patrick and Will—they wouldn't like it. Sloan, neither."

Jack glanced at the old man.

"You ain't never been much help to Meggie, Jack."

"I know that, Winston."

"Maybe you could change that now, if you wanted to."

"Winston, I know what you're trying to do, and you win. I *am* going up there, okay?"

"I'm not trying to do anything, Jack."

"Yeah, I can tell that. What?" he asked, because Winston clearly had more on his mind.

"Could be we need wood cut first."

Could be I'll change my mind if I stay long enough to cut it.

But he didn't change his mind. He chopped the wood, enough for days, and when he'd finished, he was still longing to see Meg.

So he could say what?

About that time, Meg—you know, when I joined the marines and just disappeared. Well, I had a lot on my mind then, Meg. I'm thinking maybe I forgot to tell you a few things. Like I'm leaving. Like I'm doing this for your own good.

Like you're the love of my life.

Ah, Meggie, I'm not like him. I'm not like your old man.

"Here," Winston said to him when he'd finished carrying in the wood.

"What is it?" Jack said, holding out his hand.

"It's turquoise. It's for Meg. I'm thinking maybe she's going to need it."

Jack didn't particularly like the ominous sound of that, but he took it.

"Don't lose it," Winston said as Jack put the turquoise into his pocket and lifted his sleeping bag out of the hall closet.

"I'm not going to lose it, Winston."

"You have a hard time holding on to things, boy," Winston said.

Now, that's the truth, Jack thought.

"How long you going to be gone?" Winston asked.

"I don't know. As long as it takes. Now what?" he asked, because of the look on Winston's face.

"I think you're not prepared, Jack. You got no *hozro.* You don't go into the sweat lodge. You should have had a sing when you came back from the marines. You still got the enemy and his ways hanging on to you."

"Winston, how many times do I have to tell you? I don't believe that stuff."

"You are one of The People, Jack. You can't change that. There is no believing or not believing."

"Winston . . ."

"You give Meggie the turquoise," Winston said, his voice heavy with resignation. "She needs it."

Jack had no trouble finding Dolly's place. He had some general idea of the location because of all the bootleg whiskey-buying trips he'd made in the vicinity for his old man. And Meg's car was parked near enough to the road for him to see it.

He decided to walk in as well, and he pulled his truck in behind her car. In his mind's eye, he could already see the reaction Lucas and the Baron brothers would have if one of them happened to come up this way and see it.

The sun was bright, but it gave little warmth. He carried the sleeping bag on his shoulder. It was hugely presumptuous on his part, to walk in announced and expect to stay, but there was no help for it. He had to find out what was wrong with Meg, and he really did plan to stay as long as it took to get it out of her. Dolly would be there, and Dolly was the closest thing to a decent female relative he'd ever had. Between the two of them, they should be able to persuade Meg to explain why she'd come home.

He kept thinking about Will as he walked along. It was true that Jack had rather enjoyed getting in Patrick's face. He would even admit that the visit from the Baron brothers had prodded him into making this trip to see Meg sooner than he might have if he'd been left alone. But Will had been wrong about Jack's wanting to defy Lucas. If that had been the case, Jack never would have left the reservation in the first place. He would have stayed, and he would have tried to marry Meg or live with her. At the very least he would have gotten her pregnant, and married or not, her dream of going to school and really doing something with her life would have ended.

For as long as he had known her, Meg had been making plans. She had always wanted to learn to do something that would help people. She was too tenderhearted to be a nurse like Sloan, but there were other things, she told him earnestly—social work, psychology, teaching.

Do you think I could be a teacher, Jackie? he remembered her once asking. They'd been climbing one of the monoliths behind her house, and when she'd looked at him, the sun had turned her hair to flame. He'd thought she was beautiful.

You're white, he'd almost answered. *You can do anything.*

But he hadn't, because it was Meggie who asked, and he had loved her even then. He'd loved her enough to want to protect her from the resentment he felt. She didn't know anything about his kind of justified animosity toward the supposedly superior race. She probably still didn't.

What was that movie line? Love means never having to say you're sorry?

Wrong.

Love means not ruining Meg Baron's life.

The sun was in and out now. Occasionally he could see footprints ahead of him, ones he thought must be Meg's. He hadn't listened to the weather report before he left. If he'd paid attention to the things Dolly Singer had tried to teach him when he was at the receiving home, he'd probably know whether or not these fast-moving clouds coming in from the west were going to bring more snow.

Dolly Singer's homestead wasn't completely isolated. He could see a scattering of hogans and house trailers in the distance. But he followed the small footprints until they finally disappeared in an area of rocky ground. There was a small prefabricated house beyond and a log-and-mud hogan. He could see a corral behind that, and the "summer" house made of standing saplings and brush, where the family cooked and slept in warm weather.

But the weather was by no means warm today. The clouds were growing heavier. He shifted his sleeping bag to his other shoulder and walked on, expecting to be met by a pack of dogs anytime now. He wasn't disappointed. They burst forth from behind the house, barking loudly. He stood and waited, giving them time to sniff his heels and make their decision as to his intent, and giving Dolly time to ready herself for a visitor.

No one came to the door. He set his sleeping bag down on the small porch, careful to keep the dogs away from it in case any of them declared it a dog bed or worse, unmarked territory.

He waited awhile longer, speaking softly in Navajo to the obvious leader of the pack, telling him what a fine watchdog he was and how much he'd scared a lowly intruder like himself. Jack was very cold from the long walk, and he tried to move around to keep from getting any colder without agitating the dogs.

"*Yá'át'ééh!*" he called finally to the silent house. No one answered him.

He picked up the sleeping bag and walked around the house, escorted en masse by the now-happy-to-see-him dogs. Someone must be at home. Dolly's truck was parked in back; he could smell food cooking. He looked about him, seeing no one. He walked closer to the hexagon-shaped hogan a traditional person like Dolly would have to have on her property.

He heard a small sound off to the left, and he stuck his sleeping bag into the low branches of a walnut tree—Dolly Singer's handy source of brown dye for her rug wool—growing not far from the back door. He began to walk in the direction of the sound, finally seeing the cause of the noise in the small fenced-in area behind the house. Someone was tossing silage to the dozen or so sheep inside the fence.

Meg.

He didn't interrupt her. She was humming softly—some popular song he'd heard on the radio but couldn't name. She had never been able to quite sing on key, and it still made him smile. After a moment she turned her attention to a single lamb standing off to the side. He could hear her talking to it as he walked closer.

"Hello, Meggie," he said, and she started violently, frightening the lamb into a bleating retreat to its mother.

"Jack! You scared me!"

"Sorry," he said. "I thought you heard me or at least heard the dogs."

"The dogs bark at everything," she said, looking up at him. "Sometimes they bark when people leave."

He couldn't keep from smiling. "Oh, well, not much call for that, is there?"

She smiled in return—finally. "No. Not much. What are you doing out here?" She came through the gate and began to walk toward the house. He fell into step with her.

"I came to see Dolly," he said, almost truthfully.

"She's not here. She's gone to a ceremony for one of old Joe Laughter's grandsons. He came and got her yesterday. I don't think she wanted to go, but he more or less insisted."

"Probably less," Jack said, thinking of the persuasive "less is more" techniques of old Winston.

"Well, whatever he did worked," Meg said. "I can't say that I blame him. If I was going to call the Holy People into a sand painting, I'd want a believer like Dolly there, too."

Jack made a small sound of agreement.

"So you're feeding the livestock while she's gone," he offered.

"That's the plan," she said as they reached the back steps.

"So can I come in for a while?" he asked.

"A while?" she said, glancing at the sleeping bag in the walnut tree. He didn't say anything, and she abruptly laughed. "It's only my hearing that's off, Jack. I can still see."

"I thought Dolly would be here," he said, more embarrassed than he would have liked to admit, and he didn't say that he knew *Meg* would be here. He got the sleeping bag down out of the tree, then opened the back door for her. The inside of the house was warm and smelled of something wonderful cooking—mutton stew, he thought, and coffee.

"Did you have to walk far?" she asked, shedding her coat and gloves. "I know I didn't hear that truck of yours."

"As far as you did," he said, tossing the sleeping bag onto the floor. "I left the truck at the same place up by the road."

He looked around to keep from staring at her. The kitchen and living area hadn't been partitioned and took up half the house, with two doorways leading to small bedrooms on the other side. The place had been paneled in a kind of white pressed wood with a green-colored grain. An easy chair, a couch and a recliner sat in a row against the far wall, arms touching like theater chairs. Their purpose clearly to accommodate whatever television viewers might be on hand. Dolly had a wood stove she used for cooking and heating, and a white enamel pot sat on top, the rising steam lifting and dropping the lid from time to time and letting more of that wonderful smell into the room.

"Am I invited for supper?" he abruptly asked, and Meg laughed.

"Good old, Jack. Subtle as ever."

He took that for a yes and removed his coat, wondering how much things between them had changed. If at some point he wanted to kiss her, would she let him the way she used to?

He pushed the thought aside and went to stand closer to the stove to warm his hands.

"How is Dolly?" he asked, because he needed something to say.

"She's getting old, Jack. It makes me very sad."

He glanced over his shoulder at her. She was ladling water from the bucket into a small pan so she could wash her hands. *Don't stare,* he thought. But, God, she was beautiful. She had on jeans and a blue-plaid flannel shirt with a long-sleeved T-shirt under it. No bra, he observed. He could see the soft movement of her breasts under her shirt when she bent and reached, and he knew he'd better get his mind on something else. Now.

Meggie dried her hands on the nearby towel and went to get another enamel pan that was sitting on the kitchen table—the dough for the fry bread. He moved out of the way when she got the iron skillet and set it on the stove to heat, watched her spoon a blob of lard into the skillet, tried harder to think of something to say. He could smell her scent—some kind of flowery soap and the out-of-doors, a combination that didn't remind him of anything but still tore him apart.

"Will you get the bowls down?" Meg asked, working a piece of dough into the necessary round shape. "They're over there."

He got the bowls, grateful for something to do, and cups for the coffee, and he set the table.

This is what he'd always wanted, he thought. This little domestic scene. He and Meg together, doing everyday things, just...living. But he hadn't known what to do to get it. He hadn't known how to be anything except what he was—wild Jack Begaye with no relatives to teach him.

He watched Meg make the fry bread; she couldn't have been very old when she'd learned. She glanced at him from time to time, and it wasn't so much that she seemed awkward around him, rather that she seemed wary.

Why?

Because he'd behaved so badly that time two years ago? He could still feel the pain of seeing her so changed, so *white*, laughing and talking with the big college friends she'd brought home with her from the University of New Mexico, all of them from a place he couldn't go and didn't begin to understand. Not long after that she'd transferred to a school in North Carolina, and he'd gotten the message loud and clear. She might love the great Southwest, but she'd had enough of him.

The stew and the fry bread were excellent—as good as if not better than what he'd had in any Navajo household. Even so, she ate very little, and he ate enough for them both. They talked. He asked her about graduate school; she asked him about the marines and the mission shelter. Both of them gave the kind of answers reserved for strangers.

"Do you know what kind of ceremony Joe Laughter was having?" he asked, so he'd have some idea of when Dolly might return.

"I don't remember," she said. "The Blessing Way, maybe. Are you going to wait for Dolly?"

"Yeah. I want to stay here tonight. That is, if your boy-friend wouldn't mind." He smiled when he said it. She didn't.

"No problem. You've got your sleeping bag and there's the couch."

She abruptly got up and began to clear the table. He helped with the dishes—she washed; he dried. The wind picked up, causing the single lightbulb that dangled from the ceiling to flicker.

"I had something in particular I wanted to ask Dolly," he said when the dishes were done.

The light blinked, then went out. Meg moved away from him, and he could hear her searching for something in the darkness. She found the candles easily and lit one, then an-other, setting them in the small tin candle holders Dolly ap-parently kept for just such occasions. Meg stood looking at him from across the room, the second candle holder still in her hand.

"I was going to ask her if she knew why you came home—if she knew what was wrong," he said.

She abruptly set the candle down on the table. "There's nothing wrong, Jack."

"Sloan and Lucas think so. Lucas came to see me at the shelter."

"Why?"

"Because he thought I might know something about why you're here all of a sudden."

"I'm sorry he bothered you. I'll talk to him."

"Patrick and Will came to see me this afternoon."

She gave a soft sigh.

"They're all worried about you, Meg. *I'm* worried about you."

"There's nothing to worry about, Jack. I just needed to think about some things, that's all. I don't *always* do exactly what people expect me to do, you know. It was hard at school this semester. I needed a break. And some peace and quiet."

"Did you tell Sloan and Lucas that?"

She didn't answer him. She suddenly smiled. "You know, I'm really tired. I think I'll go on to bed."

"Meggie, wait. I want to talk to you."

He would have reached out and caught her arm if she'd been close enough, but she backed away from him. She did look tired—and pale.

She managed another smile, this one weaker than the previous one. "Just make yourself at home. I'm sure Dolly won't mind. And if you'd bank the fire, that would be good."

"Meggie—"

"Good night, Jack."

"Wait. I have something for you." He reached into his shirt pocket and brought out the piece of turquoise Winston had given him. "Winston Tsosie wanted you to have this."

She held out her hand, and he put the turquoise into it. She looked at it a long time.

"It's beautiful," she said finally, her voice barely audible. When she looked up at him, he thought she was about to cry.

"Meggie—"

"Please tell Winston—thank you. It's very kind of him. I'll—treasure it—"

She abruptly turned away and went into the bedroom.

"Good night, Meggie," he said to the closed door.

Chapter Five

The dogs did bark when people left, and it was a good thing they did. Jack had lain awake for a long time, trying to decide how to sort through the dilemma of Meggie's homecoming. He finally fell into a heavy sleep just before daylight—what seemed like only minutes before the dogs cut loose. He came awake immediately, startled by the barking and by the sound of a straining motor and the heavy grinding of gears. He leapt up from the couch, despite the fact that it was highly unlikely someone might be trying to steal Dolly Singer's old truck.

The truck choked and died about the time he threw open the back door. Meggie was driving it—or trying to. She hadn't gotten far, and she sat now with her head resting on the steering wheel.

He stepped out into the yard in his sock feet, expecting her to look up and see him. She didn't. He had to tap on the truck window, then open the door to get her attention.

"Meggie, what..."

She looked so unwell that he forgot the question. He reached for her instead, and she leaned heavily against him.

"Where are you going?" he asked, too worried to make any attempt to hide his concern. He tried to see her face. "Meg? Are you sick?"

Whatever she said, he couldn't hear. He touched the side of her face. She didn't seem to have a fever.

"I have to... go into Fort Defiance," she said, making an effort to push away from him. "I don't... feel well. I think I need to see... a doctor."

"Well, wait—" he said. "Let me get my boots on. I'll take you."

"No!" she said. "I can just... drive Dolly's truck to where I left my car."

"You can't even drive out of the yard, Meg. Wait right here. I mean it!"

He kept looking over his shoulder as he hurried back into the house to get his boots. Once inside, he expected to hear the motor start any minute. He grabbed his coat on the way out the door, not taking the time to put it on. Meggie was still sitting where he'd left her, her head resting on the steering wheel.

"Slide over."

"Jack, you don't need to—"

"For God's sake, move over and let me drive!"

She climbed out from under the wheel. He tossed his coat onto the floorboard, then pulled the garment over her as an afterthought.

"I don't think you've got a fever," he said as he started the truck and put it into gear. "Do you have a cough? Have you been throwing up or anything like that?"

She shook her head, grabbing the door and the dashboard as the truck began to bounce over the rough track that led out onto the road. The so-called road was hardly any better, but he accelerated, leaving the barking dogs behind.

"How long have you been sick?" he persisted, glancing at her as he drove.

"A couple of days," she said. Her eyes were closed now.

"A couple of *days?* Why didn't you say something last night?"

She didn't answer him.

"Meg, what kind of symptoms are you having?"

"Jack, it's nothing."

"Oh, yeah, I can see that. Tell me, damn it!"

"I . . . hurt," she said, wincing as he bounced over another deep rut in the road.

"Where?"

Again she didn't answer. She moved closer and leaned against him instead, pulling his coat as much as she could over them both.

"Meggie—"

"I don't want to talk anymore, Jack, okay? Just let me stay here for now. I'm cold."

And scared, he thought.

When they changed vehicles, she resumed the same position, leaning against him with her head on his shoulder, even though her car had a working heater and it was much warmer. He didn't ask her anything else. He worried instead, all the way into Fort Defiance.

The hospital was not crowded this early in the morning. Meg had already been taken to be examined by the time he got the car parked. He toyed with the idea of calling Sloan and Lucas, then dismissed it. They would have too many questions—and he had absolutely no answers. He hung around the waiting area, watching it fill and empty and pestering the people at the reception desk until one of them finally went to check on Meg for him.

"She's resting much better now," the woman said when she returned. "The doctor's seen her and there are still a few tests she wants to do. Why don't you go get some breakfast?"

He didn't want to go get breakfast, and he didn't want to stay here, either. He just wanted to see Meg.

"Go on," the woman insisted. "I'll tell her we've run you off for a little while if she asks for you."

He went, because of the unlikelihood that Meg would want him with her, but he didn't stay long. He bought a burrito and black coffee at the first convenience store he saw—and a roll of sour candy for Meg, the kind she used to love and he'd always hated.

How can you eat that stuff? he'd asked her more than once, and she'd only smiled her Meggie smile and flaunted her superiority in this one thing, at least. She couldn't climb as high or run as fast, but she could certainly handle "sour."

He gave a heavy sigh. He had missed her so much.

I don't know what's wrong. I don't know if I want to know what's wrong. What if she's come home because she's sick—something really bad, something she can't get over?

The waiting area was crowded when he returned, and the woman at the desk was busy for a time, taking information from the new arrivals.

"The doctor's waiting for some test results," she told him when he finally got a chance to ask about Meg again.

"What kind of test results?" he asked, and he got two raised eyebrows for his trouble. He ignored them; raising eyebrows was his life.

"Can I go back there where she is?"

"No," she said without hesitation.

"Will you give her something then?"

She looked up from the papers she had begun to shuffle. "What is it?"

He took the candy from his shirt pocket and held it up for her to see. The woman almost smiled.

"I'll see if she can have it," she said. "Now will you go sit someplace and quit bothering me?"

"For a little while," he warned her, and she almost smiled again.

Eventually, sometime well after noon, Meg appeared. She still looked pale and sick, and she had some prescriptions in her hand and the half-eaten roll of candy. Like the receptionist, she managed to almost smile, as if she was actually pleased to see him still here.

"I'll go get the car," he said, and she nodded. It wasn't that far away, but she clearly wasn't up to walking.

She said very little when they were on their way, only that she wanted to stop at a drugstore. And she insisted on getting the prescriptions filled herself. She didn't even want him to come inside with her.

If it had been anyone other than Meg, he might have thought she was ashamed to be seen with him. But it was Meg, and as far as Jack knew there had only been one time when she'd truly been ashamed of him—two years ago when she'd been with her college friends and he'd been drunk and acting like a jealous fool. He could only conclude now that she didn't want him to know what kind of medicine she'd been given.

Once they were on the road again, she went to sleep almost immediately, out of exhaustion and probably out of her need to keep him from asking her any questions.

He waited. He had never been very good at biding his time, and he had to work very hard at it. He said nothing when she wanted to drive her car the rest of the way in to Dolly's place while he drove the truck. She did seem to be feeling better after her short sleep, and he didn't argue with her when she insisted on putting together some kind of meal for them while he fed and watered the dogs and sheep. He even managed not to make any comment when she surreptitiously took the pills that had been prescribed for her. And she didn't leave the bottles sitting out where he could see them; she put them back in her purse. One of them looked like some kind of vitamins. Why wouldn't she want him to know she was taking vitamins?

Eventually, the chores were done. The dishes were washed and the kitchen straight. The fire burned quietly in the stove, and they had exhausted every neutral topic of conversation possible. He could feel her waiting, just as he had been.

"Are you going to sit down?" he finally asked her.

"What?" she said, as if the question had startled her somehow.

"Sit down," he said, sweeping his hand around the room. "You—on the chair of your choice."

She sat, but she clearly didn't want to.

"Meg—"

She abruptly got up from the chair. "I think I'd better—"

"Meg, you're going to have to talk to me."

She didn't sit down again, but at least she didn't bolt for the bedroom and shut the door.

There was no use beating around the bush. They had known each other too long for that. "Tell me what's wrong with you," he said bluntly.

She gave a small sigh and bowed her head.

"Meg, tell me." He came closer to her. "I can see how worried you are. I know it's got something to do with why you left school. You know I'll help you. Whatever it is, I'll—"

"You can't help me with this, Jack. No one can."

"Meggie, you came to the mission shelter to see me. You wanted to tell me then. I can't stand this! You have to tell me what it is!" He reached out for her, but she backed away from him. He let his hands fall and he stayed where he was.

"Whatever it is you've got . . . I want to know. How serious is it?"

"It's nothing to worry about. It's—" She sighed instead of going on.

"Meg, are you sick or not?"

She looked up at him, her eyes welling, pleading with him, for what he didn't know. *"Nda,"* she said in Navajo, her voice barely a whisper, her pronunciation perfect. *"Sha'awéé' ná-háleeh."*

He stared at her. The breath went out of him. "What did you say?"

"Sha'—"

"Speak English!" he said, and she turned abruptly away from him, her arms folded tightly over her breasts.

How dare she tell him *this* in his own language! Did she think it would make it easier for him to hear if she said it in Navajo? He watched the rise and fall of her shoulders as she struggled for control. He could hear the wind outside, and the backdraft in the stove.

Meg turned to face him, and she looked directly into his eyes. "I'm pregnant, Jack," she said. "The father of the baby . . . he's—"

"No!" he said, holding up his hands. "I was wrong. I don't want to hear this. Do you understand? I don't want to know anything about this!" He grabbed up his coat and backed away, as if he thought she would try to follow him and force him to listen.

"Jack," she said when he reached the door.

In spite of his intense need to run, he turned to look at her. She was so beautiful even now with her sad eyes and somebody else's baby inside her.

"Thanks for the candy," she said.

Chapter Six

Meg was determined not to cry. She had expected Jack to be disappointed in her, but she hadn't expected that her revelation would wound him so. She wasn't prepared for the look in his eyes or the break in his voice.

Oh, Jackie.

She had known him far too long not to realize how much she had hurt him. He hadn't looked at her as if he were a disillusioned friend. He had looked at her as if he were a betrayed lover, when he was the one who had ended their relationship. She would never have left the reservation if he hadn't. She would have stayed here—with him.

She knew perfectly well that there was no point in agonizing over the abrupt departure the announcement of her pregnancy had precipitated. There had been no other way to tell him except to just *say* it. The only alternative would have been to put him off until it became obvious to everyone that she was going to have a child. It was better that he heard it from her than from the reservation grapevine.

The grapevine.

How long would it take before someone told Sloan or Lucas that she and Jack had been to the hospital in Fort Defiance? All the personnel at the reservation medical facilities seemed to know each other. And everybody knew Lucas. While they might not specify the reason she'd needed medical care, they might certainly ask if she was better.

I'm going to have stop hiding, she thought. *I'm going to have to tell the truth and I'm going to have to stand my ground.*

She tried not to think about the car from California or the shock of seeing it. She hadn't expected the woman to be so persistent.

It's her grandchild, the only one she'll ever have.

The thought came unbidden, making her sigh.

"But you're *my* child," she whispered. Until now she had only known Navajo grandmothers, and because of that, she was perfectly comfortable with the ideals and principles of a matriarchy. But she had never met a grandmother-to-be like this one. There was no reality for the woman except her own will. She simply refused to believe that Meg didn't want to go live in California with her until the baby was born or that she wouldn't leap at the chance to have the "best" prenatal care. It was inconceivable to this woman that Meg only wanted to be surrounded by the people who loved her, even if that happened to be on an Indian reservation.

What mismatched parents you have, little one, she thought sadly, gently smoothing her hands over her belly. *She* had been essentially abandoned and unwanted, and *he* had been all but smothered by a parent's love. Meg still had an aversion to saying—even thinking—his name. And it wasn't so much all those Navajo warnings that she might cause his *chindi* to return as it was a desire not to do anything—however illogical—to impede his long journey to wherever the lost ones go. She hadn't been able to help him when he was alive, and his mother would be interfering enough. In her mind's eye, Meg saw the woman beating her breast and crying his name, giving him no peace even beyond the grave.

Meg managed to get through the rest of the afternoon. It took a great deal of concentration on her part not to jump every time she heard the dogs bark. She had no reason to think that Jack would return. He'd told her plainly enough that he didn't want any part of this, and she knew better than anyone that she couldn't chase after him to try to make him understand. He had always needed to be alone to come to terms with whatever troubled him. And the truth of the matter was that there was really no reason why she should want to explain the situation she was in, even if she could. Whatever love Jack might have had for her was clearly gone.

She was so tired, mentally and physically. Her back and her belly still hurt. Nothing to worry about, the doctor had said. A common problem during pregnancy. Drink plenty of liquids, be sure to take all of the antibiotic, and her "plumbing" would be good as new.

But not her heart.

Don't cry. It's not going to help.

She lay down on the couch, wrapped up in the sleeping bag that Jack, in his haste to get away from her, had left behind. She slept fitfully for a time until someone rattled the back door.

Meg crept to the window, trying to make sure there were no cars with California plates in the yard. But it was Dolly, who only had to look at her to know her state of mind, whether the tears were showing or not.

"What's wrong?" the old woman asked as soon as Meg unlatched the door.

"I—it's—Jack knows about the baby," she said. In spite of her resolve, she was going to cry.

It was such a relief to just say it. She felt no constraint with Dolly Singer. Dolly was her Navajo grandaunt-grandmother. She had always been kind, even before Lucas married Sloan. She had taught Meg how to make fry bread and how to weave a rug, leaving one gray thread to the outside so that her spirit wouldn't be trapped. She had taught her exactly what it meant to be Navajo, and she had taught her how to understand Jackie Begaye. If anyone could help her find her harmony now, it was Dolly Singer.

Even so, Meg turned away and went to carefully fold Jack's sleeping bag. It still smelled of him, familiar and masculine, and once again it was all she could do not to cry.

Dolly said nothing, busying herself with pouring a cup of coffee to ward off the chill from being outside. It wasn't her way to rush to comment. She took time to digest the announcement and to see if there was any more information forthcoming.

"He ran," Meg said without looking at her. She held the sleeping bag clutched tightly against her breasts for a moment, then put it aside.

"Running is all Jack knows," Dolly said, sitting down at the kitchen table. Her fingers were gnarled with arthritis, and she held the coffee cup in both hands to warm them. "It was the only thing that saved him from his father's drunkenness."

"I tried to tell him what happened. He wouldn't listen to me."

"He had no relatives to teach him," Dolly said.

No relatives, Meg thought. To Dolly that explained every bad and thoughtless thing Jackie Begaye had ever done. She pulled out a chair and sat down at the table next to her. "He had us, Dolly. He had you and me."

"It's not the same, is it?"

Meg gave a small sigh. She supposed that it wasn't the same. A loving family's influence would have been constant and early, and she and Dolly had come along much too late.

"I think he . . . hates me now."

"He doesn't hate you," Dolly said, taking Meg's hand. "He doesn't hate you and he doesn't hate your little one. He just has to get used to what's happened."

Get used to what's happened. Now there's a challenge. Even she hadn't been able to do that.

"He's not the boy he was when he left here. He is a man now," Dolly said. "He has to find his own way."

Meg agreed entirely. She herself had noted the change in him. He was a man and he was a stranger. She had no idea if anything of the boy she had loved with all her heart still remained.

"Meggie," Dolly said. "Do you remember what I told you a long time ago? There is a wildness in Jack. Sometimes a wild creature can be tamed and sometimes it can't."

"I remember."

The dogs suddenly burst off the front porch in a frenzy of barking, for once getting the sequence right. Meg went to the window, hoping to see Jack's old truck in spite of everything.

But it wasn't Jack's truck; it was one of the Navajo tribal police utility vehicles.

Lucas.

Dolly came to stand behind her. "Your uncle is very worried," she said quietly.

"I know."

"He needs to know what your trouble is, Meggie."

"I know," she said again.

"He can help you if that woman comes."

Lucas was still outside, waiting now by the back door for his mother to let him in. Meg took a deep breath as Dolly called him into the house. As always, he was the consummate policeman, immediately taking in everything without seeming to do so—Meg's teary eyes, the folded, camouflage-print sleeping bag that wouldn't be Dolly's or hers.

But he said nothing.

Not yet, she thought. *I can't tell him yet.* She simply couldn't bear any more looks of bitter disappointment today.

Jack told himself that he really wouldn't have abandoned Meg. He wouldn't have left her alone when she was sick *and* pregnant. He would have gone back to the homestead eventually when he'd calmed down.

But he saw Dolly returning in Joe Laughter's truck about the time he reached the main road, and suddenly he didn't have to decide anymore. Dolly had relieved him of that, and Dolly would take good care of Meg. He didn't have to worry. He could just—go. Everything was back to normal. He could live his life, and Meg and her baby could live theirs. She would be fine and so would he.

Who was he kidding? There was that one small matter he couldn't get around no matter how hard he tried. He couldn't think about anything else. It stayed with him night and day.

I love you, Meggie—no matter what.

It was someone she'd met while she was in college—he was certain of that. Someone who didn't want Meg or the baby now that it was made. Or maybe *she* was the one who didn't want *him*. He liked that scenario better. Meg was strong. She would never take a man who wasn't good enough for her.

Jack gave a short laugh. And who would know that better than he did?

Just don't think about it. It's not your worry. It's got nothing to do with you.

Not his concern. Not his problem. Not his woman.

I won't think. I won't feel.

He forced himself to do what he was supposed to do at the shelter, all the while trying to dodge Winston's imminent inquiries. It was apparent to him that the old man was dying to ask him about his visit to Meg, just as it must be apparent to Winston that he didn't want to be asked.

Oh, yeah, Winston, I saw her. And you know what? She's pregnant. Our little Meggie is pregnant, Winston. What do you think of that? The father of the baby? Well, we didn't exactly get around to discussing him.

Why?

Because I don't want to know about the sonofabitch, that's why. She's pregnant. That's all I have to know.

And sick. And scared...

I don't care what I said—I can't help her.

Won't. Won't *help her.*

Ah, Meggie. What can I do? I can't just stand by and pretend it's not killing me to know you love another man.

Jack gave a sharp sigh, one loud enough to turn the heads of any number of the shelter residents in his direction. But he made no attempt to justify his agitated state. No harmony, he would say if he was asked. No *hozro.*

He sidestepped Winston in the hallway and went into the office, searching in the phone book until he found the Window

Rock number. He dialed it; someone eventually answered. He made his request and waited, giving Winston plenty of time to get into eavesdropping position.

"Mary Ann!" Jack said finally, ignoring Winston's shocked and incredulous look. "I'm glad I caught you. How much longer have you got to work? Yeah? You ready to go dancing at Benny Joe's?"

"What?" he said pointedly to the old man after his plans were made and he'd hung up the phone. "You want to go dancing, too?"

"Yes," Winston said, immediately setting his broom aside and untying his apron. "I'm ready."

Jack laughed. "Winston—"

"Let's go," he said. "If we're going, let's go."

"You think you've got the time to wait until I change my shirt and put on my go-to-town boots?"

"Yes," Winston assured him.

"So are you planning to bring a date or what?"

"No. I'll get mine after I get there."

"Winston, have you ever been to Benny Joe's?"

"No."

"Do you even know what they do there?"

"Sure. Eat chili, drink beer and line dance," he said mildly. "I can do those things."

"You can line dance?"

"Sure," Winston said. "Us Navajo been line dancing for years."

Benny Joe's was hot. So was the chili. So was Mary Ann. But a lot of good it did Jack. The place was typically crowded for a Friday night. He let Mary Ann and Winston out while he circled the dirt parking lot several times trying to find any empty place to park. By the time he got inside, the two of them were out on the dance floor, Winston totally at home with the complicated line dances, primarily because he did the exact same heel-first Navajo step to all of them.

"He's so cute," Mary Ann called once as they went bobbing by.

Oh, yes, Jack thought. *Mr. Tsosie is cute all right.*

"I thought you were going to find your own woman," Jack said when he finally took a break.

"I did," Winston said, and Jack laughed.

"Yeah, well, from now on I'm leaving you at home. There are some things this *semper fi* marine-buddy stuff won't cover."

The place was poorly lit and smelled of hot grease and french fries, cigarette smoke and hair spray and celebrity perfume. He saw a few people he knew—some of them Navajo, some not. He and Mary Ann and Winston ordered chili and cold beer. Jack tried to follow Mary Ann's giggling conversation. He even managed to get past Winston and have a dance or two.

This is what I need, he kept thinking. *Some fun—no complications. This is really good.*

Then why did he feel so bad? Why weren't the beer and Mary Ann helping?

Mary Ann and Winston went off dancing again, but this time he was more relieved than irritated. He sat at the table alone, breathing somebody else's cigarette smoke, nursing another beer. He watched the dancers march and stomp and twirl around the floor. People out having a good time—some of them desperate about it. Just like he was.

Winston came back to the table alone; Jack didn't ask him what he'd done with Mary Ann.

"You any good at saying you're sorry?" Winston asked after a long silence.

"Hell, no," Jack assured him, intending to take another swig of beer. "Why?"

"Meggie's here."

Jack faltered slightly in his reach for the beer bottle, but other than that, he thought he handled Winston's newest gorilla pretty well. His immediate indignation at the old man's notion that he'd done something that made it necessary for him to apologize to Meg flared and quickly died. He gave a quiet sigh.

"Did you know Meg was going to be here tonight?" he asked after a moment, Winston's sudden penchant for hitting the dance floor with *his* date now making some kind of sense to him.

"Yes."

"Yes?"

"I heard about it," Winston informed him, and Jack shook his head.

"You going to tell me just how you managed that?"

"Eddie Nez."

"The Eddie Nez Lucas brought to the shelter?"

"Yes. The boy Will—he told Eddie about it."

"And you heard him."

"I heard him," Winston agreed.

"So you were helping me, I guess," Jack suggested. "Coming along tonight."

Winston neither admitted nor denied it.

"Okay, never mind that. Where . . . is she?"

"Other side of the dance floor."

"Is she . . . with somebody?" he asked in spite of all he could do.

"Yes—no. It's Will's birthday. It's the family celebration."

"Ah, yes," he said. "The *family* celebration." She wasn't with the father of her baby then. Just two brothers and an uncle. Jack stood abruptly. He could handle that. He finished off the beer and set the bottle down. "Let's see if the bastard can crash the wedding."

"You're not a bastard, Jack—legally," Winston said.

"Yeah, thanks for pointing that out, Winston."

"Jack," Winston said, waiting until Jack looked back at him.

"She's still worried, Jack. She's still looking for the *hozro*."

He made no reply, and he took the most direct route to get to her—straight across the dance floor in the direction Winston had indicated, dodging couples as he went, or rather making them dodge him. He spotted Meg as he reached the middle of the floor. He could see her plainly. She was almost directly under one of the small ceiling spotlights.

Someone grabbed his arm—Mary Ann, smiling and having a good time with a big, light-footed cowboy. "Come on,

Jack!'' she said, giggling, and she hung on to him and danced with him and the cowboy both for a moment before she let the cowboy twirl her away.

Jack located Meggie again. The Baron-Singer table was crowded against the railing at the edge of the dance floor. She was talking to Sloan. Every now and then she laughed. When she finally saw him, he was less than twenty feet away, and her laughter immediately disappeared.

But he wasn't deterred in the least. He wondered if he was drunk. He didn't feel drunk. He didn't feel anything except the long-familiar emptiness that had been with him all his life. There was only one person in the whole world who had ever been able to fill it up, and she was looking right at him.

Yeah, it's me, Meggie.

He walked up and leaned nonchalantly against the railing.

''*Yá'át'ééh,* Will!'' he said, greeting the birthday boy first. ''I hear it's your birthday. How many does this make?''

''Hey, Jack. Seventeen.''

''Yeah?'' He bent down closer. ''You watch out for Eddie Nez,'' he said quietly in Navajo.

''You watch out for my uncle,'' Will countered. ''When he sees whose name is in that sleeping bag Meggie brought home, your butt's *had* it, man.''

''Don't worry about it.''

''Ditto,'' Will said.

''Patrick,'' Jack said loudly, moving on to acknowledge the next Baron. This time he didn't make the mistake of offering Patrick his hand, nor did he wait for a response.

Two brothers down and one uncle to go.

''Lucas,'' he said finally, getting the biggest threat out of the way. Jack didn't wait for him to say anything, either; he nodded to Sloan, who looked a lot more worried than she should.

That left Meg, who clearly didn't know what to do. But he knew. He had to get her off to himself.

''How about a dance, Meggie? That is, if you're not afraid I'll stomp on your toes.'' He remembered to smile. He remembered to look into her eyes and pray.

Please.

"I don't think I can get there from here," she said.

"Sure you can," he said, reaching over the railing to take her by the hand. He pulled her to her feet and lifted her up and onto the dance floor, clearing the railing in one easy swoop, ignoring the glares from the brothers and the uncle, but acknowledging the round of applause that rippled from the nearest table.

Meggie was smiling when he sat her down. "You *are* crazy, Jack," she said.

"No, ma'am," he said. "Resourceful is all. A good Navajo marine is *always* resourceful."

But he thought, *Yes*. He had always been crazy where she was concerned.

Benny Joe's music player had put on one of those upbeat, "I'm-a-sonofagun-and-proud-of-it" cowboy marching songs.

Again.

"Do you feel up to this?" he asked as he led her into the parade of dancers. He would be perfectly content to sit this one out with her someplace.

"I feel fine," she assured him, smiling still.

"You look fine, too," he said, because it was true. She was beautiful.

Her smile slid away. "Jack, what are you doing?"

"Dancing, Meggie. Or trying to."

"You know what I mean," she said, stopping dead so that the couple behind them stepped all over his heels.

The song ended, and they stood staring at each other on the dance floor. She abruptly turned away from him.

"Meg, wait," he said, catching her by the hand and hanging on. Lucas got up out of his chair. "Meggie," Jack said urgently, because people were beginning to look at them.

The lights suddenly dimmed, the cue for a plaintive song about lost love and and the desperate yearning for a second chance.

He still held on to her hand and he bent closer to her. "Don't. Don't run away from me."

"I'm not the one who runs, Jack."

"I know. Meggie, I'm sorry. I'm *sorry*."

She looked up at him, and when he reached for her other hand, she didn't pull away. Then she was in his arms somehow, and they began to move to the music, unclogging the flow of dancers they had bottlenecked behind them. He caught a glimpse of Lucas over Meg's shoulder. He was still standing.

"If you don't look like you're enjoying this pretty soon, Lucas is going to come out here," Jack said, only half-teasing. "Lucas is okay, but I'd much rather dance with you," he added, and she abruptly laughed. He took it as permission to pull her closer.

The sadness of the song swirled around them. After a moment, she rested her head against his shoulder. She felt so good! He could smell the sweet, clean scent of her hair. He could feel her breasts warm and soft against his chest.

Meggie—I love you, Meggie.

"Are you all right?" he asked.

"I'm all right, Jack. You don't have to worry about me."

"I love you, Meg," he said simply, surprising himself and her. But it was the truth and always had been, and she might as well know it. She leaned back to look at him, worried still, her eyes searching his face.

"I'm not asking for anything," he said. "I just wanted to tell you, in case you didn't know."

Her mouth trembled, and she suddenly leaned against him, her hand clutching the back of his shirt.

"You did know, didn't you?" he whispered against her ear, and she shook her head.

"Always," he said, pressing his face against hers. "I can't even remember when I didn't. It's still the same for me. Do you understand? Nothing's changed. Nothing."

"Jack—"

"Don't cry. I don't want to ever make you cry."

The song played on, but they had stopped dancing. She slid her arms around his waist, clinging to him hard. He could feel her trembling.

"Meggie—"

She suddenly broke away, slipping from his grasp and leaving him standing in the middle of the dance floor. She dodged between the swaying couples until he lost sight of her in the darkness. He tried to follow, but some woman with a camera was taking pictures. The flash went off, blinding him for a moment. When he could see again, the Baron-Singer table was empty and Meggie was gone.

Chapter Seven

This was not a good time for an unannounced visit. Jack could tell because the back door flew open before he got to it.

"What do you want?" Lucas asked bluntly.

Jack walked as close as he could before he answered. "I want to see Meg."

"No," Lucas said, attempting to close the door again, but Jack grabbed it.

"Lucas, we can stand here fighting over the door if you want to, but unless you plan to shoot me, I'm going to see Meg."

"She doesn't want to see you."

"Then let her tell me that."

"Damn it, Jack! Haven't you done enough?"

"What have I done, Lucas? What? You've been accusing me of things since I was twelve years old."

"I never accused you of anything you didn't do. I am telling you right now, Jack—turn around and get out of here!"

"Lucas, don't!" Meg said behind him, but he didn't move so she could get by.

"Meggie, you don't have to talk to him."

"I want to talk to him. I told you. Jack hasn't done anything."

"Then why were you crying last night? He did *something* at Benny Joe's."

"He was kind to me—when I needed a little kindness. Now, please. Let me out."

Lucas stood for a moment longer, then stepped aside. She managed a small smile to reassure him that she knew what she was doing, but he was clearly not reassured.

"What's going on?" Jack asked when they'd walked a few paces along the flagstone path that led away from the house. The wind chimes on the front patio tinkled softly behind them. He looked toward the monoliths, remembering the long-ago climb up to the top and his burning desire to impress her with his incredible daring. She'd been daring, too, following right behind him, and in the end, he was the one who had ultimately been impressed.

"I told them I was pregnant," she said, and he looked back at her.

He made a small sound of understanding, but other than that he had nothing to say. She abruptly put her face in her hands.

He stood there, not knowing what to do, particularly with Lucas and any number of concerned parties likely watching from the window.

"Is Sloan okay with this?" he asked. He had already seen Lucas's state of mind.

She looked up at him and gave a heavy sigh. "She won't stop crying."

"She's not going to throw you out or anything, is she?"

"No, nothing like that. She's just . . . disappointed. She thought I would know better, I guess. She thought I understood how hard it was for a woman to raise a child alone because I'd been through it. She had a terrible time making enough money to take care of Patrick and me after my father took off and left us with her. And Lucas, he's—" She broke off and shook her head. "I'm so tired, Jack."

He put his arms around her then, in spite of the probable audience, and she leaned against him. She looked tired and defeated. And he couldn't stand it.

"Go get your things," he said, holding her away from him.

"What?"

"Go get your things. I'm going to take you back to Dolly's. You can rest there and think. It'll give Sloan and Lucas time to get themselves together. You don't want to stay here right now, do you?"

"No," she said, but she still wasn't convinced.

"Then let's get your stuff and go. You need to give everybody a chance to settle down. Everything is out in the open now, right?"

She gave him a pained look, and he could feel her trying to make up her mind. "All right," she said after a moment. "But I'll drive my own car."

"Meg, I'll take you. You're exhausted. You need to rest and you might as well start right now."

"Jack—"

"Let me do this for you, okay?"

"It will just cause more trouble. Lucas isn't convinced you're not the one who . . ." She stopped, and he reached up to stroke her cheek with his fingertips.

"I don't care what Lucas thinks, Meg."

"I don't want him to blame you."

"It doesn't matter," he insisted. And it didn't. If anything, he was used to taking the blame for things whether he deserved it or not, which, as Lucas had pointed out, he usually did. And the real truth of the matter was that he wished he *was* "the one." Then he'd take Meg away and marry her—a traditional Navajo ceremony first because she had told him once that she wanted a Navajo wedding, and then the other kind if her white relatives insisted. They'd live together and take care of the baby together. She could teach at one of the schools or the community college. He could find something in one of the clinics. He could stand paperwork and keeping the clock for Meg and his baby.

And Lucas and the Baron brothers could just get over it.

He walked back to the house with her. She looked doubtful when he followed her inside, but she didn't object. Sloan was sitting at the kitchen table, her eyes red from weeping. And Lucas—Lucas had the look of a man whose women desperately needed his help, but he didn't have the slightest idea what to do for them.

Meg said nothing to either of them; she disappeared into her bedroom at the back of the house. Jack stood and waited, completely neutral. He hoped.

"What do you think you're doing?" Lucas asked him.

"I'm taking Meg out of here," Jack said, because there was no use putting off the inevitable and because that was the bottom line and because he'd never been overburdened by tact.

"The hell you are!"

"Lucas!" Sloan cried, jumping up from her chair and moving in between them.

"Meg is *not* going with him!" Lucas yelled. "The last thing she needs is Jack Begaye!"

"Stop it!" Meg cried from the doorway. "Stop it! I can't take any more!"

"Meggie," Sloan said, reaching out for her, but Meg moved away, only allowing the briefest of contact.

"I'm going to stay with Dolly," Meg said. She struggled hard for control. "Jack's going to take me. I'll be back when I feel better. Please! Please . . ." she said, her voice gone quiet now. "I love you both and I'm sorry about all this. But I have my baby to think about, and right now I need you to—just let me be."

Jack stepped around Lucas to take *his* sleeping bag from Meg's hands. Clearly, Lucas hadn't seen the name tag in it yet.

"You got your vitamins and stuff?" he asked, because she was upset and might not have remembered the bottle he'd seen earlier. He realized too late that the familiarity his question implied was about to set Lucas off again.

Sloan put her hand on Lucas's arm to restrain him. No words, just a look and a touch. Jack marveled that Lucas responded to it, to her quiet plea for a little sanity and self-control. It was still there, he thought, whatever respect and concern they'd had for each other when they'd first married.

"Yes, I've got them," Meg said. She hesitated for a moment, then hugged Sloan and Lucas both.

But she had nothing more to say to them. She led the way out the door and all the way to the truck.

"Are you all right?" Jack said to her profile as he stuffed the backpack and the sleeping bag under her feet. "Scratch that," he said the moment she looked at him. She wasn't all right. She'd had about all she could stand.

She tried to smile and didn't quite make it.

He got into the truck and backed it around, still half-expecting Lucas to come running out of the house with a shotgun.

"Are you warm enough?" he asked when they had been on the road a few minutes. She sat watching the scenery—such as it was.

"I'm okay," she said.

"If you're cold, you can use the sleeping bag."

"I'm not cold, Jack," she said, still not looking at him. "I'm scared."

He reached for her hand. She resisted for a moment, then let her cold fingers cling to his.

"It's going to be all right, Meggie. Everybody's just got to get used to the idea, that's all," he said, and for some reason, she smiled at that.

"What about him—the guy? What does he say?" he asked after a time, because he suddenly found that he did want to know about him, after all. He wanted to know very badly.

"Nothing."

"Nothing?" he said, glancing at her as he drove. Surely the man knew Meg was going to have his kid.

"Nothing," she repeated, finally looking at him instead of the view. "He's dead."

Dead, Jack kept thinking, but he didn't ask any more questions. Meg was half-asleep by the time they reached Dolly's, and at Dolly's insistence she went to lie down immediately. Jack headed back outside, ostensibly to feed the sheep and the dogs, but in reality because he needed to think about Meggie's second revelation.

Dead. Ah, Meggie. How am I going to take you away from a dead man? Dead men had no faults, no weaknesses. Dying made them perfect.

He stayed outside a long time, chopping a pile of wood when he'd finished feeding the animals. Eventually, Dolly came to the door and called him. He went to see what she wanted, carrying a load of wood up to the house.

"You're a good man, Jack," she said of the wood, "to care if an old woman is looked after. Come in the house. You've been out here in the cold long enough."

"You got anything else that needs doing?" he asked, stacking the wood by the back door.

"I need you to come inside," she said. "Get warm. Drink some coffee. Eat something."

She had made him fry bread with honey and powdered sugar sprinkled on it, his favorite when he'd been sentenced to do his community service under her direction all those years ago. She'd seen to it that he worked hard and that he was fed well. He had never had anyone so concerned about the state of his stomach before or since.

He ate nearly the whole batch, chasing it down with hot coffee. Both tasted wonderful. He had always been able to enjoy the simple things, probably because he'd never had anything else.

"Is Meg still asleep?" he asked.

"Yes," Dolly said. "But why don't you go see?"

Go see?

He stayed where he was, not understanding what Dolly was telling him to do.

"You need to know how she is. She needs to know you're still here to help her," Dolly said quietly. "Go."

He stood up, hesitating for a moment because it seemed he should say something, explain his intent.

No, he decided. Dolly Singer knew he loved Meg Baron.

There were two doors, two bedrooms. He opened the first door, the one Meg had used when he was here before. There was a double bed in the room. It was pushed against the far wall, and it had no headboard or footboard. Meggie was lying on top of the bed, a Southwestern-type blanket pulled over her, her head near the window. He stepped inside and walked closer. The daylight was almost gone, and she was sleeping quietly.

So beautiful, he thought, as he always did when he looked at her.

He wanted to touch her, but he didn't. After a moment he sat down carefully on the side of the bed, and he stayed there, trying to see her face in the fading light.

What are we going to do, Meg?

He had no idea how long he'd been there when she opened her eyes, and if she was surprised or alarmed to see him, it didn't show. She simply made room for him and held out her arms.

He unlaced his boots and lay down beside her, sharing her pillow and her blanket and the warmth of her body. He put his arms around her and held her close, realizing that she had immediately dropped off to sleep again. Outside, the wind had picked up. He could hear it moaning around Dolly's small house.

Listen, Jackie. Listen to the wind....

What *chindi* was this? he wondered. His grandfather? Meg's lover?

He closed his eyes. And, for the first time since he was a little boy, he let himself cry.

Chapter Eight

Meg woke up alone. She sat up on the side of the bed, feeling rumpled from having slept in her clothes, but rested. The sun was just coming up, and she made her way carefully to the tiny bathroom. She cringed at her reflection in the mirror over the sink. Pregnancy and sleeping twelve hours had done nothing for her looks. She washed herself quickly in the cold room, changed her clothes and tried to do something to tame her hair. When she came out, someone else was awake and moving around.

Jack.

She had no idea how long he'd stayed with her last night, held her, but his strength and his closeness were exactly what she'd needed. He looked up when she came into the warm kitchen, but he didn't say anything. He took down a cup and poured her some coffee.

"Is it okay for you to have this?" he asked when she didn't immediately take it.

"Not really," she said, trying to see his eyes so she'd know what he was feeling.

"I'll drink it then," he said, turning away so that she couldn't. Was he sorry he'd said he loved her? she wondered. She hadn't exactly welcomed the revelation, and neither of them had mentioned it since. She stared at him. He looked so different to her. Part of it was that he wore his hair short now, in a kind of modified military cut. Part of it was that he himself was different. She knew that beyond a doubt, but she really couldn't determine in precisely what way. His self-assurance, perhaps. He had decided immediately that she needed to give Lucas and Sloan some time, and he had been right.

"Where's Dolly?" she asked.

"She's out doing her morning chant—greeting the day."

"Jack, I want to tell you what happened," she said abruptly.

"Why?" he asked, finally looking at her.

"Why? Because..." She stopped, because she suddenly couldn't bear the look in his eyes.

"Are you going to tell me because you want me to go or because you want me to stay?"

"Jack—"

"You know where we are now, don't you? This is it, Meg. This is where we decide. Am I going to be in your life or out of it? I don't know, because I don't know what *you* want. The only thing I know for sure is that I can't stand things the way they are now."

She looked at him for a long moment, afraid suddenly, because they *were* at the crossroads. And she saw no hope at all of their ever getting past the obstacles to their being together.

"I'm going to go out with Dolly," she said, getting her coat and putting it on. "We can talk later, okay?"

He didn't answer her, and she hesitated for a moment before she went out the back door. She really didn't expect him to come with her, but he did, neither of them saying anything as they walked over the cold ground away from the house. They found Dolly standing in front of the hogan, deep in concentration, her face turned toward the pale golden edge of the horizon.

Meg waited quietly, listening to the chant, understanding many of the Navajo words. Even so, she had forgotten a great deal of the language both Dolly and Jack had tried to teach her. She only remembered the ultimate goal: to find harmony and to walk in beauty.

She had always wanted that, for herself and for Jack. Now she wanted it for her child.

Dolly's morning prayers ended, and she smiled at them both. "Are you hungry?" she asked, patting Meg gently on the cheek.

"Very," Meg said.

"I don't have to ask you," Dolly said to tease Jack.

He actually smiled in return. He was so handsome when he smiled, Meg thought. And what a shame life had given him so few opportunities to do so.

"I'll go cook now," Dolly announced. "A big breakfast. And I don't want any help," she added pointedly. "I'll call you when I want you underfoot again."

"But I want to help," Meg began. She stopped when Dolly held up her hand to stop her.

"I will call you," the old woman said firmly.

Meg stood and watched her make her way back to the house. Meg was afraid again, and she could feel Jack waiting, feel his unhappiness and his determination to endure.

"So let's talk," he said immediately. He had never been one to prolong the suffering, she remembered. Get it over with or get out had always been his first directive. And perhaps their talking would give him the opportunity to do both.

"What do you want to know?" she asked, turning to face him.

"What do *I* want to know? This is your idea."

"Jack, I can see the question every time I look at you. I just don't know what it is."

"All right. Did you love him?"

"No," Meg said quietly.

"Then what are you doing having his kid?"

She gave a quiet sigh. This was going to be much harder than she'd thought.

"What? Have we hit a wall already?" Jack said.

"I don't want to make excuses."

"Then let's go for the truth."

"All right. He reminded me of you," she said bluntly and without apology.

"Ah, God, Meggie!" he said, turning away from her. "Don't tell me something like that!"

"It's the truth."

"I don't want to hear it!"

"That's what you asked for—the truth."

"Okay! Okay, then. What was it about him that reminded you? Was he Navajo—?"

"No."

"Was he poor? Orphaned? Was his old man a drunk?"

"No."

"What was it then?"

"He was lost. Like you."

He shook his head and gave a bitter laugh. "Meggie, Meggie—what was it Patrick always said? You and your damn strays."

"He reminded me of you, Jack, because he was always so sad. But he and I were never lovers. There was only that one..." She stopped. She did *not* want to make excuses. "I had just talked to Patrick and I thought you were getting married," she said, trying to sound calm and matter-of-fact, when she had been nothing of the kind at the time. She caught his arm to keep him from walking away. "Or you were married already. I was very upset, and he understood...."

Jack swore and pulled his arm free. "Yeah, I just bet he did. You should have known. You should have remembered!"

"Remembered what?"

"Us, damn it! You should have remembered *us.*"

"Like you did, Jack? Why wouldn't I believe what Patrick said? Why wouldn't I think you'd found someone else? You knew how much I loved you, and it didn't stop you from leaving."

"Yeah, well, you showed me, didn't you?"

"It wasn't like that!"

"No? It sounds *like that.*"

"He and I were friends," she said, refusing to be upset. "We understood each other. He knew about you—"

"You told him about me?" he asked incredulously, as if her betrayal was even worse than he'd first thought.

"I wanted him to know why there couldn't be anything between us."

"Well, so much for that."

She abruptly began to walk toward the house. "This is hopeless."

"No, wait," Jack said, catching up to her. "Wait. Meg, I didn't...it's just..." He put his hands on her shoulders to make her stop walking. "It hurts, that's all. What you said is true. *I* left. I don't have the right to parade my hurt feelings now, but I can't help it."

They stood looking at each other.

"So you felt sorry for him," he said after a moment.

"Yes."

"Like you always felt sorry for me."

It wasn't quite a question, but she answered it anyway, taking the chance that she would offend him more than she already had. "Yes."

"I never wanted your pity."

"And I never wanted *yours,*" she countered, remembering only too well how very pitiful she had been when they had first met.

"I couldn't help it," he said.

"Well, neither could I."

He almost smiled.

She began to walk toward the sheep pen and he walked along with her. `

"People were trying to make him into something he wasn't," she offered.

"What people?"

"His family. His mother was very...ambitious. She came from money and she thought she'd married beneath her. She tried for years to manipulate her husband's career. He worked for some government law-enforcement agency. He kept being transferred, and she hated it. So she was always telling him what to do, trying to get him promoted so he wouldn't be transferred anymore. She used to write letters to his superiors—petty, irate complaints about the unprofessional behavior of some his co-workers, how it reflected badly on the agency and everyone associated with it, herself included. I guess she thought it would make *him* look better. Of course, he was always passed over for promotion, and she never understood that *she* was the reason.

"Finally, she gave up on him and began to concentrate on her son. *He* would have to 'be somebody.' At first she wanted him to be a doctor. He knew he couldn't handle that at all, and he tried to pacify her by going to law school. He thought he could stand it, but he couldn't. The classes and the work were so hard for him. His mind just didn't work that way. He wanted to build things with his own hands. He worked all last summer as an apprentice bricklayer. I think it was the happiest he'd ever been in his life."

"I don't see the problem here, Meg."

"He wasn't strong like you, Jack. He didn't know how to go his own way no matter what. And I think his mother always made him feel responsible for her unhappiness."

"So what happened to him?"

"He was sick for a while and he'd been staying up late at night trying to make up the work so he could pass his final exams. He was driving on the interstate. The police said he fell asleep. He hit a bridge abutment."

"He knew about the baby?"

"No."

"But you were going to tell him."

"I don't know. I guess I would have had to at some point."

"You didn't want to marry him?"

"I told you. We were friends." She didn't say "just" friends, because it had been more than that. They had cared about each other, tried to help each other. She had been devastated when he died.

Jack looked at her for a long moment, his eyes searching her face. She was leaving out things and he knew it. "I have to go," he said abruptly, and he began walking toward his truck.

"Jack—"

"I have to go," he said again, and he didn't look back.

Knowledge Is Power.

The motto had been taped to the wall in one of Jack's grammar-school classrooms, the piece of paper it was printed on tattered, one corner missing and the remaining ones riddled with thumbtack holes from all its previous relocations.

Knowledge Is Power.

An uplifting platitude to inspire the children to greatness. It should have read Knowledge Is Pain.

When he had first awakened this morning, he hadn't realized where he was. When was the last time *he* woke up with a woman in his arms? There had been only one while he was away in the military—the discarded girlfriend of one of his marine buddies. He couldn't even remember her name. And yes, damn it, she had reminded him of Meg. For a brief moment, in the heat of passion, she had been Meg.

But this morning, Meggie was really with him. She stirred in his arms, sleeping still, her body spooned against his. The room was very cold, and he pressed her closer. He lay there, savoring her warmth, afraid she'd wake up and ask him to go.

Eventually, he forced himself to move away from her, and it had been so hard to leave. They had slept the whole night together, as innocent as children. He wanted to crawl back under the blanket with her. He wanted to touch her and make love with her until they both forgot everything except each other.

I still love you, Meg.

It had hurt him to know about this other man, but Jack had listened. In Meggie's brief telling, he had understood him as a person who always carried his sadness around with him, always let it crawl up from his belly and look out his eyes.

Another one of Meggie's strays, he thought again. *Just like Jack Begaye.*

But how could he fault Meg for being herself? For the first time he made a conscious effort to think of the child she carried as *hers,* not the child of some stranger.

Knowledge Is Power.

Perhaps it was the truth, after all, because he knew exactly what needed to be done now, what should have been done a long time ago. And he felt such profound relief in finally knowing which path to follow. His spirit soared with it. For the first time in his life he felt like singing the songs of The People—a warrior's song, because he would need it. The words swirled in his mind, words he had never intended to learn or remember:

> *Lo, the Flint Boy, I am he . . .*
> *Clearest, purest flint the heart*
> *Living strong in me, heart of flint . . .*
> *Living evermore*
> *Feared of all evermore*
> *Lo, the Flint Boy, I am he!*

Now he had a plan. An impossible, all-or-nothing one, yes, but a plan nevertheless, and he had to find Winston Tsosie. He needed the old man's counsel. There were things he needed to ask about before he could proceed. Winston would know, and Winston had foolishly offered to help him.

You may regret that big talk, Marine, he thought.

He found Winston at the shelter, sitting outside on the back steps in the sun, the morning chores done, the residents either checked out to go home or sleeping. For once Jack was reasonably sure that Winston didn't have any startling announcements of his own to make. This time *he* was the one with the announcement.

"I'm going to get married," he said without prelude, sitting down on the step beside him.

"Who to?" Winston asked.

"Who to? You know who to. Meg."

"How am I going to know that, Jack? Meggie ain't the one we went dancing with last Friday."

Jack frowned, but he made no comment. He sat there. And waited.

"Lucas will probably kill you," Winston observed after a time.

He gave Winston a look, but again he made no comment.

"Or Patrick," Winston added. "Young Will I'm not sure about. Maybe he wouldn't mind it so much, but you never know."

"Will you stop trying to scare me? Are you going to help me or not?"

"What you want me to do, Jack?"

"I want you to do whatever needs doing. Meg told me once that when she got married she wanted a traditional Navajo wedding."

"What does she say now?"

"I don't know, I haven't asked her. Don't look at me like that."

"If you think Meggie is going to marry you Navajo when she ain't been asked about it, *somebody* better look at you."

"Winston."

"She seen you dancing with Mary Ann at Benny Joe's the other night. All kinds of people seen you. This wedding thing will be a *big* surprise."

But Winston didn't mean "all kinds" of people, he meant Lucas and the Baron brothers.

They both sighed.

"When did you ask Meggie to get married to you?" Winston said after a time.

"I didn't," Jack said, obviously confirming Winston's worst fear. "I want you to do that. If we're going to do it Navajo, then Dolly's the head of the family, right? She's the one we talk to—we don't have to bother Lucas with any of this. I want you to be my uncle and make the arrangements, go talk to Dolly."

Winston sat there.

And sat.

"You got any money?" he finally asked.

"What for?"

"For the horse, Jack. You going to get married traditional, I got to offer a horse."

"Yeah, I can swing a horse."

"A good horse," Winston qualified.

"Yeah, a good horse. Two or three of them, if it takes that."

"Where did you get that kind of money?"

"It's my marine pay, okay? I never spent much of it. It's in the bank in Gallup. If you want a good horse, you got one. What?" Jack said, because Winston clearly had something else on his mind.

"You must be serious about this, Jack. You even sound like a man trying to get married—nerves shot all to hell."

"You just get this show on the road and don't worry about my nerves, okay?"

Winston smiled. "I'm glad I decided to mind your business, Jack. Boy, things are sure picking up now."

Jack left locating and purchasing the horse to Winston, a task the old man accomplished in much less time than Jack would have imagined—less than a day. And while he found the price more than reasonable, he did have some problem with the seller—Eddie Nez.

"It's a fine horse," Winston said. "It will make Meggie smile."

"Yeah, but is it his to sell?"

"No problem with that, Jack."

"You didn't tell him what it was for, did you?"

"No," Winston said. "But you know as good as anybody you can't keep secrets from The People. Somebody always knows."

"Well, nobody knows right now but you and me," Jack said pointedly. "And we're going to keep it that way."

"You didn't mean what you said, did you?"

"About what?"

"About not bothering Lucas with this."

"Winston, I have to find out if Meg will marry me first. Then I'll worry about Lucas."

"Well, she ain't going to have nothing to do with you trying to leave him out of it."

"I *know* that, Winston. First things first, okay? There's no point in getting Lucas all stirred up until I know something, is there? He's stirred up enough as it is. So when are you going to see Dolly?"

Whatever Winston answered, Jack didn't hear. The old man left him standing and got busy elsewhere for a time, eventually returning as Jack was finishing some of the paperwork he had earnestly led Lucas Singer to believe was beneath him. It wasn't that he found the record keeping difficult; it was that he'd rather be doing something else.

"It's ready," Winston said from the doorway.

"What's ready?"

"The sweat lodge."

"Winston, are you going to see Dolly today or not?"

"Yes."

"Do you think you have time for a sweat bath?"

"Not me, Jack. Us."

He looked up from the sheet of paper he had been adding figures on. "Sorry, Winston. I have every respect for your belief in the ritual, but I don't do sweat baths."

"You do today, my son," Winston said.

"No, I don't."

"Yes, you do."

"Winston—"

"You said traditional, so we'll do it traditional. We got to get ourselves ready—pure—to talk marriage."

"You're the one that's supposed to do the talking."

"And you get to sit there—in harmony—while I do it. You don't want to make me say 'or else,' do you, Jack?"

"Winston," Jack said, but the old man was already out the door. "Winston!" he called after him, finally following him outside.

"What, Jack?"

"Winston, it's too cold out here."

"You sound like them people that come rolling into Window Rock on the tour bus. Every time they get off, it's too hot or too cold. You won't be cold long, Marine. You said you wanted my help—I'm helping. You want this traditional or not?''

"Yes, I want it traditional," he said after a moment. He just didn't want anything to do with a sweat lodge.

But nobody could deal with Winston Tsosie when he was determined, not Eddie Nez when he didn't want to be put to bed in a shelter, not Jackie Begaye when he didn't want to double-date, and, Jack hoped, not Dolly Singer.

He could see now what Winston had been doing the past hour or so. He'd built a fire on the ground and he'd been heating a pile of large stones. The sweat lodge had been dug into an upward slope of ground, the low doorway braced with logs and covered with a piece of canvas and a striped blanket. The residents and Winston used it frequently. But not Jack Begaye.

Winston began to pick up the hot stones with a shovel and place them carefully inside.

Jack stood and waited, his mind suddenly filled with memories he thought he'd buried long ago.

"Jack," Winston said quietly when he'd finished. "Doing this for Meggie is not the same as doing it for a drunken father who only wanted to find fault."

Jack looked at the old man, both surprised and not surprised that Winston knew about that painful time in his life. He took a deep breath. And then another.

"I couldn't do it right," he said finally, hating the sudden weakness of spirit that drove him to make excuses. He'd never been able to do it the way his father demanded, and he'd been punished severely for it.

"You were only a boy," Winston said. "And what you don't remember now, I will teach you."

Again Jack breathed deeply. It was a beautiful day, bright sunshine and cloudless blue sky. A day worthy of such a ceremony. And even he would acknowledge that if he was going to succeed in his quest to marry Meg Baron, he would need all the help he could get.

No, he thought. *This isn't the same.*

"All right," he said, and he began to strip off his clothes in the cold air, waiting for Winston to do the same and to begin the ritual with his high, plaintive call.

Holy People, come!

Chapter Nine

"You feel all right, Jack?" Winston asked when they had almost reached Dolly's homestead.

"I feel fine," Jack said, because he did. The sweat bath had done its work. He felt rested, alive, and more than that, he felt worthy. He had even remembered much of the song that went with the ritual. Winston was certainly pleased with the result, and so was Jack. He had done what needed to be done with only a minimal amount of emotional pain from his past.

But the closer they came to the homestead, the more anxious he began to feel. What if Meg wasn't there now? What if she'd left for who knows where and he couldn't find her? Or worse, what if she was there and she wouldn't see him?

He began to regret having let Winston drive—the old man drove too slowly. But now, suddenly, they were getting there too quickly. He kept taking deep breaths. He drummed his fingers on the door, jiggled one knee. Nothing helped.

"Lo, the Flint Boy, I am he!" he chanted under his breath, over and over. He glanced at Winston. The old man nodded in approval.

Jack could see the homestead now. Dolly's truck was there, and thank God, no vehicle from the Navajo Tribal Police or the Baron family. Winston pulled into the yard and parked to wait for Dolly to call them inside. "You okay, Jack?" Winston asked.

"Yeah." He glanced in Winston's direction. "Yeah," he said again. "Winston?"

"What, Jack?"

"You make sure Dolly knows the one horse is only a symbol. She can have more if she wants. She can have anything—everything—I've got."

"Okay, Jack."

Dolly opened the back door, beckoning to them to come inside.

"And there's something else you ought to know," Jack said as he got out of the truck.

"What?"

"Meg is going to have a baby."

He started off toward the house, then realized Winston wasn't coming with him. The old man was still standing by the truck.

"*Your* baby," Winston said when Jack looked back at him.

"No," he said, walking on.

"No," Winston echoed behind him.

Jack stopped and waited for him to catch up. "And that's all you need to know about it," he said when the old man reached him.

Winston looked at him.

"I mean it," Jack said.

"I ain't asking no questions, Jack. It's your business."

"Yeah, like that makes a big impression on you."

Winston suddenly laughed and pounded Jack on the back. "You know, boy, you pretty good at keeping them gorillas up your sleeve yourself."

Jack grinned in return, feeling infinitely better suddenly. They walked the rest of the way together to the back door together. Unfortunately, his improved state of mind was short-lived. The door opened wide when they reached it, and Dolly stepped out. About the same moment, he noticed a person walking up from the sheep pen. At first he thought it was Meg. He was on the verge of calling to her when he realized that Dolly had herself an entirely different shepherd today.

Will Baron.

Meg sat cross-legged on the floor in front of the rug loom, concentrating intently on the pattern. She heard the back door open and the muted conversation, but she didn't interrupt the task at hand until she heard Will's rather forceful announcement in Navajo.

I am the brother.

She looked over her shoulder. She could see him standing just outside the doorway, and she could see part of Dolly's back. She couldn't see who had come or the reason for Will's peculiar comment. She was mildly curious, but she immediately pushed her curiosity aside. She simply didn't have the energy these days for that self-indulgence.

She went back to weaving, thrusting the shuttle back in the other direction and pounding the yarn into place. And she kept working until she realized that Dolly was standing at her shoulder. She looked up and smiled.

"We have visitors," Dolly said so solemnly that Meg became immediately alarmed.

"What's wrong?" she asked, struggling to get up. "Is something the matter with Sloan or Lucas?" As someone who had gotten sudden bad news both as a child and as a woman, Meg didn't have to make much of a leap to expect the very worst.

"No," Dolly said. "Come over here."

In all these many years, Meg had never known Dolly to raise her voice about anything. She didn't have to. She had other ways of communicating her wants, and what she wanted right now was silence. The look she gave Meg left no doubt about it, and despite the fact that Meg was a grown woman, at this particular moment she was to be seen and not heard.

She gave a small sigh and waited in the spot Dolly indicated. Will came inside first, the expression on his face telling her that

Dolly had had to take him in hand as well. He, too, was quiet and he didn't like it.

She immediately recognized the old man who followed him— Winston Tsosie from the mission shelter, who had given her the turquoise. It was a beautiful piece. She had it in her pocket, and she would have thanked him for it but for the fact that she didn't have leave to do anything at the moment.

She looked up sharply as the third person came in—Jack, who was just as solemn as Dolly.

What in the world? Meg thought, and she didn't miss the territorial looks he and Will exchanged. Jack didn't look at her once. By all indication, he didn't even see her standing there.

"Sit down, everyone," Dolly said finally. She pulled out the chair she wanted Meg to take and waited until she did so. Jack and Winston Tsosie sat down at the kitchen table across from her.

Dolly turned to get down cups for the coffee she always had ready, and Meg would have gotten up to help her if Jack hadn't very pointedly cleared his throat.

She understood that, too.

Stay put.

She pursed her lips to put forth a question, but in the wake of the looks she got from both Jack and Winston, she let it go. It was not her desire to upset whatever this was, and she certainly didn't have any pressing engagements. She could wait.

Will, on the other hand, was not quite so patient. He whispered something to Dolly, whose reply left him no happier than he'd been when he came in.

Meg contented herself with staring at Jack and employing a look of her own.

I thought you'd gone for good, Begaye.

He glanced at her, then back again as the look got through to him.

Dolly was bringing the coffee. Meg accepted her cup, but drank very little of it. The others, however, slowly drank all of theirs in silence. Will, who was still standing, fidgeted behind them, and Meg worked hard not to sigh.

A piece of wood shifted in the stove. The dogs barked briefly at something, and Winston Tsosie finally began the conversation—quietly, as Meg suspected was his way. Both Dolly and Jack responded, but unfortunately, she couldn't follow any of it. She had always known that, out of courtesy to her, Dolly and Jack spoke unnaturally slow whenever they said anything to her in Navajo. She had always had trouble understanding other people, and neither Dolly nor Jack were extending that courtesy now. She glanced at Will. She thought that even he was having trouble following.

The conversation continued. Meg stared at Jack's hands. She had always loved his hands, lean and strong and long fingered. Gentle.

She finally understood a word. Dolly said it, and the conversation abruptly stopped.

Ha'át'éegosha'.

Why?

The ball now seemed to be in Jack's court, and he was not at all happy about it. He said something to Dolly.

"Do you want Will to leave?" Dolly immediately asked Meg in English.

"Will?" she said, taken by surprise. Why should she want Will to leave? She had no real reason to hide anything from him now. He knew about her pregnancy. In fact, he had come to Dolly's to see if there was anything he could do for her. She glanced at him. It was all he could do to keep quiet.

"He's my brother," she said, using a variation of his own earlier comment. "I don't want him to go." She understood the difficulty he was having in trying to find his rightful place in the two cultures, and she had no wish for him to think that she considered him anything but her true family.

"*Shahane'—*" Jack said, but Dolly held up her hand.

"In English, Jack," she said. "Meg needs to know what you want in English."

There was more discussion, this time from Winston Tsosie. Jack made no comment, and he still didn't look in Meg's direction. He sat there for what seemed a long time before he finally began again.

"I . . ." He cleared his throat, glancing briefly at Dolly before he started again. "You asked me why, and I was going to tell you this sad story of Jack Begaye. I was going to tell about when I was a boy and I was forced to go to the receiving home in Window Rock.

"But you already know this. You know that I didn't want to be there. I *hated* being there. But in the eyes of the authorities I was a child still and I had to stay. I was full of anger, and I was very . . . sad. It shamed me for people to know about my family—to know why I had to live there." He stopped and took a quiet breath. "But one day, I looked around and I saw a little red-haired girl sitting at the table in the dayroom. She was white, but she was kind to me. She didn't call me names. She didn't look down on me. And she was filled with a kind of joy I had never known, even though her own life was just as sad as mine. She shared that joy with me and with her little brother, Will, and with the other children in that place, and I loved her for it. I loved her that day and I have loved her every day since."

He stopped again, and Meg could feel her tears welling. Her throat ached and her eyes burned. She stared at the pattern of flowers in the plastic tablecloth to try to remain in control, not understanding the reason for this outpouring. The only thing she understood was that she didn't want to make a fool of herself and cry.

"When she told me about the child she carries," Jack said quietly, "I was very angry because I've always thought of her as . . . mine. Even though we went our separate ways. Even though I haven't seen her in a long time. She was still *my* Meg and I loved her.

"At first I wished with all my heart that *I* was the father of the baby and not this other man. And I hated him because of the love Meg must have had for him.

"I don't hate him anymore, but I was still wishing that I was the baby's father. I kept thinking if only it was mine, then I'd marry Meg. We could live together and take care of this baby. We could work and help each other. We could grow old together.

"Then I realized when I look at Meg I still feel the same as I did that first day in the receiving home. And I realized that that's the important thing. I knew what I needed to do. I love Meg, so how could I not love her child? There is no reason why we can't marry, no reason why we can't be together and take care of this child together. It would be *my* child, and if Meg will agree to be my wife, I swear to you, Dolly Singer, and to her, that I will be a good husband and a good father. I mean what I say. Meg knows that I don't lie. She knows that what I think can be done *is* possible, because she grew up with Lucas and he's always treated her as if she was his own. I will do the same for this little one. Don't cry Meggie," he said abruptly. He reached across the table to take her hand.

"I didn't know you were...going to...do this...." she said, struggling hard for control.

"He didn't, either," Winston said, making her smile in spite of the tears that threatened to overcome her.

"Meggie," Dolly said. "Give Will your chair. Will, you sit here now. Meggie, you go away while we talk."

Meg got up without hesitation. She needed to find her self-control, and she needed to think. Never in her wildest dreams had she expected Jack to do this.

Well, perhaps her *wildest* dreams. She couldn't believe that he remembered. He actually recalled her saying that she wanted the ceremony and the honor of being *asked for* in the Navajo way. That she didn't think she could trust a man's intentions otherwise. If he openly declared himself to a girl's family, then surely he must mean what he said. How old had she been then—thirteen? Fourteen?

She put on her coat, and she went out the front door so as not to interrupt the kitchen-table conference. She walked in a wide path away from the house, finally sitting down on a stump at the far edge of the yard. She sat there, staring at the mountains in the distance, and she couldn't keep from smiling. She would remember that Jack Begaye had asked for her like this—now—all the rest of her life.

But the smile abruptly faded. She had no room in her life for wild dreams. She was pregnant with another man's child, and

Jack deserved better than that. He deserved someone who would come to him with no distractions and no prior loyalties. How could they ever marry?

How?

"Stop beating yourself up," Jack said from behind her, making her jump.

She looked up at him, her eyes searching his.

I do love you, she thought. *I love you with all my heart.*

She abruptly smiled. "I wasn't beating myself up."

"Sure you were," he said. "If you weren't, then I have a question for you."

"What question?" she asked, making room for him to sit down on the stump beside her.

"Who are you and what have you done with Meggie Baron?"

She laughed, and he put his arm around her.

"You know, I was thinking the same thing about you," she said.

"Yeah, it's a hell of a note, isn't it?"

"Is it?"

"Well, it's not exactly the way either of us planned."

She sighed and rested her head against his shoulder, completely at ease with him as she'd always been, even if he did claim to want to marry her.

"Are they through talking?" she asked after a time.

"No. I came out here because I was afraid you might make a run for it. Dolly's holding on to Will's shirttail so he can't follow me. You aren't going to make a run for it, are you?"

"I haven't decided yet," she said.

"Yeah, I know the feeling."

His arm tightened around her, and he took a deep breath. "I didn't say everything I wanted to say in there," he said. "I didn't talk about the other thing."

"What other thing?"

He leaned down to pick up a wood chip and immediately tossed it aside. "How much I want you. You know what I mean."

"No," she said to be obtuse, to tease him a little.

But he wouldn't be teased. He was entirely serious. "I didn't say how much I want to make love with you. I didn't say how I used to wake up in the middle of the night sometimes when I was away from here and all I could think about was being with you. I didn't say how I wake up now. I want you, Meggie. I want to make love with you and sleep with you. And in the morning, I want your face to be the first thing I see."

She turned sharply toward him. Here it was—hers for the taking—her wildest dream. And it was too late. Far too late.

"Do you remember those little children in the receiving home?" she asked quietly. "The ones who used to sit by the window and wait and wait for somebody to come and get them? Only nobody ever did? That was me, Jack—*waiting* for you. When you left here, I didn't know what had happened to you. I didn't know if you were sick or hurt or *dead*. It was a long time before I heard you'd enlisted. Do you know how hard it is to pretend everything is all right when your heart is breaking? That was me, too, until I finally realized—a long, *long* time after everyone else did—that you left like that because you wanted to and you didn't care if it hurt me."

"Meg, I didn't want to—"

"Who made you do it, then?" she cried, giving in to her anger at last. "Who, Jack? Me? Was I too clinging? Was I suffocating you with my abject devotion?" She pushed hard against his chest. "How could you just disappear without a word? How could you do that?"

She raised her hand, meaning to strike him with her fist, and he caught it, pulling her hard against him to keep her from trying to hit him again. But he said nothing.

Nothing!

"You're not even sorry, are you?"

"If I'd stayed, it would have ruined everything!"

"Oh, well, that's certainly worked out, hasn't it? Nothing ruined here."

She pushed away from him and stood up. She walked a few steps in the direction she'd come.

"Meggie—"

"Leave me alone, Jack."

"Meggie!"

She looked back at him. Tears were streaming down his face.

"I'm scared, Meg," he said, his voice breaking. "I'm scared for us. I love you so much! This is our last chance. I *know* it!"

The time it took her to finally reach out to him seemed an eternity. She stood there, gazing at him with such a look of betrayal in her eyes that it was all he could do not to turn away.

This is it, he thought. *It's over.*

But she was in his arms suddenly, clinging to him, and the joy he felt was nearly more than he could bear. He kissed her mouth and her eyes and her mouth again.

"Marry me," he said. "Marry me, Meggie."

"It won't work, Jack."

"Yes, it will."

"It's too late! Can't you see that?"

"We still love each other! Don't we?" He made her look at him. "Don't we?" he insisted.

"Yes," she said, but she said it as if it were the worst thing in the world.

"It'll be all right, Meg. I'm going to work more for the mission. We won't be rich, but I can make enough for us to live on. It'll be all right! You and me and the baby—we can make it. I promise you."

"Meggie!"

They both looked around at Dolly, calling her from the back door. Meg tried to move away from him, but he held on.

"Tell me," he said. "Tell me you'll marry me!"

"What if I did, Jack Begaye? What would you do then?"

He smiled, almost certain now, almost believing.

"What would you do?" she asked, her eyes searching his for some sign that she could trust this offer of marriage, that she could trust *him* enough to give in.

"I'd go see Lucas," he said.

Jack didn't take Winston with him to the law-enforcement building. Some things had to be done without the go-between. And he wasn't as nervous as he might have expected. Lucas was a formidable obstacle, but Meg had said yes to the marriage, and that was that as far as he was concerned. Lucas could like it or not.

The place hadn't changed much—and he'd been inside enough to know. Mary Skeets still manned the phones. He could hear Captain Becenti's lecturing voice coming from somewhere down the hall. Jack wondered idly if that man had ever been in a situation that made him happy.

No matter. Jack was happy enough for the both of them.

He stood and waited for Mary to look up.

"Jack!" she said in surprise. "What brings you here?"

"I want to see Lucas," he said.

"Lucas who?" she asked pointedly, and he grinned.

"You know Lucas who. Is he in?"

"Yes, he's in. But this might not be the best time. He and Captain Becenti have had another slight difference of opinion," she added in a whisper.

"So what else is new?" he said. "I'll wait if he's busy. No, don't buzz him," he said, when she was about to do just that. "I'd rather take him by surprise."

"Okay," she said doubtfully. "But don't say I didn't warn you. You know where his office is, I guess."

"Yeah. Thanks, Mary."

"You're welcome, Jack."

He walked down the hall in the direction of Lucas's office. He found the door easily enough, and he didn't hear any more "difference of opinion" coming from inside. He rapped lightly on the door.

"In!" Lucas called sharply.

He was shuffling papers—a task that elicited a certain amount of sympathy in Jack—and it took him a moment to look up. But if Lucas was surprised to see him, it didn't show. Much.

"What do you want?" he asked rudely.

"Nice to see you, too, Lucas," Jack answered.

"Look, Jack, I'm busy. And I know this isn't a social call."

"Well, actually it is."

"Get to the bottom line."

"Okay. I'm going to marry Meg," he said bluntly, and *now* Lucas Singer was surprised. "I've asked her. She said yes. Winston Tsosie is making the arrangements with Dolly. We're going to have a traditional—"

"No, by God, you aren't going to have anything! Not with Meggie!"

"Lucas, I'm here to tell you man-to-man. I love Meg and we're getting married. There's nothing you can do about it. The only thing you can do is try to make the best of it. I know how you feel about me, but you and I both know it would break Meg's heart if you didn't take part in the wedding."

Lucas made a noise of disgust. "And how long will it be before you leave her again, Jack?"

"Again? I didn't leave her the first time and you know it! What I did was listen to you—I listened to you until I had no choice! You were right, I know that. I would have robbed Meggie of her education, of becoming what she always wanted to be. But that was then and this is now, Lucas. We're getting married."

"Does Sloan know about this?"

"No. Nobody in the family knows but Dolly and Will."

"Will knows? I just saw him and he didn't say a word!"

"I asked him not to. I wanted to do this right, Lucas. I wanted you to hear it from me."

"You actually think I'm going to sit still and let you marry Meg?"

"Yes," Jack said pointedly. "Because there's nothing you can do about it." He picked up a pen off Lucas's desk and boldly circled a date on his calendar five weeks away. "This is when the wedding will be. You either come and give *her* your blessing, if not the both of us, or we'll do it without you."

"Get out!" Lucas said.

"Lucas—"

"Get out!"

Jack looked at him for a long moment, then turned to go, jerking open the door and startling any number of eavesdroppers who were purposefully standing in the hall. He saw Mary

Skeets look at him expectantly on his way out, but he didn't stop. He hit the door hard, the anger boiling up in him.

"Hey!" somebody called from across the parking lot. Will Baron stood leaning nonchalantly against Eddie Nez's truck. Jack gave a sharp sigh and walked over.

"So how did it go?" Will asked.

"Well, considering Lucas was wearing a side arm, I guess it went damned good."

Will grinned. "You got some nerve, man. I'll give you that."

"I love your sister."

"Yeah, well, everybody knows that by now, I guess. Even Lucas. It's a good thing you're doing."

"What is?" Jack asked, looking over his shoulder. He might have nerve, but he still didn't want Lucas sneaking up on him.

"Having the wedding traditional. I want you to know, I'm beginning to think this thing with you and Meggie might work out okay."

"Yeah, well, I want *you* to know," he said, glancing at the truck, "when I get to be your brother, we're going to have to talk some more about the company you keep."

Will grinned again. "Knock yourself out, Jack."

Chapter Ten

My wedding day, Meg kept thinking.

She had been up since dawn, helping Dolly and Sloan with the flurry of last-minute preparations. She was astounded by the number of volunteer cooks who had already come to help with the food, arriving at Dolly's homestead in vans and in trucks with campers on the back. It would have been better for everyone trying to get her and Jack successfully married if they had waited until warmer weather, she thought yet another time. But she was concerned, too, that in the five weeks since Jack's proposal, her pregnancy had become so obvious. The entire reservation must know by now that she was hardly the virgin bride. But if Jack minded, she couldn't tell.

Lucas was on hand for the arrival of the marriage gift, a sorrel gelding with a black mane and tail. It had been groomed to within an inch of its life, and Meg fell in love with it immediately. But she stood back, letting Lucas carefully inspect the animal on her behalf.

"It's a fine horse," he grudgingly pronounced, and she couldn't help but smile.

"Is it broken?" he asked Winston.

"It is."

"Is it paid for?"

"Lucas!" Sloan chided, and he gave a sharp sigh.

But Winston seemed in no way offended. It was as if such remarks were to be expected from the bride's relatives, if they were properly carrying out their duties.

"I myself put the money in Eddie Nez's hand," he assured Lucas. "Come," he said to Meg. "Let this horse get to know you. I've been telling him about you all morning."

She smiled and stepped forward, letting the animal see her straight on, letting him gingerly smell and nudge her pockets for any tidbit she might have to offer.

She had indeed come prepared, and she took out the pieces of apple from her jacket and began feeding him, speaking to him softly.

"You see?" she whispered. "It's me. You are so beautiful."

The horse gave a soft rumble.

"He's so beautiful," she said to Winston, who was grinning from ear to ear.

"I told Jack this horse would make Meggie smile," he said.

"Thank you, Winston. Thank you for bringing him."

"I'm glad to bring him, Meggie. Now Jack can't ask me what time it is anymore." He leaned closer. "He's afraid he'll be late," he whispered, and she laughed.

She was a little afraid of that herself, but she didn't say so.

"No, Meggie," Winston said as if she had. "Jack will be here. He has waited a long time to marry with you."

She looked around as Will walked up.

"*One* horse?" he asked. "*One?* My sister is worth a lot more than one horse."

"Why, thank you, kind sir," she said, latching on to him and kissing him soundly on the cheek. She had been truly amazed by his participation in this event. He seemed to know exactly how things should be done, and he wasn't the least bit hesitant about handing out instructions. The wedding basket and the water jar needed for the ceremony had both come from him.

"Don't get all complimented," he said to tease. "I just like horses."

"Well, then, take this one around the block," she said. "Tell me if *I* like him."

He grinned broadly, reminding her at once of the little boy he used to be. And he was off like the wind, riding bareback "around the block" as it were.

"Meggie," Lucas said at her elbow. "There's still time to change your mind."

"No, Lucas," she said, watching Will's progress. "I don't want to change my mind." She looked up at him. "I promise."

"Then maybe you and Jack should live with us for a while. We've got the space. There's your room or Patrick's old room."

"You and Jack under the same roof? I don't think so," she said, teasing him now so he wouldn't look so serious. "Jack and I are going to live in the house the mission owns. I like it. It reminds me of the place Sloan and Patrick and I lived in when we first came to Window Rock. Jack's going to work at the shelter and I'm going to teach some adult reading classes. It's all settled."

"Meggie, are you sure?"

"Yes, yes, yes, I am sure," she said, giving him a hug.

He sighed. "Then I guess I'd better go somewhere and do...something," he said, not precisely happy but apparently resigned.

"That's a very good idea," Sloan told him, giving him a small kiss on the cheek. She waited until he had walked away. "Meggie, you are happy, aren't you?"

"*Yes.* I'm happy. You know I love Jack."

Sloan sighed. "I know."

"I wouldn't do this if I didn't think he and I had a chance. I know what a good marriage is, Sloan. I've lived with you and Lucas all these years. I wouldn't settle for anything less—not for myself and not for my baby."

"I just want you to be sure."

"And I just want you and Lucas to *stop worrying.*"

* * *

Meg stayed busy the rest of the day, and when the shadows began to grow long, she put on her wedding ensemble. The skirt was Navajo, full and flounced, the blouse a kind of long-sleeved, high-collared Victorian with covered buttons at the neck and sleeves. Both were made of unbleached muslin that had been washed and dried in the sun. She wore Dolly's silver-and-turquoise squash-blossom necklace and earrings, and she had a lace handkerchief from Sloan tucked into her sleeve, with Winston Tsosie's turquoise piece tied in one corner. She wore a pair of fawn-colored, soft leather boots—a present from Patrick. And with Dolly's and Sloan's help, she even managed to tame her hair into some semblance of order. All she had to do now was wait for the arrival of the bridegroom.

"You look beautiful," Sloan assured her. "Stop fussing."

But it wasn't her looks that made her so fidgety. What if Jack changed his mind? She could hardly blame him. What if...?

Will suddenly appeared at the doorway. "He's here," he announced ominously, and she was ashamed of the relief she felt.

Jack was really here. He had come to marry her, baby and all.

"What happens now, little brother?" she asked, relying on Will to be her wedding director.

"We're going to give a little more time for the 'hello, how are yous' and then Lucas and I will take you to the hogan. Now when you go in, the blanket is going to be kind of diagonal and off to your right."

"Diagonal and off to my right," she repeated.

"Don't get so nervous you go wandering around like you don't know where you're supposed to be."

"Yes, Will," she said dutifully. "And I'm not nervous."

"You may not be, but Jack is. You can sure tell he don't get married every day. Lucas is going to act as the bride's father and I'm going to help—hold the pollen bag, stuff like that. Patrick is going to stay the heck out of the way. Well, actually he's going to make sure Jack goes through with it."

"Very funny," Meg said. "Isn't he funny?" she asked Dolly and Sloan.

"Funniest one we've got," Sloan assured her. "Where's Lucas?"

"Waiting for us," Will said. "So, if we could get this show on the road now. It's *time.*"

She smiled and let him take her by the hand, then give her over to Lucas when they reached the back door.

The sun was going down; the bonfires had been lit. The air was heavy with the delicious aroma of mutton stew and fry bread being cooked for the wedding feast and, under it all, the pungent scent of burning wood.

"Meggie," Lucas began, his policeman's face for once easy to read.

"Be happy for me," she said, looking up at him. He had a few gray hairs now, but he was still fit and handsome, particularly today. "Please, Lucas. I know what I'm doing."

"I just don't think you can depend on him, Meg."

"My uncle," she said quietly. "I remember all the problems you and Sloan had to get through before you could marry her. I was there when you came all the way to North Carolina to get her. I was there when *she* took a chance on *you.* Sometimes you have to do that—just take a chance. And you know that better than most."

He gave a heavy sigh. "The worst kind of curse," he said with a slight smile. "A niece with a long and perfect memory. You *are* my child, Meg. You know I only want the best for you."

"I know," she said. "And I love you for it."

He sighed again and offered his arm, and together they walked toward the gathering outside the hogan. She was surprised at the number of people who had come—friends and co-workers. Half the Navajo Tribal Police must be here, and Mary Skeets, and all the medical-clinic staff who worked with Sloan. She even saw Lucas's long-time boss and adversary, Captain Becenti, among the men.

And Lucas's wayward sister, Lillian, had arrived, dressed in her gray power suit and high heels. Meg was infinitely pleased that Lillian had taken time away from her law practice to come, and she reached out her hand to her. Lillian stepped forward immediately, stopping the procession long enough to give her an embrace.

"Go get him, Meggie," she whispered in her ear. "All that man of yours needs is a good woman—that's you, sugar face."

Meg laughed and hugged her in return. "Thank you for being here, Lillian."

"Oh, I had to be here. I love you to death. And I haven't seen Lucas trying so hard to behave since we were packed off to boarding school. That alone was worth the trip."

Meg could see Jack now, standing tall outside the hogan. He was wearing a white, traditional Navajo shirt and newly pressed jeans, and strings of turquoise pieces around his neck.

How handsome he looks, she thought.

He watched her approach, and she saw him close his eyes and take a deep breath—shoring up his courage, she supposed, for this monumental undertaking.

But then his eyes met hers, and she had no more doubts. Jackie Begaye loved her.

There was no conversation between them, no touching. He turned and went inside the hogan. She followed, led by Lucas, with Will in their wake. The blanket where she and Jack were to sit had been carefully placed on the northwest side of the hogan. He waited there now, waited for Lucas to present him with his bride.

She gave Jack a small smile as she approached. If he was as nervous as Will had led her to believe, she couldn't tell. He smiled in return, resisting the impulse to help her when she positioned herself on the blanket beside him.

The shallow wedding basket filled with corn gruel was already in place, and the small jar of water with a gourd ladle. The guests began to file in—the men to one side and the women to the other. She caught a glimpse of Winston. He had worn his marine code-talker clothes—the orange shirt with his military patches and his battle ribbons—in honor of the occasion.

She gave Jack a sidelong glance. He gave her a wink in return.

All her life, she thought, she was going to remember the outpouring of love and warm wishes she felt from her family and from The People.

Lucas and Will came forward, and Meg watched Lucas as he solemnly made a cross of white corn pollen over the top of the gruel.

East to West.

South to North.

And then a circle, starting again at the East to always follow the sun.

When he finished, she reached for the gourd the way Dolly had instructed her, filling it with water from the jar and pouring it carefully over Jack's extended hands. His hands trembled slightly; he *was* nervous, she thought.

Then she offered her own hands so that he could do the same. Water was so precious here. How appropriate that it should be a part of the ceremony.

Both of them consecrated now, Jack looked into her eyes for a moment before he dipped his finger into the gruel, where the pollen touched the circle at the East, and ate. He waited for her to follow his example and take some from the same place. They moved around the circle, he and then she, each of them eating a small pinch of the gruel and pollen, South to West to North.

And suddenly it was over and all the solemnness fell away. The marriage was done, and it was time for the celebration to begin. Meg sat with Jack on the blanket, holding court, receiving everyone's good wishes, while outside the hogan the feasting and dancing and singing was about to begin. Everything became a blur of people and noise and color.

"Are you okay?" Jack asked her at one point.

"Are you?" she asked in return.

"That's a *big* affirmative, ma'am," he said, dragging up his former marine persona to make her smile.

In time they went outside to join the others. The food was abundant and smelled delicious. Meg was cold, and she stood in the curve of Jack's arm for warmth. She made an effort to talk to everyone who had come, accepting advice from the elderly women present on how to keep her husband happy and in hand.

At one point, Patrick waited to speak to her. She knew he was not as resigned to the situation as he might have been, but he gave her a hug. He didn't offer Jack his hand.

"Happy marriage, Meggie," he said to her, still ignoring Jack.

"Thank you, Patrick," she whispered, giving him another hug.

"Jack," he said finally, "you be good to my sister."

But he didn't wait around to hear Jack's reply.

"I'm sorry," Meg said, watching her brother's retreating back.

"He thinks you've married a shiftless Indian, Meg. And he's not going to change. I don't want you to worry about Patrick. The main thing is that we're together."

"He didn't used to be like this."

She leaned against him and put her arms around his waist, savoring his masculine scent and the warm, strong feel of his body.

Together.

But she was afraid suddenly—not of beginning their life together, but of the car with the California license plates and everything it represented. She hadn't told Jack about that. She hadn't told anyone except Dolly.

He kissed her softly on the cheek, then on the mouth, ignoring the ooh's and ah's around them.

But someone was calling them to come to the place of honor that had been prepared for them and they went in that direction, hand in hand. His fingers were warm and reassuring around hers and no longer trembling.

It's going to be all right, she thought. *It's my wedding day and it's going to be all right.*

She sat there, with Jack at her side, in the center of the celebration, laughing and talking with people, but she was thinking of later on. Did Jack even guess, she wondered, how much she wanted him? Did he have any idea how happy it made her to finally be able to come to him and lie with him and make love with him? She had no idea where they would be going tonight. She had left that detail to him and he had been doggedly secretive as to their destination.

At one point, Winston came and whispered something in Jack's ear. He nodded, and Winston went away again.

She gave Jack an inquisitive look, which he pointedly ignored, his expression clearly of the ask-me-no-questions-and-I'll-tell-you-no-lies ilk.

She looked around, because Dolly was approaching, holding out her hands to make them both stand up. "It's time for you to go start your life together," she said. She hugged them both and kissed Meg on the cheek.

"Walk in Beauty," she said in Navajo.

Meg managed a brief farewell to Sloan, then to Lucas, who was still clearly trying to behave. And she hugged Will. "Take care of my horse," she whispered to him. Patrick was nowhere around.

And then Jack was pulling her along with him, finally picking her up and carrying her—much to the delight of the crowd—when she stopped to talk to yet another well-wisher. He didn't stop until they'd reached his pickup truck. Someone had already started it and had it running. The inside was warm and smelled of a bag of fresh oranges someone had given them. Jack covered her with a blanket, anyway—a new striped one that had come from Winston.

Jack drove out of the yard carefully, mindful of the other vehicles and the rough ground, but Meg still had to hold on to his arm as they bounced along. When they reached the road, she leaned out the window, waving to the people who still followed after them.

She leaned back and closed her eyes, completely content.

"You're too far away," Jack said, and she slid closer, resting her head on his shoulder.

"Thank you, Jack." she said, because the marriage ceremony had been exactly what she'd always wanted. "It was perfect." She could feel him grin in the dark cab.

"My pleasure, ma'am," he answered.

"Where are we going?"

"You'll see."

"*When* will I see?"

"When we get there. No more questions. You'll ruin the surprise."

She didn't ask anything else, but she nearly ruined the surprise anyway, because she fell soundly asleep, only waking because the truck abruptly changed speed and began to bounce over rough ground again.

"Where is this?" she murmured, trying to sit up. She had no idea where they were.

"It's not far now," he said.

"How long was I asleep?"

"A long time. See up there? We're here."

She caught a glimpse of a cabin in the headlights as he turned off the rutted road. And a lot of juniper and piñon trees.

"It's Captain Becenti's summer place," he said.

"Oh, yes. I was up here once with Lucas and Sloan when I was a little girl. Whatever made you think of it?"

"Becenti and his wife offered to let us come here as a wedding present. It was kind of strange, really."

"Why?"

"He said his wife thought it was a special place, especially for newlyweds. She's been sick a long time, and I got the feeling that he really wanted us to take him up on it to please her. So I did."

"You know what I remember? The view. If you look out that way, you can see *Tsoodzil*—Turquoise Mountain. It's beautiful in the mornings."

He parked the truck at the side of the cabin and turned off the lights.

"Wait here. I'm going to go in first, make sure everything's all right—no creatures or anything." He opened the door to get out, but then he hesitated. "Are you okay with this place?" he asked.

"Yes!" she assured him. "Mrs. Becenti is right. It is special. You're going to love it here."

"I'd love being anywhere you are, Meg."

He looked at her for a long moment, then squeezed her fingers and got out. He was gone for a while. She could see a light flickering inside the cabin, and then another and another. He must be lighting candles, she thought. He finally came back, but this time to get a large cardboard box, a duffel bag and her suitcase from the back of the truck, and his jacket from the cab.

"You know I could carry something," she offered.

"Nope. Hand me the oranges."

She smiled and handed him the mesh bag.

"Be back in a minute," he said, staggering off with his load.

This time, when he returned, he came to her side of the truck and opened the door.

"Now," he said, pulling her by the hand and setting her gently on the ground. He put the blanket around her shoulders. "It's cold out here."

She looked up at the starry sky. "So beautiful," she said. "Do you remember when we were children and we used to do this? Stand outside in the cold and look at the stars?"

"I remember," he said. "Meggie..."

She turned to him, standing close, her hand resting on his shirt front. But he didn't say whatever he had on his mind.

"It's cold out here," he said again. "Let's go inside."

He hurried her along, his arm around her shoulders. When they reached the front door, he surprised her by lifting her and carrying her over the threshold. "I always wanted to do this," he said. "Saw it in a movie one time in Gallup—at a very impressionable age."

He set her down in the middle of the floor, and she was completely surrounded by flickering candlelight. It was so intimate and romantic—he must have bought every candle in the store—and practical, given the lack of electricity.

But she didn't need modern conveniences. She only needed him.

He went immediately to check the stove, adding another piece of wood to the fire. The room was still cold and smelled of wood smoke and candle wax. She stood wrapped in her blanket.

"This is really nice," she said. "Even better than I remember." She looked up at the wagon wheel that had been suspended overhead. It had candles around the rim, all of them lit.

He glanced at her, giving her a slight smile. And both of them tried not to notice the double bed that totally dominated the room. It had been freshly made with crisp white sheets and brightly colored Navajo-patterned blankets. Someone had turned it down, so that it looked inviting and ready.

She felt so awkward suddenly.

"Well," she said brightly. "Let's see what we have in here."

The large box he'd brought inside was full of groceries, and she immediately began to empty them out on the table—cans of peaches and pork and beans, Rainbo bread, coffee, condensed milk, sugar, potatoes, cornmeal.

"Meggie," Jack said from behind her. He took the bag of cornmeal out of her hand and set it on the table, then he turned her toward him. She looked up at him, trying to appear more relaxed than she felt.

"Meggie, it's okay," he said. He rested his hands on her shoulders. "It's enough for me just to be with you. We don't have to . . . do anything if you don't—"

She reached up and put her fingertips against his lips, then her mouth where her fingers had been—softly, but with great purpose, so he would know her intent. She kissed him again, and then again, her arms sliding around him.

"Jackie," she whispered, and she gently nuzzled his smooth cheek, savoring the scent of his skin. When she touched the corner of his mouth with the tip of her tongue, his arms tightened around her and he moaned softly. She reached behind her to grasp his hand and bring it around to rest firmly on her belly. She was not going to pretend that her child didn't exist. She was not going to be ashamed of the changes in her body.

"I want to belong to you, Jack," she said, looking into his eyes. "I want *us* to belong to you."

She stepped away from him and went to sit on the side of that all-too-prominent bed. He came to her without hesitation, kneeling down in front of her, his arms sliding around her waist. He held her for a moment, his face pressed against her breasts, and then he leaned back to look at her. His eyes were dark with desire.

She reached up to unfasten the squash-blossom necklace and handed it to him. As he put it aside, she pulled the handkerchief from her sleeve and began to unbutton the row of buttons at her wrist. But he moved her hand away and undid them for her. She sat quietly, watching his face, offering him her other sleeve when he'd finished.

"What are you thinking about?" she asked, because he was so intent.

He looked up and smiled. "Christmas at the boarding school. Unwrapping the present the teachers left for us under the Christmas tree. It was underwear—*always* underwear. But it was the only time that place was ever the least bit interesting. I can't complain, though. Boarding school is the reason I didn't have any problem getting used to the marines."

She gave a soft laugh and leaned her forehead against his for a moment, then she lifted her chin so he could reach the row of covered buttons at her throat. He undid them slowly, taking his time, making his one present last.

He took the blouse from her, folding it and laying it aside with such care that it made her eyes fill with tears.

"You wore this for me?" he asked about the camisole she had on underneath. He touched the top edge of lace and ribbons, dragged the backs of his fingers across the soft swell of her breasts.

"Yes."

"I like it," he said. "Unwrapping your underwear is a *lot* more interesting than unwrapping mine."

They laughed together like naughty children, foreheads touching again.

But the laughter faded. They weren't children, and they had waited far too long.

"Meggie," he whispered, his mouth finding hers. "Meggie."

Her lips parted under his. She had to hold on to him to keep from falling.

"Jack, am I..."

"What?" he asked, looking at her, his breath ragged. "What?"

"Ugly now?" she said, the words barely audible.

"Meggie, no!" he said, cupping her face in his hands. He kissed her, hard. "You take my breath away," he said urgently. "You're beautiful. I want you so *bad....*"

She gave a wavering sigh, eyes closed, her heart aching with regret. This should have happened when she was eighteen. *He* should have been her first lover.

No, don't think about that.

She remained still, letting him undo the fastenings down the front of the camisole, letting him look and touch as he pleased, savoring the feel of his warm hands moving over body. Her head dropped back and her breath caught as he gently suckled first one breast and then the other.

She opened her eyes, reaching for him, not wanting him to stop. But he moved to take off her boots, his fingers caressing the backs of her knees and the calves of her legs as he pulled them free and set them aside. He took away her white stockings and her muslin skirt and her petticoat, still using great care with each article as he laid them in a neat pile.

She had only her camisole and panties left. His hands moved to caress her breasts again. She closed her eyes. His touch was more demanding now. His thumb stroked the tight bud of her nipple as his mouth found hers. She couldn't sit still.

"Jackie," she whispered, nearly overcome by the sudden wave of desire she felt. "Jackie ... *shitah hoditlid....*"

My body, it trembles....

He drew her forward so that he was kneeling between her thighs. She clung to him, holding on for dear life. She felt no awkwardness, no embarrassment now. His body strained against hers; she could feel his hardness, feel him trembling as she was. She locked her legs around him. They had waited so long for this.

So long!

His mouth moved hungrily over hers. She wanted to touch him as he was touching her. She pulled at his shirt until he broke away long enough to drag it over his head and throw it off to the side. She ran her hands over his smooth hard chest and arms, the sensation both remembered and new. He had been a boy when she'd last done this, and they had always stopped too soon, both of them knowing they were standing on the edge of an abyss that held nothing but unhappy consequences. Now he was a man. Now he was *her* man.

When he stood to take off his jeans, she moved to the middle of the bed, pulling the sheet and blankets farther down to make a place for them. She waited, on her knees. He came to her naked and aroused and unashamed, and he stripped away the last of her clothing, lying down with her, rolling her on top of him and then onto her back, his hands and his mouth gentle and then rough and then gentle again.

She looked into his eyes. The sadness was still there, just as it had been the first time she ever saw him, just as it had always been.

Let me take it away, she thought, holding him, kissing him. *I love you so!*

He was in a hurry now, and she gloried in his passion, whimpered aloud when he finally touched her between her thighs.

She was ready for him—more than ready. Her body arched against his hand. She reached to bring him to her, inside her.

At last!

"My wife," he whispered as he entered her. "Meggie..."

She strained against him, wanting more. "Always," she said against his ear. "I love you so. I need this... with you. I need to have you... love me like this...."

He thrust deeper, began to move, urgent and needy. The pleasure rose in her. She clung to him. She was both aware and not aware. She knew he spoke to her, but she didn't hear the words. She didn't have to.

The pleasure rose in her, higher and higher, until it finally peaked and shattered and she cried out his name.

My wife.

Jack lay with his eyes closed, tired and sated, but he wasn't asleep. He could hear the wind outside the cabin—a lonesome, jealous *chindi* sound. The wood popped in the stove and the candles burned low.

"I was going to seduce you," Meg said quietly, and he opened his eyes, surprised to find her sitting up, cross-legged, beside him. "The night you left. I was going to seduce you."

He smiled, not quite believing her.

"It's true," she said. "Lucas and Will had gone camping—something to do with his Navajo instruction. And Patrick was off somewhere. Sloan had gone to some kind of medical workshop in Flagstaff. There was nobody in the house that night but me."

"Meggie—"

"And I was going to take you to bed."

He reached for her, not knowing what to say. She gave a soft sigh and stretched out beside him, her head on his shoulder.

"You wouldn't have had to do much seducing," he said after a time.

She turned her head to look at him. "You were the one who always stopped."

"I loved you," he said simply.

"Then why didn't you answer my letters?"

He didn't say anything.

"Did you even open them?"

"Yes, I opened them. I read them all the time. I still have them, Meg."

He turned his head to look at her. She was smiling, clearly pleased.

But the smile slid away.

"Was tonight...okay?" she asked. "Were you disappointed?"

"Disappointed? Meggie, how could you even think that?"

"It's like you said. Marrying this way, now, isn't exactly what either of us planned."

"Are you telling me you're sorry you did it?"

"No! I'm not sorry. We've both changed, that's all. I just think maybe you got the worst end of the deal."

"Don't," he said, making her look at him. "Don't ever say that again. You're my wife. *Shil hózhó,* Meg—I am happy." He stroked her face and kissed her eyes. "I love you, Meggie," he whispered. "I love you."

He stopped and leaned back to look at her, then suddenly smiled. "Seduce me now," he said.

Chapter Eleven

"Meggie," Jack whispered in her ear. "Meggie, someone's here."

She stirred in his arms but didn't waken, murmuring something as she reached up to touch his face and settle deeper into the pillow. He looked down at her, marvelling still that the marriage had actually taken place. He couldn't believe the happiness he felt. The six days they'd been here in Becenti's cabin had been more wonderful than he could ever have imagined. Even the simplest of things filled him with joy—just talking and laughing with her, or watching the sun come up, cooking a meal, bathing together, sleeping together.

Making love.

He would never get enough of that. Never.

Meggie.

He kissed her gently. He could still hear their visitor walking around outside. He got up quietly, deciding to let her sleep. It was barely daylight, and they'd done a lot of exploring yesterday.

A lot of exploring.

He found his jeans and a T-shirt and pulled them on. He had no idea who it could be. Someone Navajo, he thought, because they didn't immediately come pounding on the door. He wouldn't be surprised to find Lucas outside, here to present him with some kind of marriage annulment. Or Patrick, checking to see if he'd ruined Meg's life yet.

He got his boots on and opened the door, but he didn't see anyone. It was cold out. He stood for a moment looking at Tsoodzil in all its glory, feeling a certain reverence in spite of his lack of traditionalism. Then he stepped back inside to get his jacket. When he came out again, the visitor, a Navajo about his own age, stood at the edge of the porch.

"*Yá'át'ééh*," the visitor said. He was smiling, but he sounded official, anyway. "Sorry to bother you. I know you're on your honeymoon. Mary Skeets sent me."

"Mary Skeets?"

"Well, you know Mary. If she thinks something needs doing, it gets done, one way or the other."

"I don't understand."

"No, I don't guess you do. I'm Billy Yazzie. I'm with the tribal police. I was up here taking some vacation days with my grandfather—his place is not too far from here. Anyway, one minute I'm chopping wood and the next minute I'm getting a message from Mary that's been patched through fifty different radios. She said I was to tell you first that the Alcohol, Tobacco and Firearms guys have been watching somebody named Eddie Nez and his bootlegging activity for a long time."

"And?"

"And your wife's brother got picked up in a raid. She said to tell you the kid, William, is in jail, and he says he won't talk to anybody but you."

"Me?"

"That's what she said."

"Did she say *why* he wants to talk to me?"

"No."

"Man, Lucas Singer is just going to love this."

"Oh, yeah," Billy Yazzie said.

"Are the Feds going to press charges—did she say?"

"Well, they flat caught him 'hauling water.' He was driving a pickup load of the stuff, and if he's not talking, he's not denying anything."

"Damn hard-headed little sonofa— I *told* him to quit hanging around Eddie Nez!"

"The Feds might cut him some slack if Becenti asked them to. But if you know Becenti at all . . ."

"I know Becenti," Jack said. "There is no way he'd ask for special treatment. Thanks for coming up here, man."

"No problem." The man abruptly smiled. "You know you and Lucas's niece had one of the best weddings anyone's had around here in a long time."

"You were there?"

"No, I had to work. Mary Skeets told me about it. She said the word sure got out. The day before the wedding, some tourists came by the law-enforcement building trying to find out how to get there. Mary didn't tell them, though. She said neither one of them looked like they knew how to behave. Hey, I'm sorry I messed up your honeymoon."

"You're not half as sorry as I am," Jack assured him.

He went back inside, leaving Billy Yazzie standing. He should have invited him inside for coffee, offered him breakfast, but he couldn't very well do that with Meg still asleep.

But Meg wasn't asleep. She was up and half-dressed and worried.

"What did Billy Yazzie want?" she asked immediately. "Is something wrong?"

Jack sat down on the bed beside her, not surprised that she would know and recognize a tribal policeman even in his homesteading clothes. "Yeah. Will's been arrested for bootlegging."

"Bootlegging? There must be some kind of mistake!"

"I doubt it," he said, and she looked at him sharply.

"Why?"

"Because he's been hanging around with Eddie Nez and Eddie Nez is a bootlegger. We're going to have to go back, I guess. The word is he doesn't want to talk to anybody but me."

"Oh, Lord, Lucas is going to have a fit."

He sighed instead of commenting.

She suddenly smiled and kissed his cheek. "My poor husband," she said.

He accepted her sympathy and pushed for a little more, tipping her backward on the bed. But she had other things on her mind besides kissing, and after a pleasurable moment or two, he sat up, pulling her up with him, both of them knowing without a doubt that the honeymoon was over.

They packed up quickly and took extra pains to leave the place the way they'd found it. They arrived in Window Rock well before noon. Jack drove straight to the law-enforcement building.

"I want to talk to him alone, Meg," he said as they walked across the parking lot. "I'm going to call your brother a lot of names I'd just as soon you didn't hear."

She sighed heavily. "I feel like calling him a few names myself. Why would he do such a thing? He's never been in trouble before. His grades are good in school. He's got a lot of friends and family who care about him."

"I don't know, Meggie. Money, maybe. Sometimes—"

"Jack!" Mary Skeets called as they walked through the front door. "Lucas wants to see you—he said as soon as you got here," she added, apparently guessing he was about to decline. "Actually, he said *if* you got here," she immediately revised.

Nice going, Mary, he thought. She was really good at her job. The door hadn't even shut and she'd already insulted him into doing exactly what he was supposed to do.

"Where is Lucas?" he asked.

"I'm waiting for you," Lucas said from behind him. "I want to talk to you in my office."

"Right here is fine," Jack said. He wasn't a kid anymore and his days of being hauled off to the woodshed were long past.

Lucas glanced in Meg's direction. "All right. What do you know about this bootlegging business?"

Jack looked at him a long moment before he answered. He could feel Meg's worry and Mary Skeet's intense curiosity. "I knew Will was hanging around Eddie Nez," he said evenly.

"And you didn't bother to say anything to me or Sloan?"

"No," Jack said, "I didn't. I said something to Will. Several times."

"And a lot of good *that* did, Begaye."

Jack exhaled sharply, working hard to keep his temper. Whatever the appeal was regarding Eddie Nez, it hadn't been his business to talk Will out of it or to report it to Lucas. The only reason he'd said anything to the boy at all was because he cared about Meg.

"Are you going to let me see him or not?" Jack asked abruptly.

"I want to know exactly why he thinks he's got to talk to *you* about this."

"I don't know, Lucas! And I'm not going to find out standing here. Let me see the kid."

Lucas still hesitated. "All right," he said finally. "But I want to know what he says. I mean it, Jack."

Jack made no comment. He turned to Meg instead. "Meggie—"

"I want to come with you," she said.

"It would be better if you didn't. Having you or any of the family see him right now is just going to make him feel more ashamed. I think that's why he's asking for me. I'm the stranger, the outsider, and I've been in trouble before. I can't make him feel any worse."

"I just want him to know I care what happens to him."

"He already knows that. But I'll tell him again. Okay?"

She was biting her lower lip. "Okay," she said finally.

"For better or worse," he said, taking her hand.

"We didn't say that at the ceremony," she answered.

"I did," he said, and she abruptly smiled. It was like the sun coming out.

"I feel like a little kid again," she said. "Every time we had a family crisis, I got stuck with Mary Skeets."

"Yeah, well, she's going to be dying to get her hands on you today. She's going to want to know if the honeymoon was as spectacular as the wedding."

"Don't worry," she whispered. "Your reputation is safe with me."

He laughed and gave her a brief hug, then followed Lucas down the hall to a locked door and then to a small side room.

"I'll have him sent in. You better know what you're doing," Lucas said.

"I'm not going to *do* anything, Lucas. If he really wants to talk, I'll listen. If he doesn't, he's all yours."

Jack sat on the edge of the table and waited for what seemed a long time. Finally, the door abruptly opened and Will walked in, doing his best to seem cocky and sure of himself. It was a great act, Jack thought, but he wasn't fooled. Will stood for a moment, listening to the door being locked behind him, then he pulled out the only chair and sat down on the other side of the table.

"Well?" Jack said without prelude.

"It's not what you think," Will said.

"What I *think* is that you were arrested for driving a truck full of bootleg whiskey," Jack answered. "What I *think* is that your little 'hauling water' stunt has got the whole family in an uproar. What the hell is wrong with you? You're acting like you've got no relatives," he said, laying out one of the ultimate insults among the Navajo. "Why?"

"What do you care?" Will said, apparently deciding on "hostile" as opposed to "guilty." "You don't care about me, so don't—!"

"Knock it off!" Jack interrupted. "I don't want to hear any of your poor-little-misunderstood-half-white-boy crap. I want to know what you're doing in this mess so I can do something to help you get out of it. Now if you don't want to tell me, I'll be leaving, so make up your mind. You've had more going for you than a lot of kids your age—white or otherwise. This is where you straighten up and act like you care about your family. Meg's out there waiting. She's all upset and worried. She cares about you, damn it! And what about Sloan and Lucas?"

"They're not my whole family."

"What are you talking about?"

"I've got more family than just them. I've got a mother."

"You mean Margaret Madman?"

"Yeah."

"Don't tell me you took up bootlegging for *her!*"

"She's my mother!"

"Oh, yeah? Who do you think you're talking to here? I've been in on Margaret Madman's mothering skills from the get-go. You can *call* her your mother if you want to, but we both know better than that."

Will didn't say anything else.

"So were you bootlegging for her?" Jack asked again.

"Not—exactly."

"Well, what exactly? Has she come back to the reservation?"

"Yeah."

"You've seen her? Talked to her?"

"Yeah."

"And she wanted you to help Eddie," Jack said.

"No. No, she didn't ask me to do nothing. She didn't—" He broke off and gave a heavy sigh.

"Didn't what?" Jack asked.

Will looked at him. "She didn't act like she even knew who I was, man."

"So you wanted to get her attention."

"No! Not the way you think. I just wanted her to know I wasn't ashamed of being half-Navajo. I wanted her to be proud of me. I wanted her to be . . . glad I was her son."

The last part was barely audible.

Jack sat there. Somehow he was just not getting it. Will was a smart kid. Surely he didn't think that his mother, the ex-con, would be proud of him if he was an ex-con, too?

"How were you going to make her proud?"

Will stared at the floor.

"Are you planning to answer me sometime soon or am I leaving?" Jack said.

"I was learning to be a *hataalii,* all right?"

Jack frowned. This was the absolute last thing he'd expected. He had to think about it for a moment.

This doesn't make any sense, he decided, only to immediately change his mind. It did make sense on some level. Will wanted to learn the ancient healing and harmony ceremonies so that his Navajo mother would be able to say to all her friends "my son, the *hataalii.*"

"It takes years to do that," he said.

"I've got years. Or I did," Will answered.

"How were you planning to learn?"

"Eddie Nez was teaching me."

"Eddie Nez?"

"He used to be a singer. He did the Red Ant Way and the Blessing Way and the Enemy Way. He did them for a lot of people. Everybody wanted him because the people he did them for got well."

"Eddie Nez?" Jack said again.

Will looked up at him. "Yeah."

"How come I never knew that?"

"He's been a drunk a long time, I guess. People quit coming when he wouldn't stay sober and they couldn't trust him to get the sand paintings and the chants right. The Holy People don't like mistakes. Bad things happen."

"But he's been staying sober enough to teach you."

"Yeah."

"And you trust him to get it right?"

"Yes, I trust him!"

"Are you any good at it?"

"I'm damned good," Will said with a flash of pride Jack had to admire. "Everybody says so. I can remember everything I see in the sand paintings. I never leave stuff out."

"So how did you talk Eddie into teaching you?"

The boy didn't answer him.

"What were you doing, driving him around to make his deliveries so he'd teach you the ceremonies?"

"Yeah," Will said, the relief he felt that someone finally understood the situation clearly visible on his face.

"You should have told Lucas you wanted to be a *hataalii.* You just made it worse by not telling him."

"I know that," he said.

"Couldn't you find somebody besides Eddie Nez to teach you?" Jack asked. "I don't think people are exactly standing in line to learn this stuff anymore."

"I didn't want anyone else," Will said. "I wanted him to do it."

Because he used to live with your mother, Jack thought, no longer surprised that Lucas hadn't been advised of this project. The kid wanted some tie to his actual Navajo clan, however tenuous.

"Eddie is going to tell Lucas he was teaching you the chants and you weren't 'exactly' in the bootlegging, isn't he?"

"I don't know where he is."

"You mean the Feds took him someplace else?"

"I mean they didn't catch him."

"He left you holding the whiskey?" Jack said incredulously.

Will looked at the floor again. "Is Meggie very upset?" he asked after a moment.

"I told you she was, Will," Jack said. "I haven't seen Sloan, but I doubt she's any better. And Lucas is looking for something to kill."

"What's going to happen, Jack?" Will asked, his voice trembling just enough to give him away. The boy was scared to death.

"I don't know," Jack said. "I'll try to find out."

"Hey," Will said when Jack thumped on the door for somebody to come unlock it. "Thanks, man."

"I haven't done anything yet," Jack said. "And I still want to kick your butt from here to Albuquerque. I was on my honeymoon, damn it. So don't thank me."

Meg was waiting for him when he came out. "How is he?" she asked, hurrying forward.

"He's scared. And he's done a really stupid thing for a really not-so-stupid reason." He told her about Will's quest to become a *hataalii*. "Did you know anything about that?" he asked.

"I knew he was having trouble deciding where he belonged."

He looked at her for a moment, noting once again how much he liked doing just that, and how much he loved her and how good it felt to belong to her, even if it meant coming here. "Do you know where Lucas went?" he asked.

"He's talking to the ATF agents. He and Becenti."

"Great," Jack said, meaning anything but that. "In Becenti's office?"

"Yes. Are you going in there?"

"I've got to make my official report," he said. "I don't want Lucas any more upset than he already is. Did any of them look like they spoke Navajo?"

"Only Lucas and Becenti," she said, and he smiled.

"Be back in a minute."

When he returned, Meg was no longer in the hallway. He walked into the reception area. She wasn't there, either.

"Mary, have you seen Meg?" he asked.

"Yes, she went outside."

"Thanks, Mary," he said, walking quickly out the door. He didn't see her at first, because he expected her to be waiting in the truck. She wasn't. She was just standing on the far side of the parking area. And she didn't hear him when he walked up.

"Meggie?" he said, making her jump. "Are you okay?"

"Fine," she assured him. She smiled, but her eyes didn't quite meet his. "I just wanted some fresh air. I think I stood too long. It makes me light-headed sometimes."

"Then what are you doing still standing?"

"You'll notice there are no chairs out here," she said, making a sweeping gesture with one hand and trying to make light of the situation.

"Well, let's go where there are some. Are you ready to check out the mission house?"

"I still want to see Will," she said.

"Will is going to be otherwise engaged for a while. He's got people standing in line to talk to him, and Lucas says there's no point in your waiting. Come on, Mrs. Begaye. Let me take you home." He put his arms around her and she rested her head on his shoulder.

"Jack," she said, leaning back to look at him.

"What, Meggie?" he said, tucking a loose strand of her hair behind her ear. Red. He liked it.

She seemed about to say something, but she didn't. She rested her head on his shoulder again instead.

"Are you sure you're okay?"

"I'm sure."

"Then I think we'd better go before Mary Skeets strains something trying to see what we're doing out here," he teased.

She smiled again, but then the smile abruptly faded.

"What's wrong?" he asked, worried that she might be feeling light-headed again.

"Nothing," she assured him. "Let's go."

The mission house was spotless and ready for them—Winston's doing, Jack suspected. It was small and there was very little in the way of furniture—a rocking chair, four straight chairs and a kitchen table, one easy chair, and a bed and a chest of drawers. His and Meg's clothes had already been moved here, and two belated wedding gifts sat on the kitchen table.

"I'll make a deal with you," he said when he was about to light a fire in the wood stove. "You take a nap and I'll go get some groceries."

"And then what?"

"And then we'll have supper and open wedding presents." He smiled. "Then we'll do whatever old married couples do."

"Don't light the fire yet," she said. "I'd rather go with you."

"I've got to check on Winston and the shelter, too."

"Fine," she said.

"Are you sure you wouldn't rather stay here?" he asked.

"I'd rather buy groceries, Jack," she said. "If I stay here, I'm just going to worry about Will."

"Okay," he said, pulling her to her feet. As much as he loved Meg—or perhaps because he did—he still wanted to kick Will Baron's butt. He had no doubt, however, that Becenti and Lucas both would do the best they could to get him out of this mess. The kid had had a good reason for doing what he did. It didn't make him any less guilty, but at least he was a first-time offender, and that should count for something.

The Begaye cupboard was essentially bare; they needed everything. But the store was crowded and it took a long time to get through the checkout line.

"I forgot the oranges," he said as they wheeled the grocery cart across the parking lot.

"We can get some later," she said, unlocking the truck door.

He gave her an arch look, and she laughed. She had been craving oranges; the bag they'd been given at their wedding was gone, and he'd heard enough about the no-orange situation today to know that he wasn't about to leave here without a new supply.

"Who is it who keeps saying, 'Jack, we have to buy oranges'?"

"That would be me," she confessed.

"Exactly," he said.

"Maybe I should just wait here in the truck while you go get some?" she suggested, smiling still.

"Yes, maybe you should," he agreed, putting her and the grocery bags inside and giving her a quick kiss. He chuckled to himself as he shoved the cart into the designated area and walked back across the parking lot. He was happy to go get her oranges—more than happy. Oranges he could afford—

"Are you Jack Begaye?"

He looked around at the man who'd asked the question—a white man in a suit and tie. Alcohol, Tobacco and Firearms was Jack's first thought, but he had left the two ATF agents in Becenti's office, and this man wasn't one of them. In light of the fact that Will hadn't wanted to talk to anybody but good old Jack Begaye, he couldn't think of any other government agency that might be making inquiries.

"Who wants to know?" he asked.

"My wife and I would like very much to talk to you. Now, if it's convenient."

He glanced in the direction the man indicated. A woman stood not far away, waiting beside a white car that was parked near the street.

"I'm in a hurry," Jack said, because he didn't like being accosted by strangers in a parking lot and because he didn't like this man's air of authority. He must be with some agency, because he had that governmental "we want it, therefore you will do it" attitude. *Convenient* be damned, regardless of how easily he tossed the word around or the fact that he had his wife with him.

Jack stepped past him and walked on toward the store entrance.

"It's about Meg Baron," the man called after him.

Jack turned to look at him. "What about Meg?"

"We really do need to talk to you," the man said, and he walked in the direction of the white car, leaving Jack no alternative except to follow.

"What about Meg?" he said again.

"My name is Ronald Pacer," the man said. "This is my wife, Carolyn."

Jack glanced at the woman, who nodded politely, as if they were at a country-club tea and not a grocery-store parking lot.

"Would you like to get in out of the wind?" she asked, still polite, her hand on the car door.

"No, I would like to know what you want," he said just as politely.

"Very well," the woman said, obviously taking over the conversation. "We understand that Meg Baron has a certain regard for you—"

"A certain regard," Jack repeated, not sure he'd heard right. He looked over his shoulder toward his truck, wondering if Meg could see him from there.

"—And we're here to ask your help." She went on as if he hadn't interrupted. Jack kept looking at her. The man didn't seem familiar, but she did. He just couldn't remember from where.

"We understand that you may even be the reason she came back to the reservation."

"Window Rock is her home," Jack said. "I don't see what business it is of—"

"Yes. Her home. One's roots can be very important, especially at a time like this." She stopped, apparently giving him the opportunity to make some comment now. But he chose not to make one. He wanted the bottom line, and remaining silent seemed the best way to get to it. He kept staring at her, trying to remember where he'd seen her before.

"As I said, we are here to ask for your help," she continued. "You see, we are very concerned about Meg's welfare—" She glanced at her husband "—and we would like your help in trying to persuade her to come to California. We know that a woman in her situation can feel very desperate and that she might find it difficult to make wise decisions. But for the child's sake, we think she needs to be with us until the baby is born. We'll see to it that she has the very best doctors. We are prepared to make it well worth your while if—"

Jack began to walk away, incredulous and completely at a loss for words.

"Do something, Ronald," the woman said to her husband, and Jack suddenly turned to face them.

"Who *are* you people?"

"I thought you understood, Mr. Begaye. John Thomas Pacer was my son. Meg Baron is having our grandchild. Surely she must have at least mentioned him to you."

Jack said nothing. He wasn't about to try to explain Navajo metaphysics and the taboo against speaking of the dead to these people, and what he knew or didn't know about their son was none of their business.

"We want to make sure Meg has everything she needs. Our son can't see that his child is provided for, so we must do it in his stead. Prenatal care is so important, and this place, you must understand, is somewhat . . . primitive by our standards. Meg should have the best of care and she'll get that in California with us. We're hoping you can persuade her to consider the baby if not herself."

"Look," Jack said. "My wife is staying here with me. I'll take care of her *and* the baby."

The woman paled visibly. "Your wife?" She exchanged looks with her husband.

"Carolyn—" the man began, but she ignored him.

"Well, Mr. Begaye." She took a deep breath. "I must say you've taken me completely by surprise. You and Meg are . . . married then. I really didn't expect . . ." She took another deep breath. "So be it. I have only one thing to say to you now. And that is I will never, *ever*, allow *you* to raise my grandchild. If I have to, I'll take Meg to court. And I can promise you, no judge in this country would let an innocent child be raised by somebody like you."

"Somebody like me?" Jack said. Carolyn Pacer hadn't meant "innocent child." She'd meant "innocent *white* child." He heard the word as plainly as if she'd actually said it. Meggie hadn't exaggerated in her brief description of this woman.

"Yes, Mr. Begaye. And I say that with complete justification. We know all about you. Oh, I can understand your appeal—some women can't resist a man like you. Your type is a favorite young girl's fantasy—the one about taming a wild and primitive male, the more reckless and undependable and dangerous he is, the better. Lowering yourself to *his* level—at least until you get tired of him. We used to call it slumming."

"I've had enough of this," Jack said, turning to go.

"I talked to Meg this afternoon. Did you know that, Mr. Begaye? No, I can see you didn't. I ran into her at the law-enforcement building. We talked about the baby and about her finishing her graduate degree. We talked about her job plans. We even talked about John Thomas. What we didn't talk about, though, was you. She never mentioned you—not once. And she most certainly didn't mention that she'd *married* you. Now why do you suppose that is, Mr. Begaye? If she thought you were a fit husband—a fit father for her child—wouldn't she have been happy to share her news?"

Jack walked away from her. He had to or he'd end up spending some unplanned time behind bars with Will.

"I'm going to take you to court, Mr. Begaye," she called after him, causing several passersby to turn and stare. "You can count on it."

Jack shook his head, calling up a bit of eloquence he'd only just learned from his young bootlegging brother-in-law.

"Knock yourself out, Carolyn."

Chapter Twelve

Jack was quiet on the way home. He'd bought Meg the oranges and teased her about them a little, but that was the extent of the conversation. Meg kept glancing at him. He had been talking nonstop since the day she'd agreed to marry him, as if he'd saved up all his thoughts and ideas during the years they'd been apart just to share them with her. But he wasn't talking now.

"Jack?" she said when they'd carried the groceries inside. He looked up from the bag he was emptying. "Why are you so quiet?"

"I'm not," he said, taking out a loaf of bread.

"You are."

"Meggie, have we been married long enough for this?"

"No, we haven't been married long enough, but I've known you long enough to be able to tell when you've got something on your mind. I'm a little rusty at it, but I haven't forgotten how."

He made no reply, and she looked at him until he sighed. "Is it something bad about Will?" she asked.

"Meg, give me a break here! If I knew anything about Will, I'd tell you. You know that."

She did know that, but it didn't make her feel any better.

He made a fire in the wood stove and then went to check on the shelter while she put together some ham-and-cheese sandwiches for a light supper. They ate essentially in silence and went to bed early, or rather she did. And she fell asleep alone, because Jack suddenly felt the pressing need to work on some kind of reports he'd brought back with him from the shelter, a chore that outlasted her ability to stay awake. When she woke up later, he still had not come to bed, even though the fire was out and the room dark and cold. She could hear the night wind against the house. And she could hear him rocking in the battered oak rocking chair by the window.

She slipped out of bed and walked barefoot across the cold floor. He turned his head in her direction, but he didn't say anything. She tried to see his face in the darkness. Why wasn't he saying anything?

"Jack?"

"I thought I could just let it go," he said. "I thought it didn't really matter—I could just forget about it. Meggie has her reasons, I said. And I don't have to know what they are."

She folded her arms across her chest, but it was more the coldness in his voice that made her shiver than the coldness in the room. He sounded so strange. She wanted to go to him, but she didn't. She stood and waited.

"All those years we were apart, you were worth the wait, Meg. I want you to know that."

"I don't understand."

"No, I know you don't. I don't understand, either. Not really. You see, there were a lot of times when I thought you must hate me after I left you the way I did. I had hurt you, disappointed you too much. I thought you *had* to hate me. But in all the time I've known you, there's one thing I didn't think. Not ever. I didn't think that you were ashamed of me—of who and what I am. I always knew how much you loved this place and how much you loved my people. You are more Navajo than I am, Meg."

"Jack, you're scaring me."

"When were you going to tell me about the Pacers, Meg? No—when were you going to tell *them* about *me?* The dead man—John Thomas Pacer. See? I'm not afraid to say his name. His *chindi* will never hurt me as much as you have. John Thomas's mother told me she talked to you today and you never once mentioned that you and I were married. Why is that, Meg?"

She didn't answer him.

"Did the woman lie, Meg?"

When she still didn't answer, he gave a heavy sigh. "Let's see. Maybe I can help you here. What is it exactly that makes you not want her to know about me? Is it because I'm *Diné?* Is it because I'm not as educated as you are or as white as you are? Maybe you're more like Patrick than I ever guessed."

"You know that isn't true."

"Did you know they were here in Window Rock?"

"Yes, but—"

"Then why didn't you say anything?"

"I . . . didn't want to worry you, Jack. These people are *my* problem."

"Your problem? What the hell did you marry me for, Meg? Tell me that! You love me a lot, but let's keep the dumb Indian in the dark, right?"

"No—No! I'm sorry! I should have told you."

"No, Meggie, you should have told *them.* It was hard to hear from strangers that you just couldn't bring yourself to say you'd married me."

"It wasn't like that! I'm not ashamed of you. If anyone should be ashamed of anyone in this marriage, it's you. I came to you pregnant, Jack."

"I love you, damn it! Pregnant or not!"

He abruptly got up from the chair and fumbled in the dark for his jacket.

"Where are you going?" she said, her voice trembling.

"Don't worry, Meggie. I'm not going to hit the bars or anything like that. I'm going to drive around for a while. I'm going to watch the sun come up, and then I'll be back. You see?

I'm not like I used to be. I'm not that wild, runaway kid anymore. I just need a little time to think. But before I go, I'm going to tell you what I'm feeling right now. I feel the way I did that time when you came home with your big college friends and I got arrested for disturbing the peace. All of you were laughing and talking and having a good time—and you didn't know me then, either."

"Jack, please. We can talk about this."

"Yeah, maybe. But not now. It's going to take me awhile to get everything straight. Go to bed, Meg. It's cold, and you need your rest."

He moved past her and opened the back door.

"Jackie—"

He looked back at her. "You're going to have to give me some time here, Meg."

He didn't get drunk, but he wanted to. He had plenty of experience locating bootleggers. How long would it take him to find Eddie Nez? he wondered. Eddie Nez would have a quick fix for his misery, maybe even knock off a few dollars for old times' sake. And nobody would be surprised that Jack Begaye was following in his old man's footsteps.

Nobody.

It's not what people say, it's what they do. He'd learned that piece of wisdom from Meg. And she'd learned it the hard way. No matter what she *said* now, he could only see the way she had behaved. He was good enough to be her husband in Becenti's cabin—but not in front of rich white people.

He sat in the truck on the side of the road, a thousand images crowding his mind—of riding bareback with Meggie the little girl on a horse as fast as the wind, her arms locked around his waist and her red hair flying; of making love with Meggie the woman. God, just thinking about it took his breath away. It had never been like that with anyone else. Never. He had believed her, trusted her. Even now he ached for her. How had she fooled him so completely?

He abandoned the notion of going on a quest for whiskey. The best he could do was light up a stale cigarette he found in a crumpled pack in the glove compartment. The tobacco was strong, but he smoked it anyway, coughing because he hadn't had a cigarette in a long time.

He kept thinking about one of his marine buddies, Ismael Chavez-Santana. Their paths had crossed for a time in San Diego, and they had immediately hit it off. Ismael was married, and he and his wife and three children were having to live on food stamps because his military pay didn't begin to support them all. He was always struggling to make ends meet, always on the lookout for some way to make a little extra money. Ismael was so strapped most of the time that Jack could only shake his head.

"Hey, no, man, my wife, my family—they're worth it," Ismael had assured him.

"They must be," Jack said, because he'd certainly never seen such dogged faithfulness to what seemed to him a hopeless situation. Living on the rez was better than that, and he'd told Ismael so.

"You want to know when I really knew Maria was the woman for me?" Ismael asked.

"Some other guy came around, right?"

"No, man! That don't mean nothing—getting all jealous over some other guy. See, she came to pick me up at the base one day, and she was driving on slick tires."

"Slick tires," Jack repeated, thinking he must have missed something.

"Yeah. It made me *crazy*. I kept thinking what will I do if something happens to her—her driving around on bad tires like that? So I had to marry her and get her something with a decent tread, right? That's how you can tell it's the real thing. You can't stand stuff like that. You wait till it happens to you, wild man, then you'll understand."

But Jack had understood. Only his worry hadn't been trying to get Meggie safer tires, it had been trying to get her a college education.

The sun was coming up. He stared at the eastern horizon, and he suddenly remembered where he'd seen that Pacer woman before.

Benny Joe's.

Carolyn Pacer had been standing at the edge of the dance floor, and she'd taken a picture when he was trying to follow Meg. The flash from the camera had gone off right in his face, and it seemed to him now that she must have done it deliberately. How else would she and her husband have been able to pick him out in the grocery-store parking lot? They must have been at Benny Joe's, watching. But to what end? To try to find some proof that Meg was unfit to be their grandchild's mother? And when they couldn't find anything, they switched to trying to bribe him to ''influence'' Meggie to go stay with them?

Jack sighed heavily. There was a lot about this he didn't understand. Meg had told him that the dead man hadn't known she was pregnant. So how had the Pacers come to believe with such certainty that she was carrying their grandchild? Perhaps Meg had told them, hoping to lessen their grief. If so, she had gotten a lot more than she bargained for.

They both had.

He couldn't find another cigarette. He didn't *want* another cigarette. He wanted his wife. His *wife,* damn it! He realized suddenly that Meg's death blow to his pride hadn't kept him from arriving at at least one conclusion. He needed to talk to Lillian Singer about this woman's threat of a custody suit. Lillian was the only lawyer he knew, and he trusted her to give good advice where Meg was concerned. He kept telling himself that there was nothing to worry about. What could this California woman possibly do?

Nothing.

But he kept thinking about the time when Sloan had had to give up Will. Meg had been devastated by the court's decision. Jack remembered the way she'd looked that day, standing just inside the receiving-home doors, her face deceptively calm but the tears streaming down both her cheeks. Meggie, accepting the worst, because that was what life had taught her to do, but still filled with such grief and pain. Whether she wanted him as her husband or not, he didn't want her to have to go through something like that again. This time it would be so much worse. This time the child was hers.

Ours.

No. Not ours.

What the hell am I doing in this mess?

Headlights suddenly lit the interior of the truck, another vehicle pulled in directly behind him instead of going on by. Jack could see the Navajo Tribal Police emblem in his rearview mirror.

He sighed heavily and put both hands on the steering wheel so the officer could see them. He knew the routine. Damn Coyote's sorry hide. The trickster just *had* to get in one more shot.

"Nice night," the officer said, shining his flashlight in Jack's face and around the inside of the truck.

"Yeah," Jack answered.

"What are you doing out here?"

"Nothing."

"Are you drunk?"

"No, I'm not drunk."

"Drinking?"

"No."

"Get out of the truck, please."

"Look, I'm not doing anything."

"Get out of the truck, please," the officer repeated.

Jack did as he was told. All he needed to round off a really superb day was to get hauled into the law-enforcement building in handcuffs. Maybe he and Will could share a cell.

"You think you can find your driver's license?"

"You think you can let me get it out of my wallet without shooting me?" Jack countered.

"We'll see. I'd take it slow, though."

Jack eased his wallet out of his hip pocket and removed his driver's license.

The officer looked at it. "It's dangerous sitting on the side of the road like that. I think you better move along," he said, handing the license back. "Are you the Jack Begaye who married Lucas Singer's niece?"

"No," Jack said. "I'm not."

The officer waited until Jack started the truck and drove away. There was no point in doing anything but return to Window Rock. When he arrived at the shelter, Winston was outside heating rocks for the sweat lodge. The old man had everything nearly ready, and he lifted his hand, thumb upward, to Jack in greeting.

What the hell, Jack thought, getting out of the truck and walking in that direction. He began to strip off his clothes to join the old man in his morning ritual, offering no explanations as to why he felt the need.

But Winston only nodded and turned his attention to the matter at hand, calling the Holy People to come forth, for once not prying for any information that might confirm his latest suspicions. And Winston must surely have them. Jack Begaye was a newlywed. He shouldn't be out driving around in a truck. He should be home in bed with his wife.

Jack crawled inside the lodge and sat there, watching Winston pour water until the steam began to rise around him, listening to the chant, finally joining in, until the heat and the sweating became unbearable and he burst forth from the small, womblike space, his body and mind cleansed and his heart still aching.

He dried off quickly with the scratched up earth Winston had ready. There was no point in putting off talking to Meg. He returned to the house to find her awake and clearly startled by his half-dressed state. But she didn't say anything, and neither did he. He went to finish dressing, and when he returned, she had the coffee made and most of the breakfast ready. He kept watching her move around the room, conscious of only one thought. He loved her more than he would have ever believed possible. Her welfare was the most important thing in the world to him. And if that was so, then he had better do what he'd assured the Pacers he would be doing—taking care of her and the baby.

"I want you to go to the clinic this morning," he said abruptly, startling her again, this time because he'd deigned to speak. "I think you need to be sure you're not anemic."

"I'm fine, Jack."

"I still want you to see the doctor. You were light-headed yesterday and you haven't had your iron level checked in a while."

She looked at him for a moment, but didn't argue.

The waiting line was as long as ever at the clinic, and both Sloan and Mary Ann were working. It hadn't occurred to Jack that Mary Ann might be there, or that she'd want to carry on one of her giggling conversations with him, as if he wasn't married and his wife wasn't standing a foot away.

He didn't go along when she called Meg back to the lab area. He went to use the pay phone instead, and he got through to Lillian with minimal difficulty.

"Jack!" she said, obviously surprised. "I thought you were on your honeymoon."

"I was, but now I need some legal advice. Can I come see you?"

"Well, actually, I'm coming up there. I guess you know about Will."

"Yeah. When will you be here?" He looked over his shoulder. Meg hadn't come back to the waiting area.

"This afternoon. I have to see what's going on with Will first and then we can talk."

"Could you call me at the shelter when you're done?"

"Sure. Are you going to tell me what this is about?"

"No. I'm going to tell you I don't want you to say anything to Meg—or anybody else in the family."

"Jack—"

"I'll explain when I see you, Lillian. I don't want to worry Meg until I have to."

"Well, you're worrying *me,* I can tell you that. Okay. Give me the number."

When he hung up the phone, Meg still hadn't returned.

An elderly woman came from the examination area to sit down nearby. She looked at him every time he fidgeted. "Something's wrong with her blood pressure," the old woman offered finally.

He frowned. "How do you know that, my grandmother?"

She only shrugged and pointed in the direction she'd come.

Jack waited. He kept watching the clock. Finally, he got up and wandered down the narrow hallway between the examining rooms, looking for Meg. He found Sloan instead.

"I was just coming to get you," she said. "Meg's blood pressure is up. And there's protein in her urine. She doesn't have any edema that you can see—her hands and feet aren't swollen—but the doctor wants her to lie down awhile, then we'll check her pressure again."

He took a deep breath, feeling a pang of guilt because of the confrontation they'd had last night. "Okay," he said.

"She's down there, last room on the left. Jack?" she said when he started off in that direction. "Thank you for bringing her in."

"She's my wife, Sloan," he said. "I'm going to take care of her."

"I know. I didn't mean . . . I wanted to say thank you, too, for talking to Will. I can't believe he got himself in this kind of trouble."

"It's not what you think."

"You have no idea what I think, Jack."

"You think you did something wrong. You didn't. He's trying to find a place where he belongs. It's a big problem for him, something that I can't really understand, or you, either. We know what we are. He doesn't. But I think he's going to be okay."

"I hope so. And I didn't mean that I thought you wouldn't do your best for Meg."

He nodded, trying not to show his worry. But he was worried—about the elevated blood pressure and about the parents of a dead man.

It was afternoon before Meg was finally allowed to leave. Her blood pressure had come down a few points, but it was still abnormal enough to cause concern.

"I think you and Meg should come stay with us, Jack," Sloan said. "For one thing, we've got a phone. And Meg's room has its own bathroom. It would be better for her. The doctor wants her to stay off her feet as much as possible. She'd have a lot farther to walk at the mission house and you don't even have a couch."

He agreed that the change would be better for Meg, but not just for the reasons Sloan gave. The Singer house would be less accessible to the dead man's parents. Those people could easily come looking for him at the shelter, but they wouldn't know where to find Meg.

And it would be better for both of them to be apart for a little while.

Meg didn't say anything when Sloan told her the plan. She didn't say anything on the drive to the Singer house. He insisted on carrying her inside—the resting and staying off her feet might as well start now. He took her into the bedroom and placed her carefully on the bed, wondering if this was the same one she'd meant to seduce him in. He gave a quiet sigh, trying not to look at it with such regret.

"I didn't think you'd agree to this," she said as he sat down on the side of the bed and slipped a pillow behind her back.

Their eyes met; his immediately shifted away.

"Oh, I see," she said quietly. "You only agreed that *I* should stay here. The move doesn't include you."

"You'll be closer to the doctor and the clinic," he said, still avoiding her eyes. "And Sloan will be here. It'll be better for you."

"I think you mean it'll be better for *you,*" she said. She bit down on her lower lip to keep it from trembling.

"I told you, Meg. I need some time. I've . . . got some things to do now. I'll see you later."

When he stood up, she caught his hand. He didn't pull away from her, but neither did he come closer.

"You won't see me later," she said. "Will you?" He stood looking down at her. For a moment, she thought he might cry.

"Will you?" she asked again.

"No," he said, his voice barely audible.

"Where are you going?"

He was silent.

"Tell me!"

"I don't know! I just can't be here right now. You're going to have to trust me. Can you do that?"

She looked into his eyes, trying to understand. After a moment, she let go of his hand. She had learned a long, long time ago that the only way to keep Jack Begaye was to not hold on.

It was nearly sundown when Jack arrived at the shelter. Winston was waiting by the back door.

"Did I get any phone calls?" Jack asked, wondering if he looked as out of harmony as he felt.

"You mean like from Lillian Singer?"

Jack have a sharp sigh. He could *not* get around this old marine no matter how hard he tried. "Yes. Like from Lillian Singer."

"She called a lot of times. Now she's waiting in the kitchen. She's in a big hurry, though. I said it would be better if she didn't go. If you said you'd be here, you'd be here."

Jack looked at him. "Thanks," he said cautiously.

"No problem," Winston assured him. "You going to go talk to her now?"

"Yeah."

"Good. She can help you with your trouble. Go talk."

Jack frowned and walked toward the kitchen. And he was careful to close the door behind him—not that he thought it would keep Winston from overhearing if he wanted to.

Lillian was eating a sandwich and working on some papers.

"I'm sorry I'm late," he said, sitting down at the table with her. "I got here as soon as I could."

"So why did you want to see me?" she asked, gathering up the papers and putting them back in her briefcase. "Give me the bottom line. You and Meggie aren't having trouble already, are you?"

He took a deep breath. That wasn't what he wanted to talk about. "The dead man—the father of Meg's baby—rather, his parents—want to sue Meg for custody of her child."

She looked at him a long moment. "How do you know that?"

"Last night this white man came up to me in the grocery-store parking lot. The woman was there, too. At first they just wanted me to talk Meg into coming to California and staying with them until the baby is born, because she'd get better care there. The woman said they knew that Meg had a 'certain regard' for me. That's how she put it. She said if I would help them and try to talk Meg into coming with them—for the baby's sake—they would make it worth my while."

"Not good, Jack," Lillian said. "I smell money. They must have already done some investigating if they know about you and Meg."

"Yeah, but they didn't know we were married. When I told the woman that my wife was staying here with me, I thought she was going to have a stroke. She said she would take Meg to court. She said no judge was going let somebody like *me* raise *her* grandchild."

"And you didn't tell Meg about this?"

"She knows I talked to them. She doesn't know about the custody suit."

"Why didn't you tell her?"

"First things first, I guess."

"I don't know what that means, Jack."

"It means there were...other things going on." He deferred being pinned down by telling Lillian about the problem with the pregnancy and that Meg was staying with Lucas and Sloan.

He waited for her to say something, but she began to scribble on a scratch pad. Then she sat tapping the pencil on the pad.

"So what do you think?" he asked when he couldn't stand it any longer. "These people can't do anything, can they?"

"In a perfect world, they couldn't."

"What does that mean?"

"I'm going to be blunt, Jack. It means that with you in the picture, these people have a shot at taking the baby."

"Meg and I are married, Lillian."

"Exactly. You're married and your reputation isn't exactly spotless. You've had minor scrapes with the law, and you have a documented history of being neglected and abused as a child.

Nobody has ever run away from as many social-service facilities as you have. More than likely these people can drag in fifty expert witnesses who will testify to the statistical likelihood of you perpetuating *your* bad childhood on your children—particularly on a child that isn't yours."

"I wouldn't do that!"

"They can make a judge believe you would, Jack. You want more? Aside from the fact that your skin is the wrong color, your yearly income isn't going to impress anybody, much less the court. And you and Meg are residing here on the rez, where more than half of The People live below the poverty level. And the Indian Child Welfare Act doesn't apply in this case. Meg is married to you, but the child in question isn't Navajo. That law won't prevent the baby's being given to a white couple. I'd like to reassure you, but the truth is things can get really dirty in child-custody cases. If these people have a lot of money, the outcome is anyone's guess. Personally, I'd bet on the white people with the money."

"Meg's been through this kind of thing before."

"I know. I was Sloan's lawyer in the custody suit for Will, remember? It was terrible for Meggie. This case isn't as cut-and-dried as that one was. It's just that the people with the money win, Jack. They *win.*"

"You're telling me Meg would be better off if she wasn't married to me."

"No, I'm telling you that in this kind of case you are going to be a liability. Even if you weren't married, they could probably still make a case just because she's associated herself with you."

He gave a short laugh and shook his head. "Associated herself. Is that what she did?"

"It's no secret how you and Meg have always felt about each other. They can find all kinds of people who'll say the two of you have had a long-standing relationship—one that her uncle, the respected tribal policeman, vehemently disapproved of and one that picked up again as soon as she came back here, even though she was pregnant with another man's baby. They can find people who'll say anything they want."

"Damn it, Lillian, I don't know what to do!"

"There are only two things you can do. You and Meg can go to court and take your chances. Or the two of you can make a run for it."

"Make a run for it? What kind of advice is that, for God's sake? You're supposed to be a lawyer!"

"I am a lawyer—a good one. I'm also a realist. I've done this long enough to know what can and probably will happen. And I'm telling you the truth." She held up her hands. "But maybe these people aren't fit to have the child. Maybe their health is bad. Maybe the sun won't come up tomorrow. Jack, I'm sorry. I know this isn't what you want to hear."

He looked up at her. No, it wasn't what he wanted to hear. It wasn't what he wanted to hear at all.

"Did you get this mess with Will straightened out?" he asked after a moment.

"You mean am I doing better by him than I am by you? I think it's going to be all right. I can probably get him probation and community service."

"I think here would be a good place for the community service."

"Why?"

"Because Eddie Nez has been a resident here."

"They're looking to arrest Eddie Nez, Jack."

He shrugged. "They don't have any real proof he did anything, do they? I don't think Will is going to get specific with the name. There are a lot of Eddie Nezes around. People get confused about who's who. If an old *hataalii*—whatever his name is—gets sent to live here again, it might be a good place for a kid to do his community service, especially if that kid is looking to learn the chants. And you met Winston. That old marine would work that boy's butt off. I think Will would have just enough energy left to sand paint and not much else, if you know what I mean."

"How could you get Eddie Nez to agree to it?"

"I couldn't. But if anybody can get some kind of teaching commitment out of a drunk, it's Winston Tsosie. It's just a thought. You talked to Will. You know he's serious about this stuff, and he's fixated on Eddie Nez because of Margaret Madman. Probably be better if both Will and his so-called teacher were someplace where they couldn't get in any more trouble."

Lillian looked at him thoughtfully. "If the tribal police could find the right Eddie Nez, Becenti could probably get him sent here for treatment. And, like you say, it might take awhile to get the names sorted out." She suddenly smiled. "Damn, Jack. You think like a lawyer."

He smiled in return, but the smile was short-lived. "I think like Meggie's husband," he said. "I don't want her worrying so much about Will."

Lillian stood up and re-wrapped her sandwich. "I've got to go. You let me know what you decide to do."

He sighed and got up to walk out with her. "Okay. You can send your bill to me here."

She looked at him for a moment. "Have you told me everything?"

"Everything I'm going to," he said.

"Well, you'd better tell Meggie about the lawsuit. She's going to have to know sooner or later."

"She doesn't need anything else upsetting her right now," he said, because he already knew he wasn't going to be the one to tell Meg that piece of bad news. He walked Lillian to her car, and she surprised him by giving him a brief hug before she got in. "You're a good man, Jack," she said. "I'm glad our Meggie's got you. But don't do anything stupid, okay?"

"You mean like grabbing Meggie and making a run for it?"

"That's not as unwise as it sounds."

"It is if you don't have money and your wife is pregnant and having problems with it."

She sighed. "I hope it's going to work out, Jack."

He stood outside for a long time after Lillian had gone. He'd never had much luck "hoping." He kept thinking how badly he wanted to go home. Home was wherever Meggie was, and she would be waiting for him now. He wanted to see her beautiful face. He wanted to peel her oranges. He wanted to sleep with her in that bed.

*I thought we could make it, Meggie. That's the kind of fool
I am.*

But there was more to it than his humiliation at Meg's being
unable to tell the white people that he was her husband. There
was the custody suit. Meg was strong. She and the baby would
be all right with Sloan and Lucas. He believed that. He *had* to
believe that. If he stayed with Meg, the custody suit was a certainty. If he wasn't in the picture, then at least there was a
chance for some kind of negotiated compromise with the dead
man's parents. Maybe they would be satisfied with an assur-
ance that the baby wouldn't be around somebody like him.

He heard Winston come to stand nearby.

"Do you ever have nightmares, old man?" he asked without looking around.

"Used to," Winston said. "After I come back from the war.
My uncles—they had the Enemy Way ceremony done for me so
I could get rid of all those men I killed. I don't have the bad
dreams so much now—unless I watch too much soap opera on
the TV."

In spite of his misery, Jack smiled. Only Winston would take
the troubles on a soap opera that much to heart. The old man's
love of melodrama was probably what kept him so close to Jack
Begaye.

They stood in silence, watching the orange glow of the setting sun on the horizon. And Jack had never felt so helpless in
his life.

"You been having nightmares when you sleep, Jack?" Winston asked after a time.

"No. I'm awake and living mine."

He heard Winston make a small sound of understanding.

"I want to ask you something, old man," Jack said. "I want
to ask you for a favor."

Chapter Thirteen

I'll see you later.

Meg had been looking directly into Jack's eyes when he'd said it, and they both had known the truth. He had no intention of coming back, and she didn't blame him.

The worst part was that there was no way she could justify what she had done. She was guilty as charged. However important her reasons may have seemed at the time, she had deliberately made the choice not to tell the Pacers about Jack. She kept going over and over it in her mind. She wasn't ashamed of him. How could she be? She loved him with all her heart and always had.

You're going to have to trust me.

The hard part. She hadn't trusted him enough to just go to him and ask for his help. Some part of her firmly believed that if she complicated his life too much, he would leave. Some part of her had never gotten past being a nine-year-old, abandoned little girl.

Maybe it was too late to trust him even if she could do it.

She abruptly closed her eyes. God only knew what Carolyn Pacer had said to him. Meg had encountered the woman enough times to know what her reaction would be to the news that the Pacers' grandchild would be part of a mixed marriage. Carolyn wouldn't stand for it.

Meg shifted restlessly, trying to get comfortable. She was already tired of lying in bed. She felt better, at least. But she hadn't argued with the doctor or with Sloan. If she needed to be off her feet for her baby's sake, then she would do it. If she had knowingly sacrificed her marriage to protect this child, she could certainly manage this.

"It's going to be all right," she whispered, cupping her hands protectively over her belly. "I promise."

Lucas came home—for the second time this evening—no doubt for yet another status report on the whereabouts of Jack Begaye. She could hear him in the kitchen talking to Sloan.

"I knew he'd pull something like this—damn marriage didn't even last a week," he said.

"Lucas, we don't know for sure that there's anything wrong with the marriage," Sloan said.

"Then where is he?"

"He'll be here."

"I told you it wouldn't work—didn't I tell you it wouldn't work?"

"Yes, my love, you told me. But it wasn't your decision to make."

"He doesn't know how to behave. He never has and he never will."

"Meggie loves him."

"Yes, and look at her. She's got enough to worry about. She shouldn't have to worry about where *he* is."

Meg put her hands over her ears and gave a wavering sigh. She didn't want to hear any more. Her throat ached with unshed tears. She stretched out on the bed, her face turned away from the door.

Dishes rattled; cabinet doors opened and closed. And the conversation switched to Will and his imminent release into

Lucas's custody. That at least was something to look forward to. She would be glad when Will came home.

The phone rang, and her hopes soared. Lucas answered it, but it wasn't for her. She lay there for what seemed a long time. Finally, she thought that the conversation must have ended, because she could hear him talking to Sloan again, their voices significantly lowered this time. She sat up as Lucas rapped lightly on the door. He looked much more the policeman than her uncle.

"Meg, have you heard anything from Jack?"

"No," she said quietly. "The only thing I've heard is what you said about him."

He gave a sharp sigh. "Meggie, I'm sorry. No, damn it, I'm not. I can't pretend I think this marriage of yours is ever going to be anything but trouble. But . . ."

"But what?"

"That was Dolly on the phone. She said Jack sent Winston Tsosie to ask her to come stay with you during the day while Sloan is working. She says he doesn't want you to be by yourself. And . . . she'll be here in the morning."

She didn't say anything. It wouldn't do for Lucas to know that they were both surprised.

The household settled into a kind of routine. Dolly stayed with friends in town at night, but during the day she came to the house to keep Meg company. She brought about an immense lifting of Meg's spirits, simply because she had always believed in Meg and Jack. The days grew warmer, and Meg began to spend much of her time on a redwood chaise longue out on the patio—often with Winston Tsosie, who also came every day to take Will back to the shelter with him as soon as he got home from school. Sometimes Winston arrived early and helped Dolly with whatever she was doing. Sometimes he joined Meg, and they would sit quietly in dappled sunlight, eyes closed, listening to the birds and the wind chimes. Today he arrived bearing gifts—a photograph and a basket of oranges.

"This is from me," he said, handing her the picture. It was one of Jack—his official marine photograph, part of Win-

ston's collection of fellow Navajo who had joined the Corps.
How splendid he looked in uniform, Meg thought, staring at his
handsome, determined face. This was the warrior, the Jack
Begaye she had never had the pleasure of meeting.

"And these are from...somebody else," Winston said,
whispering the last part and placing the oranges in her lap.

"Thank you, Winston," she said.

She sighed. She needed Jack, not his oranges. "Do you know
where he is, Winston?"

"You know Jack," he said, neatly evading the question.
"Who knows what he's doing? That's why I gave you the picture—so you could throw rocks at it."

She smiled in spite of herself.

"If Lucas doesn't beat me to it," she said. They both looked
around at the sound of a car pulling into the drive. Two people, a man and a woman, got out. Meg recognized them immediately and tried to get up off the chair, but Winston reached
out his hand to stop her.

"Jack said they would come here. We don't want to run from
them anymore, do we?"

Meg took a deep breath and stayed where she was, understanding Winston's daily vigilance suddenly. He was somebody else Jack had recruited to take care of her. And Winston
was right. There was no point in running away. She had let
these people cause her enough trouble.

The Pacers saw her and began walking in her direction.

"You got your turquoise?" Winston asked quietly.

She nodded.

"Don't let them take your harmony," he admonished as
Ronald Pacer stepped onto the flagstone path.

"My harmony is long gone," Meg said.

"Then we'll work on that later," he said. "Maybe let Will
help you find it with a chant. *T'áadoo baah níni'í.*"

Don't be afraid.

She took a deep breath. Ronald stood for a moment and
waited for his wife to catch up. They walked together the rest
of the way to the patio.

Meg offered no greeting. She simply waited. They were here for a reason, and there was no point in pretending that this was a social call.

As usual, Ronald Pacer deferred to his wife. Meg wondered again about the dynamics of their relationship. He was supposedly a successful, professional man, and yet he seemed to always be following his wife's lead. Was he weak or did he just not care enough one way or the other to be contrary? She had no sense that he and his wife were of like mind, and to his son, he had been a kind of shadow man, a father who was never physically or emotionally there. She thought now that John Thomas had looked a little like him—a little like them both.

Carolyn Pacer forced a smile and pointedly ignored Winston. "Meg, we came as soon as we heard. How are you? I was so afraid this would happen."

Meg still didn't say anything. Winston noisily moved a wooden chair closer to her and sat down. Neither of them offered seats to the Pacers.

"Meg, are you all right?" Carolyn asked, stepping closer.

"What is it you think has happened, Mrs. Pacer?" Meg said finally.

Carolyn glanced at her husband. "Well, we—heard—that you might not be . . . feeling well."

"Do I look like I'm not feeling well?'" Meg asked.

"Actually, you do look a little tired. But in any event, we wanted to see you. We wanted you to know that my—our— offer still stands. Particularly now."

"I don't understand."

"Well, you seem to have no place to live, really. It has to be very crowded here."

"Mr. and Mrs. Pacer, how many times do I have to say this? I don't need or want your help. I don't want to go to California with you. I don't even know you. This is where I belong. I have my family here. I have my husband."

"Your . . . husband?"

"Yes! My husband. I didn't mention him to you the other day because my personal life is none of your business."

"Meg, please. There's no use pretending with us. We know why you've moved back here. And I really think leaving is for the best—for you and the baby. Hasty marriages, well . . . you don't have to worry. We're here to help you. A change of scenery could be just what you need now."

Meg stared at them, realizing that she had been mistaken. It wasn't her problem with the pregnancy that the Pacers had heard about. It was her problem with Jack. "I think you should go now," she said quietly.

"But we need to discuss this, Meg," the woman insisted.

"There is nothing to discuss."

"I'm sure John Thomas would disagree."

"John Thomas is dead!" Meg said sharply.

Will had better find a really good chant, she thought. She could feel herself trembling. She attempted to stand up and might not have made it if Winston hadn't risen with her and subtly offered her his hand.

"I don't have to be reminded of that!" Carolyn cried as Meg began to walk toward the back door. "He was my son! And I can see now why he never mentioned you!"

Meg looked at her. *You poor woman,* she thought. She wasn't insulted. She was not in the least surprised that John Thomas hadn't mentioned her to his mother. He didn't mention to her anything that mattered.

"Goodbye," Meg said. "Please don't come here again."

"Did they say anything about trying to get custody of the baby?" Jack asked, pacing around the kitchen. It was late; everyone in the shelter was sleeping. He could hear the snoring all the way in here.

"No," Winston said.

"Is Meg all right?"

"Her harmony is gone—it left with her husband."

"I told you why I couldn't stay."

"Yes, but you don't tell *her.*"

"I'm trying to do the best thing here."

"And after you do, those people will still be going to the court and asking the judge to give them the baby. And Meggie will have to suffer through it by herself instead of with you."

Jack gave a sharp sigh. He didn't want to think about that. "You think they know Meg is having problems with the pregnancy?"

"Hard to say, Jack. They know something, but I couldn't tell what."

"How could they know?"

"They found somebody to ask. Somebody who needs the money."

And that observation, while true, didn't exactly narrow the field. Everybody here needed the money.

"Did you find out where they were staying?"

"No. I lost them. Too far back at the traffic light."

"Did you get their license-plate number?"

"I thought you got it."

"No, I never could get close enough, and I wasn't planning on having to look for them. They've been all over Window Rock for days—until now. Maybe they went back to California."

"I'm thinking they went into Gallup," Winston said. "The white woman—she's got to have the right place to stay. One of them motels that cost a lot of money, I think. We need to look for them there."

Jack stopped pacing and stared at the floor.

"So when are we going?" Winston asked.

"*We* aren't going anywhere," he said. He was so tired suddenly. He pulled out a chair and sat down.

"You said you wanted to know more about these people."

"I didn't say I wanted to lead a war party."

"This is what we can do, Jack. We check the motel parking lots in Gallup. We go just before dawn, when they'll be in the room and we can find the car—but it's close to time for breakfast, so they'll be leaving soon, see? And then I'll watch for you while you pick the lock."

"Pick the lock? Winston, I just want to find out about these people. I don't want to help their case. We're talking jail time here."

"Maybe not—if you don't get caught and you don't take nothing. Just look around and see what you can find out. You're always picking the cabinet locks around here when nobody can find the key. You told me you learned to pick locks when you were in boarding school so they couldn't keep you where you didn't want to be. You told me you were really good at undoing door locks."

"I was good at it."

"Then what's the problem?"

"You're the problem! I'm not taking you breaking and entering."

"You can just make like you're taking me dancing," Winston said. "You got to take me with you, Jack. If I'm along, then *you* don't look so damn suspicious."

"I don't want to break into their room. I want to talk to them."

"You can talk, but I don't think these people listen. And you know what Lillian said."

"Yes, *I* know what Lillian said—maybe we ought not get into how *you* do."

Winston shrugged. "She said maybe these people had bad health and couldn't get the baby. You could watch them and see if you see any sickness. Or if you could get into the room, you could look for medicine, maybe. You would know the names and what it was for."

"She also said maybe the sun wouldn't come up."

"She didn't mean that. We got to think of Meggie."

Jack gave a heavy sigh.

Trust me, Meg.

He abruptly got up from the chair.

"Where you going, Jack?"

"This crazy plan of yours is starting to make some sense to me. Hopefully, if I get a couple hours sleep, I'll get over it."

* * *

He didn't sleep long. There was too much to think about. So far he'd been able to keep up with his job at the shelter by coming in after midnight and taking care of the paperwork. He reviewed and assessed the health status of the men shortly after daybreak, before they had breakfast and left for whatever work project they'd managed to find during the day.

Then he disappeared. He slept, he ate, he worked on a worn-out Norton motorcycle—anything to keep him from losing his resolve or running into Lucas Singer. He was staying in a trailer that belonged to Winston's grandson. The grandson was a late bloomer, going off to the University of New Mexico in Albuquerque when he was twenty-nine. He would be surprised when he came home and found somebody living in his house, his motorcycle fixed.

When Jack wasn't playing mechanic, he was already doing some of what Winston had suggested. He was watching—the Singer house, Meggie's lit bedroom window, the Pacers when he could find them. He had completely lost track of their comings and goings since they had shown up to bother Meg.

I need to know about these people, he thought yet another time. Carolyn Pacer couldn't be as perfect as she tried to appear. Nobody could. And her son hadn't seemed to hold her in high regard.

Jack had gotten the motorcycle running, and that helped. There was nothing like riding fast and free down Route 12 when he couldn't sleep or when the thoughts he didn't welcome crowded in.

Meggie. Sometimes he could actually taste her, smell her soft, sweet woman smell. Sometimes he could feel her tight and hot around him. Loving him . . .

He groaned in frustration. He had to stay away from her now. He just had to learn to stand it.

Trust me, Meg!

But this morning he couldn't stand it. He left the trailer and rode the Norton into Fort Defiance, stopping at the first pay phone he could find. He took a handful of quarters out of his pocket. And he took a deep breath.

Then he dialed the telephone number and waited. Meggie answered, and the very sound of her voice was nearly his undoing. The desperation and the loneliness he'd managed to keep at bay all this time suddenly washed over him. It was all he could do not to cry.

What am I going to do, Meggie?

"Hello?" she said again. And then "Jackie?"

"Yeah, Meg," he managed to say, his voice sounding strange even to himself. "How are you doing—both of you?"

"We're . . . okay. How are you?"

"Oh, holding it in the road, I guess," he said, thinking that she would laugh if she knew he meant that literally. "Your blood pressure staying down? What does the doctor say?"

"He doesn't *say* anything. Sloan says he's getting even for having to pay back his student loan by working out here. He's going to do his entire assignment without talking."

"Maybe you need a better doctor."

"No, he knows what he's doing, he's just quiet about it. Sloan would tell me if she thought he wasn't competent."

"Meggie?" He sighed and paused. Some passing cowboy stopped to look at the motorcycle.

"A Norton 850 Commando, right?" the cowboy asked, regardless of the fact that Jack was on the phone. "Touring bike—you're restoring it, right? They're great, man. You want to sell it?"

"It's not mine," Jack said, holding his hand over the receiver. He gave the man a pointed look.

"Oh, yeah, right. Sorry—you think whoever owns it would want to sell?"

"No!"

He turned away and uncovered the phone. "Meggie?"

"I'm here, Jack."

"Meggie, I . . ."

He could feel her waiting, but he didn't know what he wanted to say. Yes, he did. He just couldn't say it.

"I love you, Jack," she said, and he closed his eyes. His hand gripped the receiver. The cowboy was still hovering.

"I . . . know," he said finally.

"Are you coming home?"

"I'm . . . it's not—"

He broke off. He'd run out of excuses. There were none left, only the truth.

The silence lengthened.

"Never mind, Jack," she said. "Forget that I asked. It's just a little . . . hard being here. I don't seem to belong anymore. Well, not your problem, right? I'm glad you called."

"Meggie—"

But she had already hung up the phone. He sat there, hanging on to the receiver, as if by doing it he could hang on to her. The cowboy still tiptoed around and coveted the beat-up Norton. Sign of the times, he thought. White men don't want the land anymore; they want motorcycles.

The sun was shining, the traffic moving. The world was going along just fine. But there was no doubt in his mind that he was going to have to do something and soon.

He abruptly dropped the receiver back into its cradle. And, even if it broke a cowboy's heart, he took the motorcycle back out on the road.

He managed to get to the shelter at the usual time. Winston was like a spider—waiting in the far corner of the web but ready to pounce at the first sign of unsuspecting prey.

But Jack wasn't unsuspecting.

"You see Meg today, old man?" he asked, deliberately twanging the silk.

"I saw her."

"How was she?"

"She was quiet, Jack. Didn't talk much. We got to take her some more oranges."

If only it was that simple. He had asked for time, and he was very afraid that he was going to get it. She hadn't quite hung up on him, but she wouldn't suffer his seemingly trying to find himself forever. She'd move on. She had to, for herself and for her baby.

Jack went to work, reviewing the mail and the menus. Then he checked the pantry, made out the grocery list, counted the medical supplies. He made rounds, looking carefully at each man in the shelter to make sure he was all right and hadn't been drinking.

Eddie Nez was still there, he saw halfway through his inspection. This was good. Will was already doing his community service here when Becenti, or whoever, had found the *hataalii*. Hopefully, it would keep the two of them out of any more trouble.

By the time Jack had finished, Winston was asleep in the recliner. Also good, he thought. No further pestering from him. Now all Jack had to do was wait a few hours and he'd leave for Gallup. He had to hand it to the old marine, though. At least part of his plan was reasonable. Jack needed to see the enemy camp. He wanted to talk to Ronald and Carolyn. He wanted to find out once and for all what it was they planned to do.

He went into the dayroom and sprawled on the couch, tiptoeing around Winston, who snored his old man's snore in the recliner. Jack closed his eyes and tried not to think about Meg. He might as well have tried not to breathe.

She's ashamed to be married to me.

If he could keep that thought to the forefront, then maybe he could endure their separation. But he had come to realize something in the past few days. He had been taken by surprise by Carolyn Pacer's reaction to the news of his and Meggie's marriage. But Meggie knew her, both from personal experience and from the things the dead man had told her. And she would know that the woman's response to the news would likely not be favorable. Meggie had to protect her baby, even if she didn't know precisely from what. Carolyn Pacer was a living, breathing threat, and what champion did Meg's little girl or boy have but Meggie herself?

He lay there in the semidarkness, cataloging every little sound to keep his mind occupied. And he must have slept, but he had no idea how long. He woke suddenly, not knowing where he was. The room was dark. Somebody had turned off the hall light and it took him a moment to get his bearings. The generalized snoring seemed to have tapered off, but as far as he could tell, nobody was up and moving around.

He didn't want to wake up Winston, and he tried to get off the couch without making noise—not easy with the bad springs and the stiff vinyl upholstery. But after a few false starts he managed to find his way into the kitchen relatively unscathed.

He flipped on a small lamp and looked around to make sure the room was empty. Then he got his jacket and took an apple out of the refrigerator.

Got to get Meggie some oranges, he thought as he stepped outside. Or maybe her craving had changed now. Maybe she needed something else. Some*one* else.

The night was cold, but not unbearably so. He looked up at the sky, at the millions of stars. Meggie loved a starry night. He took a deep breath and walked around to the side of the building where he'd left the Norton.

Winston Tsosie was sitting on it.

Chapter Fourteen

"**I** am *not* taking you," Jack said for the third time. Thus far, he was having this argument all by himself. Winston hadn't said a word. And he hadn't moved, either.

"Well, say something!"

"Okay, Jack. Whose motorcycle is this?"

"Not *yours.*"

"You're wrong. It is mine. I traded a whole bunch of stuff for this thing."

"Damn it, Winston!"

"Let's go, Jack. We're wasting time."

Jack looked around as a truck pulled into the parking area, one he didn't recognize in the dark. It circled around and parked heading out toward the road a short distance away. He stood watching as the headlights went off and the door on the passenger side opened. Someone came walking toward them.

Will Baron.

"What are you doing here?" Jack asked, immediately alarmed. "Is something wrong with Meg?"

"No, man, she's okay. I'm going with you and Winston."

"The hell you are! And what makes you think we're going someplace?"

Will sighed. "I heard you two talking. I guess Winston didn't tell you."

"Tell me what?"

"That I stayed here in the dayroom night before last so I could work with Eddie before I went to school yesterday morning. Only I wasn't asleep and I heard you and Winston talking about those people wanting Meg's baby—"

"Who's in the truck?" Jack interrupted, because he suddenly realized that somebody had come with Will.

"Dolly."

"Are you out of your mind!"

"She caught me when I was trying to get out of the house, man. What could I do? How many times did *you* ever get around her? You know she's got some kind of radar. She thought I was up to something and she spent the night at the house so she could catch me at it. I had to tell her where I was going and why, didn't I? She's coming, too," he added.

"No, she's not," Jack said, walking off toward the truck.

"Wanna bet?" Will called after him.

But Dolly didn't give him the opportunity to vent his many objections to her being here.

"Something has to be done, Jack," she said as soon as he reached the truck.

"Dolly, I'm going to try to be respectful here—"

"What is the matter with you? You should have told Meggie what these people are planning," she said, ignoring his offer of civility.

"She's got enough to worry about!"

"Is that so? How is it you men can never see the wrong way of behaving when it's right in front of your eyes? Meggie doesn't need you to try to save her from trouble, Jack. She needs you to be there with her when it gets here."

"Dolly—"

"I'm not done talking, Jack. I agree that you need to speak to these people if you can find them. Maybe if they understand that all of us care about Meggie and that she'll be all right with us, they'll stop this custody business. But when you come back from Gallup, I want you to tell Meg why you left her. You are breaking her heart. How many times do you think you can do that?"

"She understands."

"She understands that she loves you, and she will try to give you whatever you say you need. And she understands that you can be like a sandy riverbank. The very first time the river gets rough and wide, the bank is washed away. I want you to tell her because it's the right thing to do. And I want you to tell her the truth. Say you're afraid of what will happen if you stay with her. Say you think these people will try to take her baby, and if they do, it would be your fault and she would blame you."

"There's more to it than that."

"Then say that you forgive her for shaming you in front of people who don't matter."

He stood there, glad that it was too dark for Dolly to see his face. He glanced over his shoulder. Winston still sat on the Norton. Will was dropkicking pebbles into the dark.

"Aren't you going to tell me I behave like I don't have any relatives?" he asked.

"From this gathering in the middle of the night, I would say you have more relatives than you know what to do with. You're going to have to stop making your decisions as if you are the only one, Jack. You're not. You have a wife and you have a child coming. Can I believe the promise you made when you asked to marry Meggie or not? It's time to start being the husband you said you would be."

"I'm trying not to hurt her, Dolly."

"You can't stop trouble and pain when it comes from some other place, Jack. The only hurt you can prevent is the hurt you yourself would give—and sometimes even that is impossible. You let *her* decide if she wants you with her or not. I mean this, Jack."

"All right!" he said. He gave a sharp sigh and looked up at the stars again. They were rapidly fading. "I'll tell her."

"Good," Dolly said, opening the door and getting out. "You drive the truck to Gallup. I will explain to Winston and Will that you have to go without their help."

"Dolly—"

"If you want to go alone, drive the truck, because you are never going to get that old man off that motorcycle."

The plan was to check all the motels on Old Route 66. It would be a simple matter to ride through the parking lots, one quick pass to look for a white car with California license plates, hopefully without arousing suspicion among the guests. There were no events going on in or around Gallup this time of year; Jack didn't expect any of the motels to be crowded. He didn't anticipate any problem at all, until he found two cars that could have belonged to the Pacers, in different parking lots.

He located the first one almost immediately, but there were people milling about and he left, riding farther down the street to turn around in yet another motel parking lot. The second white car was parked there, and he had no idea which was which or if either of them belonged to the Pacers. He managed to look through the windows of the second one, but there was nothing to identify who might own the car. Short of making inquiries at the front desk, there was nothing to do but pick one of them and wait. Given Winston's observation, he drove back to the first motel, because he thought it more in keeping with Carolyn Pacer's uncompromisingly high standards.

He coasted Dolly's truck—he'd driven armored vehicles that were easier to handle—into an empty parking space near the white car. It seemed pointless trying to be subtle about it. He had no idea where their room might be or from which direction they would eventually come. They wouldn't be expecting him, might not even recognize him if they saw him, unless one of them had the Benny Joe's picture in hand.

The sun came up. The streetlights went out. He ate the apple. And two people came out and went directly to the white car—an elderly man and woman, the man wearing a plaid sports jacket and a golf cap. He was smoking a big cigar.

Jack swore and started the truck, heading back to the second car.

It was gone.

There was nothing to be done but return to the original plan of cruising motel parking lots. But he couldn't find any more white cars with California license plates.

He tried the restaurants and fast-food places.

Nothing.

He was ready to give up when he finally saw the car at a stoplight. It was heading in the opposite direction, back toward the motel. He made a ten-point turn—the best he could do in Dolly's truck—and followed them at a safe distance. The car turned in exactly where he expected and pulled into the same parking space. He drove by slowly, watching Ronald and Carolyn Pacer get out. He stuck his arm out the window, giving a left turn signal and making an abrupt maneuver into the motel parking area at its second entrance. When he came back around the building, the Pacers were climbing the steps to the second floor, both of them carrying bags that looked like they contained take-out food. He stopped and watched them go into the room exactly in line with where they'd parked.

Okay, he thought. *So far so good.*

But when he was about to open the truck door, another car drove in and parked nearby. A man wearing a suit and carrying a briefcase got out, and he walked purposefully up the steps to the second floor. He knocked on the Pacers' door and was immediately allowed inside.

Jack waited. It was a long time before the man came out again, and there was no farewell at the door. He made his exit and hurried down the steps, tossing the briefcase into the back seat before he got into his car and drove away. After a moment, the door opened again and the Pacers came out.

Jack got out of the truck and walked quickly toward them, intercepting them before they reached their car. Carolyn was the first to see him, and to say that she looked alarmed would have been an understatement.

"What are you doing here?" she asked immediately, her voice loud enough to make the boy who was watering the motel yucca plants look around and stare.

"Waiting my turn," Jack said. "I want to talk to you about Meg."

"There's nothing to talk about," Ronald said. He opened the car door for his wife.

"Look, man. I want to know what you're planning to do."

"We told you what we were planning to do, Mr. Begaye," Carolyn said. "I won't leave the only grandchild Ronald and I will ever have—the only thing we have left of our son—here."

"I understand how you must feel—"

"You do *not* understand how I feel!" she said, snaring the attention of the boy with the watering cup again. "How could you possibly understand?"

"You're right, Mrs. Pacer," he said. "I won't get it until after you take off with Meg's baby, will I?"

"I want you to stop bothering us," she said.

"Bothering you? You people came to me."

"If you persist in this, Mr. Begaye," Ronald said, "I will have you arrested—and believe me, I can do it. You have upset my wife all you're going to. Do you understand?"

Jack stood there, aching to throw a punch. "Yeah," he said, meeting the man's gaze. "I understand."

"Then get out of the way. And don't come back here."

The man pushed past him and got into the car, backing out without looking and speeding away.

Lo, the Flint Boy, I am he, Jack thought. He was a pitiful excuse for a warrior. He stood staring after the car, and after a moment he walked back to the truck. When he got behind the wheel, he could see the motel maid with her cart, moving along the row of doors on the second floor. She stopped two rooms up from the Pacers. He watched her take out the ring of keys and unlock the door. He watched her push the cart inside. He watched her leave the door open behind her.

Okay, he thought. Okay.

He waited. It took her twenty-seven minutes to clean the room. She moved the cart to the next room and unlocked it.

Seventeen minutes. Eighteen. Twenty. Then she was backing out of the room with the cart again and pushing it to the Pacers' door.

He waited, drumming his fingers on the steering wheel.

Come on, come on—

The watering boy called up to her and she leaned over the railing.

"Come on, come on!" Jack whispered as the conversation lengthened. Something funny had happened and they both appreciated the humor in it.

Finally, she turned back to the door and took out her keys.

Jack had to force himself to wait after she went inside, because the boy was still hanging around.

Let her get busy first, he thought, watching the boy. *And wait until the kid finds another yucca plant.*

The boy picked up his cup and walked around the corner of the building. Jack immediately got out of the truck, then decided to take off his jacket. If this went wrong and it got down to descriptions of the suspect, there was no use deliberately matching the one the Pacers themselves would give. He rolled up his shirtsleeves and put on his sunglasses. And he walked toward the Pacers' room.

Rule Number One in the Boarding School Survival Manual, he thought as he climbed the cement stairs. *Never look guilty, even if you're caught.*

"Good morning," he called to the maid, who was bending over the trash can when he stepped inside. "I forgot something," he said.

She smiled. "Oh, am I in your way here?"

"No, ma'am. I know where I left it. Could I get some extra towels this trip?" he asked, trying to keep an eye on her and search the room.

"Yes, sir!" she said brightly. She put a plastic liner in the trash can.

He pulled open a drawer as if he had every right to do it. The maid went into the bathroom. When he closed the drawer, he saw a briefcase sitting on the floor. He picked it up carefully and put it on the bed.

Locked.

He could hear the maid running water in the tub, and he quickly reached for the small rake pick and torsion wrench in his pocket. He had planned for every eventuality, even having to follow Winston's extreme plan. Jack got down on his knees and stuck the pick and the wrench into the left lock, manipulating the inner workings he visualized in his mind's eye. It popped open almost immediately.

He moved to the other lock. This one was slightly dented, and he couldn't get a feel for the pin mechanism. He kept working. The flow of water in the bathroom stopped.

Don't panic, he thought. *You've been in worse situations than this with a lock that won't give.* He kept moving the pick and the wrench, methodically, minutely. The maid came out of the bathroom at the same moment the lock popped open.

He palmed the pick and the wrench.

"Did you find it?" she asked.

"Yes and no," he said, flipping the briefcase open. "I could have sworn I put it here...."

He lifted the top papers by the edges, his back to the maid. A letter and some pictures slid out—ones of him and Mary Ann, him and Meg, at Benny Joe's. He turned the papers around—legal papers. He began to read, immediately seeing Meg's name. Megan Baron, not Megan Begaye. A petition for custody that had been in the works for a long time, obviously, even before Meg had come home so abruptly.

By damn, they're going to do it, he thought in a panic. And it didn't matter whether she went with them to California or not.

"Extra towels, did you say?" the maid asked.

"Yeah," he said over his shoulder. He turned over the letter. It was addressed to Meg.

"What?" he said out loud. Why would the Pacers have a letter that belonged to Meg, especially one that was postmarked?

"Did you say something, sir?"

The maid was taking towels off the cart. He closed the briefcase and wiped it clean with a corner of the bedspread.

Then he pushed it off the bed and used the toe of his boot to slide it back where he'd found it.

"Ah, no," Jack said, stuffing the letter into his shirt pocket. "Okay. I'm out of your way now."

He slid past her, and he walked the length of the building to the other stairs in case the Pacers returned. He could feel the letter in his pocket.

I don't understand.

He didn't take the time to read it once he was in the truck. He shouldn't be reading it in any case. It wasn't *his* letter.

Apparently, that hadn't stopped the Pacers.

He pulled out onto the street and headed toward Window Rock. And he had no idea at what point he made up his mind, but by the time he arrived there, he knew what he needed to do. He drove straight through downtown, past the rock formation that gave the town its name, to the Singer house. There were no cars in the driveway, he noted with relief. Except that meant Meggie would be alone and she probably shouldn't be.

If she was here at all.

He stepped up on the patio and looked into the kitchen windows. He couldn't hear anyone moving around. The back door was locked, but he didn't ring the bell. He went around to Meggie's bedroom window instead, trying to see inside by cupping his hands to shade his eyes when he peered through the glass. He could hear music playing, and he could see her lying on the bed. He tapped on the windowpane.

"Meggie?" he called. "Meg?"

"Jack!" she said, attempting to get up and go let him in.

"No, wait. Unlock it," he said, tapping on the glass again. "I'll come through the window. Is anybody here?"

"Winston and Dolly were here," she said as she helped raise the window. "They went to the grocery store. They should be back soon. Why?"

He climbed over the sill, and he reached for her as soon as he was inside. She came to him, wrapping her arms around him. She felt so good to him.

So good!

He held her tightly, nuzzling her cheek, kissing her eyes and mouth. She'd just had a bath. Her hair was still damp. Her skin smelled of lavender soap.

"I've missed you so much," he said. "Oh, Meggie."

"Jack, what's wrong?" she said, trying to see his face.

"Nothing—everything. If I asked you to come with me right now, would you do it?"

"Jack, what—"

"Would you come with me? We need to get out of here."

"Tell me what's wrong."

"This is killing me, Meggie."

He looked at her, his eyes searching hers for some sign that he was doing the right thing. But she was scared, worried, and it was his fault. "I'm sorry. I didn't mean . . ." He gave a sharp sigh. "It's such a damned mess."

"You can tell me, Jack. You can tell me anything. You know that."

He rested his head on her shoulder and pressed her against him. How much time had they had together—a week?

He heard the back door opening. Dolly and Winston, he thought. He was glad they were back. He would need them when he told Meg about the legal papers he'd found.

But it wasn't Dolly and Winston. It was Lucas.

"Let's go, Jack," he said, standing in the doorway, and Meg turned sharply in his arms.

"Why?" Jack asked, still holding on to her.

"You know why," Lucas said. He glanced at Meg.

"Lucas, what is it?" she said, her voice betraying her alarm.

"I have to take him in."

"He hasn't done anything," she said, and Jack had never loved her more than he did at that minute. How easy it would have been for her to assume the worst.

"Let's go, Jack! Don't make this hard on Meg."

He stood there, caught, trapped.

"Meggie," he said, making her look at him. "I haven't done anything wrong." Illegal, perhaps, but not wrong.

"*Now,* Jack!" Lucas said.

Jack put his arms around her, holding her close as if to say goodbye. "Take the letter out of my shirt pocket," he whispered against her ear. She stiffened slightly, but she gave no other sign. He kissed her then, and her fingers slid into the pocket.

"Trust me," he whispered. "Please, Meggie." And he held her a moment longer, giving her time to hide the letter under her cardigan before he let her go.

Her eyes met his. "What you asked me earlier," she said. "The answer is yes. I'll go wherever you want."

He kissed her one last time, and Lucas had the handcuffs ready.

"You don't need those," he said.

"Yes, Jack, I do. Turn around."

He hesitated. There was no way out of this. None. He glanced at Meggie's face. She was about to cry.

He took a deep breath and turned around.

Chapter Fifteen

"Empty your pockets," Lucas said. "And stop acting like you don't know what this is all about."

"I don't," Jack said. He took out his wallet, placing it and everything else he had on the counter. The pick and the torsion wrench he removed last.

"The hell you don't," Lucas said, turning over the wrench. "What are *these* for?"

"Picking locks," he answered. "Somebody's always losing the keys at the shelter." Both statements were true; Lucas only believed the first one.

"We shouldn't have gone off and left Meg," Jack said. "She shouldn't be by herself. She's upset."

"Yeah, and a lot you care about that."

Jack bit down on his bottom lip to keep from answering back. "How long is this going to take?"

"Look! You are in serious trouble here!"

"Yeah? Well, when are you going to get around to telling me what that serious trouble *is*, man?"

"Lucas," Mary Skeets called across the room. "Captain Becenti wants to see you and Jack. *Now.*"

Jack swore under his breath. He did not need a trip to the woodshed with Becenti.

"Let's go," Lucas said, pushing him along. They met Becenti in the hall and he led the way.

"Shut the door," he said when they were in his office. "Sit down, Jack."

"I'll stand."

"Sit down!"

He sat—with the help of Lucas's hand on his shoulder.

"They're saying you broke into a motel room in Gallup," Becenti said without prelude. "You're aware of that."

"No, I'm not," he answered, giving Lucas a look.

"What the hell did you think this was about?" Lucas said.

"I'm driving Dolly's truck. I figured *you* thought I stole it."

"I did," Lucas said.

"Dolly loaned me the truck!"

"Which you used to commit a crime!"

He tried to stand up. Lucas pushed him back down again.

"That's enough!" Becenti said. "Both of you. Sit down, Lucas." He picked up a pencil and began tapping it on the desktop.

Jack shifted in the chair.

"You were sent to the desert when you were in the marines, right?" Becenti said.

Jack looked at Becenti doubtfully, wondering where *that* had come from. This conversation was coming from an oblique direction even by Navajo standards.

"Yeah," he answered, because if there was a trap in the question, he couldn't see it.

"I'm surprised. The military actually sending somebody desert raised to the desert."

"It wasn't anything like it is here. Look, could you call Sloan or somebody to go see about Meg?" he asked.

"That's been done, Jack," Becenti said. "You don't have to worry about her right now. You have to worry about yourself." He tapped the pencil. "You know, I really didn't think I was going to see you here like this again. You've got a beautiful wife. You've got a decent job. You've got everything going for you. I thought you finally had yourself on the right path. Was I wrong?''

Jack didn't answer.

"These people—the ones who accuse you. They say you stole money—a lot of money—from their room.''

"They're damned liars!''

"They say you've been following them around—here and in Gallup. They say you accosted them in a grocery-store parking lot.''

"Oh, yeah? Did they say they're trying to get Meg's baby?''

"What are you talking about, Jack?'' Lucas said.

"You heard me! Ronald and Carolyn Pacer's dead son was the father of Meg's baby. They don't want the baby raised here. They're going to sue for custody.''

"Meg hasn't said one word about this.''

"She doesn't know!''

"But you do?''

"Yes!'' Jack cried, and he didn't miss the exchanged looks that said now we're getting somewhere.

"What makes you think they want the baby?'' Becenti asked.

"I don't think, I *know* they want it.''

"And you went into Gallup to see them today?''

"Yes.''

"Why?''

"I wanted to talk to them. When the woman found out Meg and I were married, she threatened to take Meg to court. I wanted to know for sure what they were planning to do.''

"But you didn't bother to mention any of this to Meggie?'' Lucas asked.

"No, I didn't.''

"Why not?''

He didn't answer.

"Why not, Jack!''

"Because we had a disagreement that same day. I didn't tell her about it, and then later her blood pressure was up and everything. I didn't think it would be good for her to know what these people wanted to do."

"But it was okay for you to fight with her?"

"It was a misunderstanding. What? You and Sloan never misunderstand each other and say things you don't mean?"

"We're not talking about me and my woman. We're talking about you!"

"That's enough!" Becenti said again. "Did you talk to these people today or not?"

"I tried to."

"And?"

"And they'd done a complete about-face. The last time I saw them, they stopped *me* in the grocery-store parking lot. They wanted me to talk Meg into coming to stay with them in California, this isn't a fit place for the Pacer grandchild. But today they wouldn't talk to me. They told me to stay away from them, like I was the one who had started this."

"Is that why you stole their money?"

"I didn't steal any money!"

"But you were in their room."

He exhaled sharply. He'd gone too far now. There was nothing to do but tell him. "Yeah."

"Damn it, Jack! What in the hell were you thinking?"

"I was thinking I wanted to know what these people were going to do. I was thinking I wanted to find something that would tell me why they changed all of a sudden from tracking me down to running away. But I didn't break into the room."

"You just happened to have your lock-picking kit with you," Lucas said.

"No, I didn't just 'happen' to have it. I might have used it to get inside if I'd had to. I don't know. But I didn't need it. The maid was in the room and the door was open. I just went inside and looked around."

"What did you find?" Becenti said.

"I didn't find any damn money, I can tell you that!"

"What did you find, Jack! You must have found something, or we wouldn't be here!"

"Legal papers, the petition for custody of the baby, pictures of me and some of Meg. The question is who's been following who?"

"They were just lying around for you to see."

"No, they were in a briefcase."

"Which you opened."

"Yeah."

"You broke into it."

"Yeah."

"The money was in it."

"There wasn't any money! Who would be dumb enough to leave money lying around a motel room?"

"Then what did you take!"

"I . . . took a letter. It was addressed to Meg."

"What were *they* doing with it?"

"That's what I wanted to know. It was Meg's. They didn't have any business with it."

"Who was it from?"

"I think it was from their dead son."

"What did it say?"

"I don't know. I didn't read it."

"You stole the damn thing, but you didn't read it?" Lucas said.

"No, I didn't read it! I didn't have time to read it. I took the letter and I got out. And I drove back here to get Meg and tell her about these people. And then *you* showed up with the handcuffs."

"Where is the letter now?" Becenti asked.

Jack didn't answer him.

"Jack?"

He took a deep breath. "I didn't read the letter," he said again. "But I think it must be something they need for the custody hearing. I'm not going to tell you where it is."

"What did you do? Did you tear it up, burn it? What?"

"I'm not going to tell you."

"Damn it, Jack!"

Someone knocked on the door.

"In!" Becenti said, but given his tone, whoever it was would have to be desperate or crazy to turn the knob.

Or Mary Skeets.

"Sorry to bother you, Captain," Mary said pleasantly. "Those people keep calling. Well, actually, the man's on the phone with questions and the woman's in the background directing." She glanced at Jack. "Anyway, he wants to know why the law-enforcement agency where he reported the crime isn't handling the investigation."

"I just bet he does," Jack said. "He's not going to want Meg's uncle to find out what they're up to."

"Is he on the line now?" Becenti asked, giving Jack a hard look.

"Yes, sir."

"Then tell him you've advised me of his . . . interest and I'll get back to him. Tell him the investigation is still under way and it's none of his damn business how the case came to us."

"You want me to say *that?*"

"No. Ask him for a list of all their missing property."

"I told you, they don't *have* any missing property," Jack said, and Becenti gave him another hard look.

"There's one other thing," Mary Skeets said, glancing at Jack again.

"Which is?"

"Jack's lawyer called, and he's not to say anything else until he's been properly instructed by counsel, which should be within the hour, barring any citations for speeding."

"Anything *else,* Mary?"

"Ah, no, sir. That's about it."

"I guess I should be thankful for small favors," Becenti said as she went out. "Okay, Jack, if you didn't take the money, I'd be really interested to hear why you were so sure you'd need a lawyer."

"I don't want to talk anymore," he said. He didn't know exactly how he'd come to acquire legal counsel, but for once he was going to listen to unsolicited advice.

"That's just like you, Jack. Stir up a hornet's nest and then walk off and leave it. Okay. You don't want to talk anymore, then you can sit in a jail cell."

A sigh was the only comment Jack allowed himself to make.

"Let's go," Lucas said.

"Captain Becenti," Jack said as he stood up. "Will you let Mary find out if Meg's okay? Please," he added, meeting the older man's eyes. He was surprised to find a certain empathy there.

His wife was sick, too, Jack thought. And he and Becenti were both helpless.

Becenti glanced at Lucas. "Somebody will let you know."

But no one came to tell him anything. Jack had always hated waiting like this. It was too reminiscent of his boarding-school days and having to wait for somebody to come and administer the latest punishment. It was all he could do to just sit there, and there was no room to do anything else. After a time, he paced the holding cell as best he could, stepping over the drunk and disorderly as he walked around and around the barred perimeter.

What was taking so long? Surely Mary could just dial the Singer phone number and ask whoever answered if Meg was all right. She could even talk to Meg herself.

Or maybe Meg didn't want to talk to anyone making inquiries on his behalf.

Supper came and went, such as it was. He went back to the holding cell and back to pacing. Two of the drunks got into a fight. It took Jack and three officers to break it up. He got a torn shirt for his trouble and not much else.

He finally gave up pacing and resigned himself to sitting on the floor in the corner; the benches were all taken.

"Hey!" he called to one of the guards passing by. "What time is it?"

"What do you want to know for, Jack? You ain't going nowhere."

"Humor me," he called.

"Seven-fifty-two," the man called back.

But he *was* going somewhere. Lillian arrived—his mystery lawyer. And to talk to her he was taken to the same small room where he'd had his conversation with Will.

"I see you didn't follow my advice about telling Meggie everything," she said without prelude.

"I was going to tell her, but your brother the tribal cop showed up."

"With good reason, from what I hear. Now I want *your* version of what happened. Everything. And God help you if you leave anything out."

"I want to know about Meg first. Is she all right?"

"I haven't heard anything, Jack. I assume she is. Now, let's get to the matter at hand."

"How did you get here, anyway?"

"My mother, the irrepressible Dolly Singer, called me. And she didn't give me much of a choice about whether or not I wanted to come. To tell you the truth, I'm a little cranky about it. I'm getting tired of running up here because the men in this family can't stay out of jail. I want you to start at the beginning."

"You know the beginning."

"Tell me again, Jack!"

"All right!"

They talked for a long time. Lillian treated him as if she were the prosecutor and not the person responsible for his defense. When she was finally satisfied, she left to go talk to Becenti. She was gone only briefly.

"Well, they don't have any evidence and they don't have any witnesses. All they have is the word of people who need to make you look bad."

"So I can go, right?"

"Wrong. There's still the small matter of the briefcase, which you just *had* to tell them about."

"Lillian—"

"I know you thought you had just cause—"

"The letter belonged to Meg."

"It was still burglary."

"And?"

"And I don't know. They're going to have to come up with charges soon or cut you loose. In the meantime, you stay here."

Somebody rapped on the door. In a moment the lock scraped and the door opened. Becenti stood in the hall.

"I need to talk to you, Lillian," he said.

"Right now?"

"Now," he assured her. He made no effort to look at Jack.

"I meant to ask you, Johnny," she said as she got up from the table, "how is Mae?"

"She's . . ." He stood back to let her come out into the hall. "You need to go see her while you're here," he said as the door closed. He didn't actually say it, but Jack heard the words anyway: *Before it's too late.*

Jack waited. And waited. Lillian finally came back. To say that she looked upset would have been an understatement.

"What's wrong?" he asked. "Lillian?"

She looked at him. "They found the money."

"Good. Where was it—Ronald's back pocket?"

"They found the money, Jack," she said pointedly.

He waited, trying to understand what she expected him to say.

"What's wrong?" he asked again, because he certainly wasn't getting any help from her.

"You know what's wrong!"

"No, I don't!"

"They found the money in Dolly's truck, Jack. It was in the headliner. Now you tell me how it got there!"

"I don't know how it got there. Maybe it's Dolly's stash!"

"No, it is not Dolly's stash! What would she be doing with that kind of money—the exact amount of money those people say is missing?"

"Lillian, I didn't take any money from that motel room!"

"For Meggie's sake, I wish to God I believed you." She grabbed her briefcase.

"Where are you going?"

"I've got to go think about this. I told you not to lie to me."

"No, you told me not to leave anything out. And I didn't! Lillian!"

She held up her hand. "You're wasting my time, Jack."

* * *

He spent the night sleepless and staring at the ceiling, trapped like an animal in a snare.

I have to get out of here, he kept thinking, knowing perfectly well that there was no way to get out. He had to talk to Meg. He had to tell her what these people planned. He needed to explain about the letter. And she needed to hear it all from him, not from Lucas.

He didn't expect to see Lillian again, but she returned early the next morning. She was still upset.

"I didn't do this," he tried to tell her again, but she wasn't interested in hearing his declarations of innocence.

"The bottom line is you got caught with your hand in the cookie jar," she said. "You can't explain it away, Jack. The only thing you've got going for you is that, for some insane reason, Dolly and Meg believe you."

"Did you see Meg?"

"No. I stayed in Gallup last night. Window Rock gets on my nerves. I haven't talked to any of the family this morning."

"I just don't understand this!"

"Well, you better understand it—"

Someone rapped on the door, then put the key into the lock. Captain Becenti came in, looking as haggard and sleepless as Jack himself must look.

"I've got a message for your client," he said to Lillian.

"What kind of message?" Jack asked.

"I'm sorry. It's not good. It's Meg. She's having some kind of problem. The clinic doctor sent her to the hospital in Albuquerque—the Medical Center—"

"What kind of problem?" Jack demanded.

"I don't know."

"Lillian, you've got to get me out of here!" he said, standing up so abruptly that the chair fell over. "Lillian—"

"I can't, Jack," she said.

"You have to! I need to be with her! Her old man died in there—she hates that place. You have to get me out!"

"Sloan and Lucas have gone to Albuquerque," Becenti said. "He'll keep you posted."

"The hell he will!"

"He will, Jack. He understands a whole lot more about this situation than he did. I want you to take it easy. You're in enough trouble—don't make it worse."

But Jack made a rush for the door, and Becenti grabbed him, slamming him hard against the wall.

"Damn it, Jack! I want you to use your head for once in your life! You can't help Meg by acting like this!"

"You don't understand!"

"Yes, I do!" the captain said, restraining him from trying to get out the door again. "I understand, Jack! You're not by yourself anymore. You've got people trying to sort all this out for you. But for right now, you're going to have to be patient."

"I want to see my wife," Jack said, and he was appalled that his voice broke. There was nothing he could do about it. He was going to cry, right here and now, like a little kid. And the harder he tried to hold on to his control, his dignity, the more it seemed to slip away.

"Terry!" Becenti called loudly over his shoulder. The officer was there immediately. "Take him back to his cell. No cuffs," he added when the other man reached for his.

"You sure, Captain?"

"I'm sure. Jack, you behave yourself. I'm going to tell Mary to bring you anything—*anything*—she hears about Meg. Okay?"

He didn't reply because he didn't trust his voice.

"Okay?" Becenti said again.

"Okay," he whispered.

Chapter Sixteen

Someone came for him shortly before 10 a.m. He was taken to shower, given a change of clothes—his own, which somebody must have brought in.

"What's going on?" he asked the jailer.

"Beats me," the man said.

Jack didn't ask any more questions. There was nothing more frustrating than trying to get information out of somebody who wasn't supposed to say and didn't know anyway. Becenti had kept his word; Mary Skeets had given him several non-bulletins about Meg. Meg had been admitted. She was resting and, Mary said pointedly, she'd been advised that her husband, Jack Begaye, was being a model prisoner and there was no reason for her to worry on that account—he would not do anything to make his situation worse.

"People really are trying to get you out," Mary assured him.

"People really are trying to get me *in,* too," he'd told her.

His eyes burned from lack of sleep; he couldn't think about anything but Meggie. Who knew what state of mind she was in?

Perhaps she still believed him, trusted him. Or perhaps she'd written him off altogether.

Lillian waited for him in the side room.

"What's going on?" he asked immediately.

"There's was a meeting with one of the tribal judges. He's agreed to review the mitigating circumstances of this case."

"And?"

"And I'm waiting for him to make up his mind about whether or not he's going to let you post bond."

"You think there's a chance?"

"I don't know. I looked at your police record—it's not *that* bad. You were rowdy and you were a runaway, but you were never a thief. You're employed and married. Hopefully, that will help."

He wasn't offended by her bluntness, because at least something was happening. This was far better than sitting in a cell. "Thanks for getting me a chance, Lillian," he said.

"Don't thank me. I don't have the clout to get you any kind of special review. Thank Johnny Becenti and Dolly."

"Dolly? How could she . . . ?"

"I just hear and obey, Jack. I don't know how either of them did it. Oh, and I tried to talk to Meg."

"Damn it, Lillian, why didn't you tell me that first?"

"Because you didn't give me a chance."

"What did she say?"

"Nothing. I said I *tried* to talk to her. I couldn't get her on the phone. I'll try again later. Maybe I'll have something to tell her after the judge does whatever he's going to do."

"Like what?"

"I don't have a clue. This is all unusual, to say the least. Are you ready to hear it—whatever he decides?"

"Yeah—no."

"Tell me about it," she said with a sigh.

The decision came much sooner than he expected. He was taken back to his cell while Lillian went to get the details. Waiting for Lillian was the part that took so long. He had no idea what she could be doing. He was standing by the door when the jailer came to get him again, but this time Jack didn't ask any questions. They didn't stop at the side room; they kept going into the unlocked hall. Lillian was standing at the end of it.

"Okay, you're getting out," she said, and he gave a tremendous sigh of relief.

"Right now?"

"As soon as you hear the catch."

"What is it?"

"There's a condition to your release. The judge set bail, and it's been paid, but you're going to have to be placed in the custody of the person who is paying. For some strange reason, the judge thinks you're a hothead. He says the person risking his money has the right to make sure he doesn't lose it."

"Who are we talking about here?" Jack asked.

"Winston Tsosie."

"Winston put up the money to get me out?"

"He did."

"And I'm in his custody? He goes where I go?"

"And vice versa. That's the deal. Can you live with it?"

He laughed. "Lillian, the only place I've been lately without Winston at least trying to come along is my honeymoon. It's not like I'm not used to it."

"Okay, then. Let me square away the paperwork."

Lillian came back with forms for him to sign, which he did without hesitation. He couldn't believe that Winston had pulled this off. And Dolly. And Becenti.

When Lillian returned again, it was to tell him he was a free man, at least for the moment.

"Was Becenti in his office when you came by?" he asked her.

"Yes."

"I've got something to say to him."

"Now, Jack—"

"I know how to behave, Lillian, regardless of what you think."

She held up her hands. "Okay! Winston is waiting out front with Mary Skeets. You come out there when you're done—if you're able."

He walked down the hall toward Becenti's office. The door was open; Becenti sat staring at the papers on his desk.

Jack waited until he looked up. The man was surprised to see him and it showed. "What is it, Jack?"

"I just wanted to say that I . . . won't forget what you did."

"All you have to do is act like you've got some sense. Winston Tsosie can't afford for you to screw this up, and neither can I."

"I'll . . . try."

"You'd better do a damn lot more than that. Now get out of here. I'm busy."

Jack started to go, then turned back. "I never did tell you . . . How much Meg and I liked your place in the mountains. If you could tell Mrs. Becenti that we did, I'd appreciate it. Tell her that I said thank-you for letting us stay there."

"I'll do that, Jack. Now get going before I have second thoughts."

He didn't have to be told again, and Winston was indeed waiting for him.

"Let's go, Jack," the old man said without prelude. "I got the truck—yours. I don't think mine will make it to Albuquerque."

"Winston," he said, but the old man was already halfway out the door. "Winston!"

"What, Jack?" he said, looking over his shoulder.

"How much bail did you have to put up?" He swore when Winston told him. "Where did you get that kind of money?"

"Sold the motorcycle—it runs real good now. Let's go."

"What's your grandson going to say?"

"I told you, Jack. The motorcycle was mine."

"You shouldn't have sold it."

"Maybe," Winston said with a half-smile. "But this way, I *know* I don't miss nothing. Now let's go before those people come along and see you got out."

They walked to the parking lot. The wind kicked up the sand, and the shadows were long. Jack looked up at the sky for a moment, thinking, of all things, that he needed to go to the sweat lodge after being locked in that place. The truck was parked close by, but it wasn't empty. Will and Eddie Nez both sat on the tailgate.

"Will wants to go along to see Meg," Winston said before he could ask.

"He's not cutting school," Jack said. "And he's not cutting his community service." The last thing he needed was to be a party to something else that would upset Lucas Singer.

"No. Tomorrow is one of those teacher walk days."

"Workdays."

"Whatever. And Eddie—he says he feels like he shouldn't be left to wander around by himself. I'm thinking Will can keep him straight—sort of take his community service with him."

Jack looked at him; Winston shrugged. "Can't be helped, Jack."

"Well...it's okay, I guess. As long as nobody asks who's got custody of who."

Meg lay on her side, her body and her mind turned away from the door and the people who came and went with their questions and their good intentions. No one seemed to understand, not Sloan or Lucas, and not the relentlessly soothing nursing staff. She didn't need to hear a litany of possible consequences if she didn't "settle down." There was only one thing she needed.

Jack.

She was so worried about him. She couldn't just stop worrying because people told her to, even though the burden of her wellness fell entirely on her own shoulders. She understood that she needed to be admitted, but it was hardly comforting to know that she was here not so much to be cured but in the event that the worst happened.

There apparently was no cure for this blood-pressure thing except delivery. There was no medication for her to take. No special diet. She was instructed to lie on her left or right side, not on her back. She could get up to go to the bathroom. She could stir around in the room occasionally. But other than that, there was nothing to do. Her life had suddenly become a series of blood-pressure checks, urine samples and being weighed.

Between times she ate, she slept, she rested, and the best she could hope for was that being in the hospital would somehow bring her pressure down until she was closer to term.

She spent all morning trying to make herself believe that she didn't really mind being in *this* hospital. And she tried hard to keep from noticing that the hospital still smelled and sounded the same as it had all those years ago. She hadn't been in the room five minutes before she was back in that place in her life when her stray-away father had died without seeing her or wanting to. She thought she had let go of the past and that she had moved on, and yet she had all this unrest because of these surroundings. She remembered everything—Sloan's mental and physical exhaustion, Patrick's anger and her own sadness.

Meg felt so isolated now, in spite of the fact that Lucas and Sloan had come with her. She loved them, but neither of them were substitutes for Jack. She needed *him*. And all the while she was perfectly aware that she never should have married him. She had underestimated the Pacers, and Jack was paying for it. When would she learn not to believe in happily ever after? She had fervently hoped that everything would be all right. Yet the person she loved most in the world was suffering for her mindless optimism.

She realized now the lengths to which Carolyn and Ronald would go. She knew at least part of the reason Jack had left her. Even as hurt and angry as he was, he still loved her enough not to want to be the reason she might lose custody of her baby.

"I don't know what to do," she said out loud. And she couldn't find out lying here. She sat up on the side of the bed and began looking for a phone book. She would call the Pacers and talk to them. Anything was better than this.

But she couldn't find the phone book. She picked up the telephone receiver and tried dialing the standard number for information. It wouldn't go through. She was going to have to find a pay phone.

She got out of bed and slipped on her shoes, and she was glad now that she'd chosen leggings and a big T-shirt instead of an invalid's gown and robe. She had a much better chance of looking like a visitor instead of someone who ought to be in bed. She got her purse and dug out a handful of change, standing for a moment and looking at it in her open palm. She took a deep breath. It was so hard to concentrate sometimes, and she needed to think clearly. Sloan and Lucas would be back soon, and she doubted whether they would approve of her undertaking. Neither of them had mentioned the Pacers since she'd confirmed their existence. She had tried to tell them that she hadn't known for sure that they were here until the day she and Jack had gone to the law-enforcement building to see Will, but they were clearly determined not to discuss anything that might cause her distress.

She slung her purse over her shoulder and stood in the doorway a moment, hands protectively over her belly before she went into the hall. She waited until no one was in view, then walked purposefully out of the room, trying to guess which direction the pay phone might be. She walked past the nurses' station. No one looked up from their paperwork.

She turned the corner, and she immediately saw the waiting room some distance away. She kept walking. She could hear voices coming from that area, and she didn't realize until it was too late that the voices belonged to Lucas and Jack, who were involved in a heated argument. Jack had the receiver of the pay phone in his hand and he thrust it at Lucas.

"Call him," he kept saying. "If you don't believe me, then call him and ask him!"

Jack saw her first, and he immediately dropped the receiver.

"Meggie," he said, starting in her direction.

But she backed away from him, away from them both. "No," she said. "I can't stand any more of this—this *anger* all the time! You and Lucas, the Pacers—it's my fault. I should never have come back here."

"Meggie," Jack said, still advancing.

"I never should have married you, Jack!"

"Don't say that!"

She was close to tears, and she abruptly turned and began to walk away. She didn't look back.

"Meggie!"

She kept going. When she turned the corner near the nurses' station, she realized something was wrong. Her head hurt all over and she was having trouble seeing. She grabbed for the railing along the wall and missed it.

"Meg," Jack said, taking her arm. "Wait. Let me help you."

She knew that he meant emotionally, not physically, but she was in real danger of falling. She could feel herself sway; his arms were around her suddenly and her head lolled against his shoulder.

"Meggie, what's wrong?"

She didn't answer, didn't hear anything else that he said. She stood there, hanging on to him, wanting so desperately to give in to her need for him.

"Here you go," a nurse said from behind her. "Park it right here, baby," she said, patting the seat of a wheelchair. "Let's get you back where you belong."

Meg sat down gratefully. Jack knelt in front of her to put down the foot supports. Their eyes met; she looked away. He stood up and moved aside as the nurse rolled her down the hall, but he came along, and he helped her back to bed again. The nurse moved her onto her left side.

"I'm going to give you a second, and then I'll check your blood pressure," she said, putting the blood-pressure cuff on Meg's arm. "Take some deep breaths now. You're wound up way too tight. That's good. Do it again. Excellent! What is it the Navajo say?" she said to Jack. "She needs to find her harmony? I don't know what you did with it, baby," she said to Meg, "but I don't see it anywhere around here. So do you want him in or out?" she asked, jerking her head in Jack's direction.

Meg took a long time to answer. "In," she said finally.

"You sure?"

"Yes," she said.

"What about the other one? Uncle Lucas."

"Out."

"Out?"

"I don't feel like being a referee," Meg said, and the woman laughed.

"And I don't blame you. Okay, out it is. But he's not going to like it."

The nurse left the room for a moment, then returned to take Meg's blood pressure.

"Is it up?" Meg asked.

"It is," she said. "You rest now. One side or the other, preferably left, but not on your back." She glanced at Jack. "Rest," she said again. "Period."

When the nurse had gone, Jack pulled up a chair by the bed. He reached for her hand, and she let him take it. She closed her eyes, savoring the feel of his warm smooth fingers around hers. When she opened them again, he was waiting.

"How did you get here?" she asked.

"Lillian and Becenti worked something out with the judge. Winston put up the money for the bail."

"Oh," she said, trying not to let her disappointment show. Nothing had changed then.

He leaned closer. "What's wrong, Meg? Tell me."

"It's no use, Jackie," she said sadly. "We aren't going to make it."

"That's not true."

"It is true! Can't you see that?"

"I see how much I love you and how much you love me."

"It's not enough. It was a mistake for me to marry you." She gave a wavering sigh. "I feel so . . . guilty, Jack."

"Meggie—"

"You were arrested because of me, did you know that?"

"It's not the first time I've been arrested."

"Don't!" she cried. "It's not the same! I know how serious this is! I should have told you everything about these people. I should have told you everything I suspected. One of the reasons I came back here was because they wouldn't leave me alone."

"Did you suspect that they wanted custody of the baby?"

"No."

"Then what could you have told me that you didn't?"

"I could have told you more about the relationship between John Thomas and his parents. I could have told you I thought I saw them around Window Rock."

"You weren't sure?"

"No. Not until we went to see Will. I've let them hurt you, Jack, when that's the last thing is this world I ever wanted to do."

"I could have told you that I knew they wanted your baby, but I didn't. Dolly said..." He stopped and bowed his head for a moment. But he was silent when he looked up at her again.

"What did Dolly say?"

"She said I couldn't keep trouble away from you. I could only stand beside you when it came. She said I was acting like I was still alone when I had you and the baby to think about. Maybe I don't know how to be married yet, Meg, but I can learn. We both can learn."

"The Pacers are *my* problem. I should have gotten everything all straightened out with them a long time ago. I didn't and now I've dragged you into it."

"You didn't have to do much dragging, Meg."

"You didn't know what these people were really like."

"Neither did you," he insisted.

She closed her eyes. Her head still hurt and her chest felt tight and heavy. "No," she said, looking at him again. "I didn't. But I know now. I know that they must have hidden that money in Dolly's truck so they could blame you for it. And I know they're going to make me choose."

"What do you mean, choose?"

Her eyes filled with tears. "I'm not going to give them my baby, Jack."

"Meg, I know that. We can leave here if we have to."

"You don't understand! At first I thought they meant if I gave them the letter back, they'd drop the charges."

"You've seen them, talked to them?"

"They came to the house again, right after Lucas arrested you. Carolyn never says straight out what she means. She kept telling me that she knew I'd sent you to Gallup to break into their room. I thought she wanted the letter back, but that wasn't it. She wants custody. If I give it to them, they'll drop the charges against you. I can't do it, Jack. I love you with all my heart and I can't!''

"Meggie," he said, pulling her into his arms. "They're not going to get the baby."

"Didn't you hear me?" she cried. "They're making me choose!"

"Okay, this is *not* good," the nurse said from the doorway. "Sir, maybe you should leave now."

"You have to understand, Jack!" Meg said. "Tell me you understand!"

"Sir," the nurse said again. "This is not good for her. He can come back in a little while," she said to Meg. "We need to let you settle down."

That phrase again, Meg thought wildly. She didn't want to "settle down"!

She ignored the nurse. "They'll make sure you go to prison, Jack. It's my fault and there's nothing I can do about it!"

"No," he said, making her look at him. "Listen to me, Meg. Listen! All they can do is try."

She stared into his eyes, seeing the pain and the misery she herself had caused. And for the first time in her life, she was sorry that Jack Begaye loved her.

Chapter Seventeen

"What's happening?" Lucas asked the minute Jack stepped into the corridor. Jack felt distracted, disoriented. Will stood nearby, with Eddie Nez and Winston.

"Jack?" Lucas said when he didn't answer, grabbing his arm.

Jack looked at Meg's uncle, trying hard to focus on his well-founded concern. Lucas Singer was the only father Meg had ever really known, and he owed the man some kind of response.

"Her blood pressure is still up. The doctor did an ultrasound to check on the baby," he said, simplifying the situation in the extreme. He tried to walk away. He needed to think, to try to understand.

I never should have married you, Jack.

But Lucas wasn't so easily fobbed off. "And?" he said, with all the certainty of a man who'd spent half his life perceiving the existence of withheld particulars.

"Where's Sloan?" Jack said abruptly. He needed to talk to her, to find out if she knew anything about Meg's condition he didn't. He began to walk toward the waiting area. Everyone went with him.

"I want you to tell me what's happening, Jack."

He stopped dead in the hall. "You want to know what's happening, I'll tell you. I'm going to take Meggie out of here."

"The hell you are!"

"You don't make decisions for her anymore!"

"And neither do you!"

"I'm her husband!"

"Right! The one going to jail!"

Winston abruptly stepped between them, frail but determined. They both looked at him. The hostilities had escalated, and clearly, he did not approve.

"How much do you help Meggie by fighting with each other?" he asked quietly.

It was a good question, one that immediately grounded the conversation where it belonged.

"Jack?" Lucas prompted. "I'm asking you to tell me what's going on."

"The dead man's parents came to your house right after you hauled me in," he said after a moment. "Meg thought they wanted the letter back. They didn't."

Lucas looked at him a long moment. "You gave that stolen letter to Meg?"

"It was *her* letter, Lucas."

"If they didn't want the letter, then what did they want?"

"I think they wanted to hide the money in Dolly's truck, for one thing."

"How convenient for you to think that," Lucas said sarcastically.

"The truck was right there, damn it!" he said, rapidly losing what little of his patience remained. "They had to walk by it to get to the front door. And while they were there, they made Meggie an offer. If she gives them custody of their son's baby, they'll drop the charges against me."

"Are you sure?" Lucas said.

"Meg is sure. That's why she's so upset."

"These people—if they're so concerned about their grand-child, why are they doing this to her?"

"I don't know."

"It's extortion. Surely they realize that."

"Well, *he* should. He's supposed to be in some kind of law-enforcement agency."

"He told you that?"

"No, Meg did. But I don't think it's him so much as his wife. He's the one I need to talk to—without her."

"No, he's the one *I* need to talk to," Lucas said. "You're in enough trouble."

He stopped because Sloan walked up.

"Jack!" she said, clearly startled to see him here.

"I didn't go over the wall, Sloan," he said before she could ask. "I'm out on bail—Winston put up the money."

She glanced in Winston's direction, then frowned at the presence of Will and Eddie Nez, but she didn't say anything.

"What did *I* do?" Will asked defensively. "I'm the only one in the family who knows how to behave. You can't take these two anywhere," he said of Lucas and Jack.

But Sloan didn't want to hear about it. "Jack, have you seen Meg?" she asked.

"Yes."

"How did she seem to you?"

"Not good."

"We have to do something."

"He wants to take her out of here," Lucas said.

"Here we go again," Will said.

Sloan looked at Lucas. She took a deep breath and Jack could feel her willing herself not to say what she thought about her husband's last statement. "The doctor has suggested mar-riage counseling," she said instead. "If you and Meg need a referral, he could arrange it."

"We don't need marriage counseling!" There was no coun-seling for the cause of Meg's distress, no support group for victims of the Pacers.

"You left her a week after the wedding, Jack."

"Not because I wanted to."

She looked at him. He could feel her trying to decide whether or not she believed him. "I'm sorry," she said. "I'm just telling you what might help."

"The only thing that would *help* isn't legal," he said. He moved away and went to stand at the window, leaving Lucas to explain his remark. He stared out at the parking lot. After a moment, he realized that Winston had come to stand with him and that he had said something. "What?" Jack asked. He was so tired, that he had to force himself to pay attention.

"Did you talk to Meggie's doctor?" the old man asked.

"I talked to him. He thinks the high blood pressure is all because she's pregnant. He doesn't accept the concept of man and nature needing to be in a balanced and universal harmony."

"Neither do you," Winston said.

"Meggie does," Jack said, glancing at the old man. "How can she be in *hozro* with everything that's happened? It's tearing her apart! All this trouble with the dead man's parents and me. And Will and his bootlegging. And being *here*. This is a bad place for her, Winston. Her father was brought here and he didn't live. I don't think she would have come here if people didn't keep telling her it was the best thing for the baby." He gave a sharp sigh. "I want to go to Gallup and find those people and make them stop this!"

"Yes," Winston said quietly.

"I don't know what to do for her."

"Maybe you should ask Eddie Nez."

"Eddie Nez? About having a ceremony, you mean?"

"Can't hurt."

"Yeah, that's just what Meggie needs—an alcoholic, bootlegging *hataalii* doing a ceremony, assisted by his number-one boy driver."

"He's not drinking now. And he's got Will to help him if his hands shake. I saw Eddie Nez do a ceremony once. People called him The One Still Learning then. He wasn't much older than Will. He *knew*. He had the gift, and he was the best singer I ever seen. It was sacred, powerful, the way he did the chants. You could feel it when the Holy People came into the sand painting. The air in the hogan changed, like it was full of static electricity. Might be a good thing for everybody if Eddie Nez did a ceremony one more time."

"What makes you think he could remember how? The man's a drunk."

"Some things he don't remember, like where he was last night, but he remembers the chants and the sand paintings."

"Meg isn't Navajo, Winston."

"That's what you think," Winston declared, and Jack smiled in spite of himself. It was true, he himself had said it many times. Meggie was more Navajo than Jack Begaye would ever be.

"You have to tell Meggie it's the same, Jack," Winston said.

"What is?"

"These two things. If they took the baby because she is married to you, she wouldn't blame you for it, because it wasn't your doing. It's *them*. So you don't blame her for this trouble with the stolen money. Now you go talk to her about it. You see?"

"Yeah, old man," he said, giving Winston a pat on the back. "I do."

But Meg wasn't listening. She lay on her side, her eyes closed. They had brought her lunch tray while he was gone. It sat there untouched. He coaxed her into eating a little bit of everything. She even smiled once or twice at some of his lame jokes. But he had never seen her like this, and he was scared. Meg had always believed in the intrinsic good in people. It was as if she hadn't really understood, except on some kind of intellectual, academic level, that there were people in the world like the Pacers.

After she'd eaten, she went back to lying on her side, silent, unreachable. He tried not to fuss over her, and he didn't know whether it was better for him to stay or go. Did she need him, want him here? Or did she want to be left alone?

"I thought you were asleep," he said when he realized she was looking at him.

"I thought you were gone," she countered.

"Meggie," he said in exasperation, "where would I go? I don't know what you want me to do. I'll do anything you say except let you end the marriage. I won't do that, Meg."

She gave a wavering sigh and closed her eyes again.

"Did you read it?" she asked after a long period of silence.

"Read what?" he said, because he couldn't follow the abrupt shift in the conversation.

"The letter. Did you read it?"

"No. I didn't read it."

"Why not?"

"Because it was yours. Because *they* had it and *they* read it. They had no right to do that. It was an insult to you. I didn't want to be a part of that."

She looked at him. "I'm glad you didn't," she said. "It was . . ."

"What?" he asked when she didn't go on.

She gave a quiet sigh. "It was hurtful, insulting to us both. Full of accusations. I think it's the reason the Pacers are doing this."

"I don't understand."

"I never read the letter until you gave it to me."

"But it was addressed to you, postmarked. It had been opened."

"I know. John Thomas was very upset when he wrote it. He thought our being . . . together was going to change everything between us, that we'd be lovers instead of just friends. When I told him that it hadn't changed anything and that I was sorry it ever happened . . ."

She stopped, and it was all Jack could do not to get up and pace the room. He didn't want to hear this.

And yet he did.

"He was so angry," she said finally. "He wrote the letter to tell me exactly what he thought of me—and you. He was very hurt and probably a little drunk. But after he'd mailed it, he had second thoughts. He came to see me, to apologize, but I wasn't at home. He was waiting on the front steps in the rain when I got there. He wanted to know if the letter had come and he asked me to please not read it. He said he was sorry he'd ever written it and he didn't mean any of the things he'd said. He was embarrassed and ashamed, and he just wanted me to give it back to him."

"And you did."

"Yes. The Pacers must have found it in his belongings after he died. And they think I'm...like that—the way John Thomas wrote about me."

"Meg, don't tell me any more. I know you. You're going to want me to understand these people and then you'll want me to excuse what they're doing."

"People always have reasons. It helps to know what they are."

"It helps *you* to know what there are. I don't want to know. I don't want to understand. I want them to go back where they came from and leave us alone." He stopped because she looked so unhappy. "What is it?" he asked.

"You shouldn't be involved in this, Jack," she said. "You don't *have* to be involved."

"No? Then what's my choice? I'm accused of taking their money. There's nothing either one of us can do, Meg. I'm not going anywhere."

She sat up, her hair mussed. She looked so beautiful to him, and so sad.

"Even if I asked you to?" she said quietly. She stared at him across the room, her face unreadable.

"Is that what you're doing?" he asked.

She didn't say anything. He got up from the chair and came to sit beside her on the edge of the bed. He made no attempt to touch her; he could feel her resistance to that. He just wanted to be closer. He wanted to be able to see her eyes so he would know which Meggie this was—his Meggie or the stranger the Pacers had made.

"If you are," he said, "I'm not going to make it easy for you."

Her face remained composed, but her eyes filled with tears; she refused to acknowledge the one that slid down her cheek. She gave a wavering sigh, then bowed her head.

"Look at me," he said. "Meg."

She let her eyes meet his, but it took a great effort on her part to do it.

"I've been thinking about that time when we were children and I ran off from the receiving home and came to your house. It was an ignorant and pushy thing for me to do—I hadn't known you long enough to just show up uninvited like that. I didn't know if Sloan would let me in the yard and I was sure Patrick wouldn't. The only thing I knew was that I needed to be there and I knew it would be all right with you if I came. I knew I didn't have to do anything or say anything. We could just sit together on your front steps and we could respect each other's sadness and not worry so much about the bad things that had happened to us." He reached out to touch her, then thought better of it and let his hand fall. "Do you remember any of this, Meg?"

"Yes," she said, her voice tremulous.

"If you don't want me here now, you're going to have to look at me and say it, because I won't believe it if you don't. You're going to have to tell me to go right to my face if you want me to leave. Tell me I'm making everything worse."

"Jack, don't."

"Go on, Meg. Tell me. Right now."

She abruptly covered her face with her hands.

"Meggie."

She reached for him then, and he put his arms around her, holding her. He would do anything for her—anything—and he was completely helpless. After a moment, he lifted her onto his lap, gently stroking her hair, whispering to her in English and in Navajo, praying that she would understand how much she mattered to him, she and her unborn child.

She took his hand and placed it on her belly. Immediately, he felt a fluttering as the baby kicked and moved.

"It's a little girl," she said, her hand resting on top of his.

A little girl, he thought. *Meg's daughter.*

My daughter.

"I have to get her here, Jackie. I have to carry her long enough so she can make it if my blood pressure stays up and they have to take her."

"You will," he promised.

"I'm so scared."

"I know. Just let me hold you."

He was still holding her when the nurse came in.

"Would you look at this!" the nurse said in mock horror, holding up both hands. "No, don't move. Just give me an arm—preferably Meg's."

Meg smiled and did so, still resting her head against his shoulder.

"All right!" the nurse said. "Best blood pressure reading since you've been here. Somebody should have thought of this lap thing sooner. I don't suppose you rent him out?" she teased.

"I think not," Meg said.

"Just my luck. I'll be back in a little while."

"Okay," Meg said.

"You're sure I can't take him with me? I've got at least two more patients who ought to sit on his lap before I check their pressure."

"Sorry," Meg said.

When the nurse had gone, Jack waited for Meg to settle into his arms again. She didn't. She moved so she could see his face instead, her eyes searching his.

"I can't remember when I didn't want you to be my husband. Did you know that? I wanted us to be like Sloan and Lucas. I thought we could get married and live happily ever after." She smiled sadly. "But everything is all wrong, Jack—"

"Meg," he interrupted, because he was afraid of the sudden direction this conversation was taking.

She pressed her fingers against his lips to stop him from saying anything more. "I want you to go."

"No."

"I *need* you to go, Jack. And I need you to wait."

"Wait? For what?"

"For us. I want you to wait until I can make things right, until we can start again."

"Meg, you don't go back to square one just because you hit a rough spot!"

"You do when you never should have started in the first place. Everything is out of harmony, Jack. Can't you feel it? When I married you, I brought too many problems with me. You have to let me get them straightened out."

"No!" he said. "We can do it together."

"*I* have to take care of this."

"Why?"

"Because it's the only way I can make amends! It's the only way I can find the harmony. Everything that's happened is all because of *my* choices, and I have to be the one to fix it. You can't help me, Jack. I can't bear having you hurt just because you love me."

He looked at her determined, beautiful face, and he knew that the decision wasn't his. But how could he stand being away from her, especially now?

"Don't do this, Meggie. If you let these people come between us, then they win."

"I'm not going to let them ruin your life!"

"What about *our* life, Meg?"

"I'm looking at you and I'm saying the words," she said. "I want you to go. Please. If you love me, Jack. *Please!*"

Chapter Eighteen

He loved her. As far as he was concerned that was the only certainty in this mess. And he was trying to be her husband, even if he had to be an absent one.

He walked down the corridor, his hurt and his anger making him oblivious to everything but the non-choice she had given him. Go back to Window Rock or just go.

He nearly ran into a man when he turned the corner, a man who didn't seem to grasp the concept that, if they were to continue on their merry way, one of them would have to step aside.

Jack looked up. And swore.

Patrick.

If there was anything this situation did not need, it was Meg's older brother.

"This is all *your* doing," Patrick said without prelude. "I knew it would just be a matter of time until you screwed up everything."

"Hello, Patrick. Glad to see you again, too." Jack said, making no attempt to defend himself.

"Where is she?"

"Down that way. Next to the last room on the right."

"Did she tell you why she wanted me to come?"

Jack stood there without answering, hoping his surprise didn't show. He didn't know Meg wanted to see him at all, much less why.

"Well, that figures," Patrick said. "She's not going to lose the baby, is she?"

"I don't know. It depends."

"On what? What are they doing for her?"

"Nothing."

"Nothing?"

"Look, Patrick. There isn't any treatment for this except bed rest. The cure is the delivery of the baby. They want her to take it easy, and hopefully that will keep her blood pressure down until she's far enough along so they can take the baby by cesarean."

"You mean the baby might die? What about Meg? Is she in danger?"

Jack took a deep breath. "Yeah, Patrick, she is."

"So if she got worse, they'd want to take the baby now."

"If it was bad enough."

"I don't think Meg would let them do that," he said, and he walked off, leaving Jack standing.

My God, Jack thought. Patrick was right—and it had never even occurred to him.

He didn't want to go back to the waiting area with the rest of the family, and he didn't want to leave, not with Patrick here. Whatever it was that Meggie needed to have done, *he* wanted to be the one to do it. Banished or not, he was her husband, damn it!

He returned to the waiting room after all, and he sat there, trying to behave. It took a huge effort on his part. Eddie Nez and Will were having a quiet *hataalii* class, and he half listened to that.

The pay phone rang. Sloan answered it. "For you," she said to Lucas.

Lucas took the receiver and listened for a while, then abruptly turned to look at Jack.

"Whatever it is, *I* didn't do it," Jack said sarcastically.

"Whatever it is, he didn't do it," Lucas repeated on the phone. "Yes, I'm sure. He's been here. Yeah, Winston is here, too."

"Now what?" Jack asked when Lucas hung up, echoing the question in every single person's mind.

"Those California people don't like you running loose," Lucas said.

"I'll just bet they don't. What have they got missing now?"

"They say they're being stalked by some unnamed person or persons."

"Stalked?"

"That's the report."

"And I just automatically came to mind."

"Oddly enough," Lucas said.

"Well, I don't stalk. I only loot motel rooms."

"That's a good one, Jack. You keep it up and the wrong person's going to hear you being cute."

But Jack had had enough of this conversation, and he shut out whatever else Lucas said.

What could Patrick and Meg be talking about? *Hello, brother dear. Guess what? I just dumped that husband you were so upset about.*

No. Meggie wouldn't do that. She wouldn't tell Patrick their troubles. He sighed. How the hell did he know what Meg would do? She'd certainly managed to keep him permanently ambushed so far.

He could feel Winston's acute attention and he forced himself not to jiggle his knee or drum his fingers on the chair arm.

Finally, he saw Patrick coming down the corridor. Patrick stopped long enough to stick something in his wallet. He had a brief conference with Lucas and Sloan, punched Will on the arm and then went straight to the elevator, ignoring his favorite brother-in-law completely. Only when the doors were about to close did he finally look in Jack's direction.

Jack sighed again, either with relief or resignation—he wasn't sure which. He was only sure that he'd had enough of all of *this,* too. He got up and headed for the stairwell, and he didn't stop until he reached the outside. He stood in the fresh air and bright sunlight, breathing deeply to get rid of the hospital smell. Meg was right. He had no business being here.

I should be back in Window Rock, Meg, with you.

He should be working at the shelter, going home to the mission house for lunch, searching the thrift shops for baby furniture on the weekends, going to bed, waking up, *living*—with her.

He began to walk, following the various sidewalks to nowhere he wanted to go. Eventually, he wound up exactly where he'd started. His faithful bail bondsman stood waiting with an air of unconcern Jack had to admire, considering the amount of money the old man had invested in his whereabouts.

"Did you talk to Eddie Nez about doing a ceremony for Meg?" Winston asked as he walked up.

"No," he said.

"Did Meggie say what she wanted with her brother?" Winston asked next, as if one thing led directly to the other.

Jack gave him a warning look.

"I'm wondering," Winston explained.

"You're always wondering. Maybe we should get Eddie Nez to do a ceremony for *that*."

"Curiosity ain't something you can cure, Jack," the old man said philosophically. "Did she say or not?"

"No, she didn't say."

"She's worried then—probably that you'll do something rash."

"*I'll* do something rash? Yeah, that makes sense. I might do something rash, so let's call in good old, levelheaded, unrash Patrick to come take care of it."

"Patrick can't do something that will get him put back in jail. You can. Are you going to go talk to Meggie now, maybe find out what Patrick *is* doing?"

"No."

"Why not?"

"Because she doesn't want me around."

"She said that?"

"Loud and clear."

"What else did she say?"

"Winston..."

"You need to talk about this, Jack. You're too out of harmony to think it out by yourself."

Out of harmony. He was certainly that, even if he didn't believe in it. "She said she wanted me to wait," he said, giving in to Winston's pestering because there was no point in prolonging the inevitable.

"For what?"

"I don't know."

"That sounds the same to me, too," Winston said. "There's a lot in this whole business that's the same."

"Winston, you're driving me crazy. I want you to know that."

"Jack, you're not listening. It's the same as what you asked her to do a couple of weeks ago—you know, when you had to go your own way and you didn't tell her why, but you wanted her to wait until you got done doing it."

"That was different."

"Don't sound different to me."

"Winston, it was different, okay?"

"So what are we going to do?" Winston persisted.

"I don't know. Maybe go see the Pacers, find out about the stalking business."

"Bad idea, Jack."

"Have you got a better one? No, scratch that. Your last idea got me arrested."

"Yeah, but I didn't know we were dealing with such liars."

"Said the brains behind the breaking and entering."

"I thought you just walked into that room."

"I did. And I don't want to talk about this."

"So are we staying here even if Meggie don't want us to?"

"I don't know, Winston! I don't know what's going on. I don't know why she all of a sudden doesn't want me here."

Winston made no attempt to answer the unanswerable. They stood for a while in silence.

"Did anybody—Dolly or Lucas—ever give Meggie her war name when she was a little girl?" Winston suddenly asked.

"Winston, what are you talking about?"

"Meggie. I'm thinking our Meggie's gone to war, Jack."

"Did you and Jack have a fight?" Sloan asked.

"No," Meg said.

"Then what's wrong with him?"

"I . . . don't know what you mean."

"I mean, he's got that look, the same look he used to get when his father was drunk and looking for him so he could beat him again. *That* look."

"Is he still here?" Meg tried to make the question nonchalant and failed miserably.

"He was the last time I looked."

She closed her eyes, both relieved and disappointed. She had to do something about the Pacers and he couldn't be involved. She had to do what she should have done before she ever came back to Window Rock. If she had dealt with the Pacers then, Jack wouldn't be in this trouble.

"Meggie?" Sloan said.

"I told him I didn't want him here," Meg said.

"I . . . see. Well, if that's the case, I don't think he's listening."

"He has to listen. I'm not going to change my mind."

Sloan reached out to take her hand. "Meg, are you sure this is what you want? He really cares about you—anyone can see that. And you need all the caring you can get right now."

"It's what I have to do."

"I don't understand."

"I know you don't and I can't explain it. Would you go talk to him, Sloan? Be subtle. Make sure he's all right."

"He'll think I'm meddling."

Meg smiled.

"Okay, okay. So what else is new, right?" Sloan said. "I'll go talk to him."

Jack had just closed his eyes, meaning to only skirt the edges of sleep. When he opened them, Sloan was sitting across from him, waiting. She handed him a cup of coffee—not the vending-machine kind, but some of the real stuff she'd managed to get from somewhere. It smelled good, tasted even better. He glanced around the waiting area, wondering where everyone else had gone.

Oh, I get it, he suddenly thought. *A little heart-to-heart discussion/official dismissal.*

"Thanks," he said, taking another sip of the coffee. He set the cup aside, because Sloan was still waiting. "Meg told you, didn't she?" he said, deciding to get it over with.

"Yes."

"I guess you're glad she finally saw the light."

"Jack, that's not true. I want Meg to be happy, and I've known for a long, *long* time that a lot of that depends on you."

"Okay," he said abruptly, deciding to be completely candid. "This is how it is. I don't know what to do. I don't want to leave her here. I don't want her upset because I stay. *You* tell me what I should do."

Sloan shook her head. "I don't know, Jack."

"I love her," he said, staring at the floor. He looked up, meeting Sloan's eyes. "I love her," he said again. "I just want us to be together—Meg and me and the baby. It's a little girl. Did you know that?"

"Yes."

"I'm glad it's a little girl. Maybe she'll have red hair like Meggie." He suddenly smiled, thinking about it. "Couldn't beat that—*two* of them." But his smile faded. "It's not going to happen, is it? Even if the baby gets here okay....'"

"Jack—"

"I can't fight those people *and* Meg! And Lucas, and maybe even you. I don't know what to do, damn it!"

"Maybe..." Sloan began, but she didn't go on.

"What?" he asked.

She gave a quiet sigh. "Maybe you should do whatever Meggie asked you to do. You know her better than anyone, Jack. Do you think she'd ask you to do something, especially if it made you unhappy, if she didn't have to or need to?"

He thought about this. There was a lot of truth in what Sloan said.

"If I leave, will you stay with her so she won't be alone? She hates this place, Sloan."

"I'll stay as long as she's here, Jack. I've already made arrangements to do that. A former co-worker of mine works in the hospital. She doesn't live too far away and she's offered me a bed as long as I need it."

"Good. That's good. And will you call me every day? More often if there's something going on?"

"Where do you think you'll be?"

He gave a small shrug and a resigned half smile. "At the shelter . . . or in jail," he said.

"Okay, Jack," she said, giving him a slight smile in return. "But let's hope it's the former. I give you my word. I'll look after her for you the best I can."

"If she changes her mind about . . . me being here, you'd tell me that, too?"

"Yes, Jack."

He stood up when she did, and she gave him a brief hug before she walked back down the corridor toward Meg's room. But he didn't leave right away. For one thing, he'd lost Winston. He couldn't find him in any of the places he should have been. When the old man finally returned, it was nearly sundown.

"Winston, where have you been?" Jack said, sounding like his father instead of his ward.

"The flea market," he answered.

"*Why?*"

"Had to get something for Meggie." He pulled a purple suede pouch out of his shirt pocket—a tourist version of a medicine bag. "I found the bag okay, but the things she needs to have in it took awhile. You go give it to her, Jack."

He tried his best to be annoyed with the old man and couldn't do it. He took the purple bag. It was hardly authentic, but it didn't matter about the bag itself. The contents were what mattered, and he had no doubt that those would be exactly right.

"Thanks, Winston."

"She's going to need it," he said.

Maybe she would, Jack thought. It couldn't hurt. He walked to Meg's room, prepared to explain to her and Sloan why he was still here. But Sloan wasn't there and Meg was sleeping. He stood and watched her for a long time. He wanted to touch her, to wake her, to tell her they could work this out somehow if they just stayed together. But he didn't. He quietly laid the pouch on the bedside table.

If you love me, she'd said.

"I love you, Meggie," he whispered.

Chapter Nineteen

Meg woke to the trilling of the telephone. She looked at her watch, but there wasn't enough light in the room to see what time it was. She turned over and fumbled for the receiver, dropping it once in the process.

"Hello?"

It took the caller a moment to respond. "Meg?" Patrick said finally. "Meg, I got it."

She closed her eyes in relief. "Patrick, thank you for doing this for me."

"No problem. Your friends were expecting me. It didn't take long to find it. It was right where you said. I've made copies and I sent the original to Lillian by registered mail. I can't get a flight out until late this afternoon. You need me to do anything else while I'm here?"

"Yes," she said. "Take a nice girl to lunch."

He laughed. "Oh, I can do that. In fact, I think I see one now."

"Patrick, I—"

"You're not going to bawl or gush all over me or anything, are you? You know I hate that kind of stuff. You're my little sister and I love you—pain in the butt that you always were—and that's that."

She didn't say anything. It was either silence or the kind of stuff he hated.

"I think everything's going to be all right, Meggie," he said.

"I won't forget this, Patrick. And I'll pay back the money for the airfare."

"I don't want the money. And if I stay on the line, you're going to bawl or bust. So I'm going. You take care of yourself—you and what's-his-name."

"You, too," she said. "Patrick . . . about Jack—"

But he had already gone, and she lay there for a moment before she hung up the phone.

So far, so good.

When she reached to put the receiver back, she noticed the leather pouch. She knew immediately what it was for and who had likely put it there. Without hesitation she hung it around her neck. She closed her eyes, trying to draw strength and courage from its symbolism and from the love she knew was behind it.

She picked up the receiver again and dialed information. She didn't have that terrible feeling of not being able to concentrate this morning, and the call went through immediately. She made a mental note for future reference—she'd know when her blood pressure was too high if she had a major headache, tightness in her chest and couldn't handle a telephone.

She held the leather pouch in the palm of her hand for courage.

"Gallup," she said after a moment. Then, "Chamber of Commerce."

The Chamber of Commerce person was extremely helpful, giving her the names of the motels and their telephone numbers with cheerful expertise. Meg started at the top of the list. On her third attempt, she finally located the right motel and asked the switchboard operator to ring the room.

Carolyn Pacer answered.

"Mrs. Pacer," Meg said. "This is Meg Begaye."

The telephone immediately clicked in her ear as Carolyn hung up.

Jack had no intention of confronting the Pacers again—or at least not much of one. He tried to stay busy at the shelter instead, but the fifth morning after he'd returned to Window Rock, their white car was waiting in the dirt parking lot when he arrived.

Oh, great, he thought. He'd been expecting some kind of catastrophe ever since he woke up—Eddie Nez falling off the wagon or taking Will to "haul water" again or the two of them participating in some other illegal endeavor. Jack didn't dare let his mind go to the possibility that something might happen with Meg.

And he did *not* need whatever this was with the Pacers.

Winston must have been watching for him, for he immediately came out the side door to meet him before he even got out of the truck.

"Any phone calls?" Jack asked without looking at the white car, "any" meaning ones from or about Meg.

"No," Winston said.

"How long have *they* been here?"

"Long time, Jack."

"Did they say what they wanted?"

"They asked where you were and if you'd be here."

"I don't need this, Winston."

"Coyote's been busy lately," Winston offered as an explanation for Jack's recent tribulations.

"Yes, damn his sorry hide. Well, I guess I'd better see what they want now."

"Don't let them make you do something that will get you back in jail," Winston admonished when Jack was about to get out of the truck. "You got to be able to go if Meggie needs you."

He got out of the truck and walked toward the white car. When Winston began to chant behind him, Jack looked over his shoulder.

"You need all the help you can get," Winston said in Navajo. "And you need a witness."

Jack supposed that he did. What Winston had said before was true—they hadn't known the Pacers were such liars.

He stopped walking a little more than halfway to their car. He remembered their last meeting, and if Ronald and Carolyn had something to say, they would have to come to him.

After a moment, the front car doors opened and they both got out.

Winston's chant got louder. Ronald said something to his wife, and she reluctantly got back into the car.

Jack stood waiting. The man looked tired—persecution evidently took a lot out of a person—and he kept glancing at Winston, as if he categorically did not approve.

"What is he doing?" Pacer asked.

"War song," Jack said. "He thinks I need it."

Pacer didn't approve of Jack's somewhat feeble attempt at levity, either. "I want you to know right now that my wife and I aren't going to be intimidated," he said, jabbing the air with his finger.

Jack made no reply, even though it was obviously his turn to speak.

"We know what you're doing," Pacer said. "Both of you."

Jack thought at first the man was including Winston. But then he realized he meant Meg.

"I don't want my wife upset any more," Pacer said, his voice rising. "She's been hurt enough."

"So has mine," Jack said.

"I want you to stop this now!"

"Mr. Pacer," Jack said quietly. "What is it exactly you think I'm doing?"

"You've got those people following us everywhere we go."

"Following you?" Jack looked around him. "What people? I don't understand."

"Oh, you understand! We're always being watched. They're outside when we leave the motel in the morning. They're at the restaurants, the stores—everywhere we go! I know you and that girl are responsible!"

"What do these . . . people look like?"

"They're Navajo. Old women, young boys, women carrying babies—people you've put up to doing this!"

"Mr. Pacer, I don't know what the hell you're talking about."

Winston said something behind him in Navajo.

Jack frowned and looked over his shoulder.

Winston said the word again, and this time Jack understood. "You knew about this?" Jack asked him in Navajo.

"Yes," Winston said.

"Why didn't you tell me?"

"Because you'd be thinking you got to help," Winston said. "And next thing me and Meggie know, you'd end up back in jail."

"What is he saying?" Ronald asked, his annoyance obvious.

"He said it's the 'killing with the eyes.'"

"Killing with the eyes? What is that?"

"It's a Navajo thing, Mr. Pacer. We're a subtle people. When we think another person has done something hurtful and wrong, then we watch everything they do all the time. We do it until the guilty person finally asks why. And then we can sit down and talk about it. We can say exactly what was done and why it's a problem. And the other person can explain his reasons for doing it. There aren't many secrets on the rez, Mr. Pacer. The People know what you and your wife are doing to Meg and me. They know you want Meg to give up her baby. They know you lied about the money to make her do it. And somebody in my or Meg's clan has decided to call you on it."

"This is ridiculous!"

"Is it? You're here with the question, aren't you? You want to know why it's happening. Well, Winston says it's the 'killing with the eyes.' I can't stop it. I wouldn't if I could. The only thing that will stop it is our sitting down together and trying to come to some kind of agreement. We could go to Peacemaker Court and talk—try to understand each other." He made the offer for Meg's sake. He personally would have preferred hand-to-hand combat.

"If you think for one minute we're going to let ourselves be railroaded into some kind of biased, kangaroo-court proceedings..." Pacer abruptly turned away and began walking toward the car.

"I'm sorry for you," Jack called after him, but Pacer didn't stop walking.

"I'm sorry for the son you lost. And I'm sorry you never learned how to behave. But you know who's being hurt the most by what you're doing? The baby, Mr. Pacer."

"What do you mean?" Pacer said, finally turning around.

"Meg is having complications with the pregnancy."

"What kind of complications?"

"The kind that are made a whole lot worse by the hell you and your wife are putting her through."

"I don't believe you."

"If she loses that baby, you and your wife are going to have a lot to answer for. You don't know what kind of person Meg is. She's kind and gentle. She wouldn't hurt anybody if she could help it. You don't know what this is doing to her. You could stop this, Mr. Pacer, even if your wife doesn't agree. What you're doing is wrong, man."

"It is not wrong! That baby needs a chance!"

"Planting evidence is okay where you come from? Making Meg choose between her husband and her baby is okay? What kind of people are you?"

"There was no evidence planted, Begaye! You simply aren't a very accomplished thief. And as for Meg Baron's qualifications as a mother *or a wife*—"

"Don't you say *anything* about Meg!" Jack ordered, taking a step toward him.

"Jack," Winston said quietly behind him. "Don't."

Jack glanced in his direction and took a deep breath.

"One of you put that money in the truck," he said to Pacer, reaching deep for some remnant of self-control. "If it wasn't you, then maybe you should try to remember just when it was you let your wife out of your sight."

"I've had enough of this," Pacer said, walking toward his car again.

It took everything Jack had not to follow after him, not to grab him and *make* him listen.

Pacer turned back to him before he got into the car. "We're going to court. You might as well accept that. None of your stories about planted money or so-called problems with the pregnancy are going to stop it."

"Meg is in the hospital!"

"No! She's at her uncle's house in Window Rock!"

Jack stood there, stunned. *It's not true,* he thought. *Sloan would have told me.*

Unless Meg wouldn't let her.

The car backed around and spun out of the dirt parking lot. He looked up at the sky. Winston came and stood at his elbow.

"Did you know she was home?" Jack asked.

The old man didn't answer him.

"How long has she been home?"

"Since yesterday."

"And you didn't tell me!"

"It's not my place, Jack."

"Since when?"

"Meggie asked you to wait. She must not be done yet if she don't send for you."

"I'm her husband, damn it!" He walked rapidly to the truck and jerked open the door.

"Where are you going?" Winston called after him.

"I'm going to go tell her that!"

Chapter Twenty

He held on to his anger all the way to the Singer house. He still had it when he walked up the flagstone path. But when Sloan opened the door, it immediately dissipated.

"Is Meg all right?" he asked, communicating every bit of the worry that had abruptly taken its place.

"Let's talk out here," Sloan said. "She's asleep. She hasn't slept much lately, and I don't want to wake her."

He was in no state of mind to take a tour of the grounds, but he stood back to let her come outside. The wind was up and the wind chimes clanged loudly. Her face told him absolutely nothing.

"Meg signed herself out of the hospital. I tried to talk to her, Jack. She wouldn't listen."

"What about the doctors? What did they say?"

"Actually, I think they unofficially agreed with her. There's been a lot of progress in the holistic approach to treating an illness since I was in school. She can be monitored here just as well. The doctor at the clinic knows her case, and Meg knows the consequences. You said it yourself—she was miserable in the hospital. It couldn't be good for her. To tell you the truth, I had forgotten what a really terrible time it was for her when her father died. Knowing Meggie, the stress she felt from being there was undoing whatever good she got from being hospitalized in the first place. So, here we are."

"And when were you going to get around to telling *me* that?" he asked, finding that some remnant of his anger remained, after all.

"I tried to call you before we left Albuquerque. I tried again just now, right before you came. No one at the shelter answered the phone."

"I was busy with the Pacers."

"You've seen them?"

"Oh, yes. They were good enough to come and let me know my wife was here."

Sloan looked at him, and, clearly, she refused to be put in the wrong. "What did they really want, Jack?"

"They wanted me to make The People stop looking at them."

"Am I supposed to know what that means?" she asked in a tone of voice that suggested that she wasn't going to be toyed with, either.

He sighed and explained the killing with the eyes.

"Do you think that's what's happening?"

"Winston does."

"Then I suspect Dolly is right in the middle of it."

"It doesn't matter," Jack said. "They think I'm the guilty party, and believe me, nobody is going to change their minds."

"Wrong, Jack. Lillian is about to change their minds all over the place."

"What do you mean?"

"I mean Meggie's finally turned her loose. No more kid gloves. No more begging to see them and trying to be reasonable. I believe she's doing the right thing, but it's really hard for her."

"I don't understand."

"And I can't explain it," she said. "Meg hasn't told me very much. I know you want to be with her, Jack, but the situation hasn't changed. Not really. Not yet."

"Sloan—"

"I'm going to be blunt, Jack. If you don't stay out of the way and give her the chance to make things right for the two of you, I don't think there's any chance for your marriage. It's not just that Meg *wants* to try to fix whatever harm she thinks she's done. She has to do it—because she's Meggie. And you have to wait."

He didn't say anything.

"Is she asking too much of you, Jack?" Sloan said quietly. "If you're going to bail out, if you're not going to be here for her, please tell me now. I need to know."

He looked at her sharply, ready to take offense. But, seeing her face, he knew the question hadn't come from any prejudice on her part, any expectation that he was about to run from yet another unhappy situation the way he had when he was a boy. The question came from her love and her concern for Meg, and he could accept that.

"I'm not going to bail out. You and Lucas aren't going to get me out of the family that easy," he said, and to his surprise, she abruptly smiled. It reminded him so much of Meg that he had to turn away.

He stood for a moment, staring at the tall rocks behind the house, wondering how it had all come down to this. He was as far from Meg as he'd ever been—when he loved her, and she loved him. Why wasn't that enough?

"I want to see her, Sloan," he said, looking back at her. "I won't wake her. I just want to... see her."

She seemed about to protest, but she didn't. She gave a quiet sigh, then nodded and moved to the edge of the patio to sit down and wait.

The house was very still when he went inside—no radio or television playing. He walked down the hallway to Meg's bedroom. She was living here now, as if she were still seventeen years old. As if she'd never married him.

The door was ajar, and he entered the room quietly, coming to stand near the side of the bed. She was sleeping soundly, lying on her left side and she was beautiful. He stared down at her, watching her for a long time. It took all the willpower he had not to reach out his hand and touch her.

I was going to seduce you....

Meggie, Meggie, if only you had.

He realized when he came back outside that he'd stayed with Meg too long. Sloan was pacing back and forth across the patio, and the relief she felt at his return was all too apparent.

"I didn't wake her," he said. "I told you I wouldn't. I love Meg. I'm going to do whatever is best for her."

"The problem is being able to tell what that is, Jack."

"Sloan..."

But he was tired suddenly, and he didn't go on. He didn't want to fight with her. The confrontation with Pacer had been enough for one day.

"Will you keep your promise?" he asked. "Will you call me if Meg needs me—needs anything?"

"Yes."

"And you'll tell me how she's doing with the baby and her blood pressure and everything. I'm her husband. I don't want to hear things from the Pacers or from the reservation grapevine."

"Yes, Jack. I'll do my best."

He looked at her a long moment. He believed her, but he still didn't want to go.

"Okay," he said finally. "Then I'll do what you said—for now. I'll stay out of the way."

He began to walk toward the truck, and, to his surprise, Sloan went with him.

"You'll tell her I was here?" he asked as he opened the truck door.

She nodded.

"But don't tell her I had a run-in with the Pacers."

"No," she said.

"It would worry her."

She didn't say anything, and he sighed. There was nothing left to do but go.

"Tell her—" He broke off and stared into the distance.

"She knows you love her, Jack," Sloan said. "She's *always* known that."

Winston was waiting for him on the back steps when he returned to the shelter, waiting and worrying. The old man wasn't wringing his hands exactly, but he was close to it.

"Did you talk to Meggie?" he called, standing up to ask, hardly giving Jack a chance to get out of the truck.

"No," Jack said as he walked toward him.

"Why not?"

"She was asleep. Sloan said she hasn't been resting very well. I didn't wake her."

"You still mad?"

"Not . . . very," Jack said, sitting down on the shelter steps beside him. He could feel the old man willing him to give the rest of his report, and he gave it, filling him in on the details of Meg's leaving the hospital and Sloan's revelation about "turning Lillian loose."

"I want you to go to the house again and look out for Meggie like you did before," he said when he'd finished.

"No," Winston said.

"No? What do you mean 'no'?"

"Meggie ain't the one that needs looking out for," the old man said. "She's got Sloan and Lucas and Dolly to do that. The one that needs looking out for is you."

"Winston, you aren't going to lose your bail money."

"I'm not worrying about the money. What are you going to do if those people come back here, Jack? If I'm not with you, maybe you'll do something rash."

"I am not going to do something rash!"

"How close did you come with that man and his wife earlier?"

Jack didn't answer him.

"You need help with this, Jack. Those people even make *me* want to do something rash. Maybe, if we stick together, we can behave. And Meggie will rest a lot easier if she knows I'm taking care of you. I know that for sure. I said I'd help you and I will. So you better get used to it."

"You're going to take care of me," Jack said, trying not to smile.

"Yes," Winston assured him.

"And I can just get used to it."

"That's right."

"Okay," Jack said. But it wasn't Winston's constant attendance that he needed to get used to. It was being away from Meggie and worrying about her and the baby and always having to look over his shoulder because he didn't know what persecution the Pacers would come up with next.

They sat for a time in silence—*he* was silent anyway; Winston still had something on his mind. Jack could almost hear him ruminating.

"What?" Jack said when he couldn't stand it any longer.

"I'm thinking about something Meggie told me," Winston answered.

"What?" Jack said again, but in a kinder tone this time.

"When you were in the marines, she said you never did write to her. Not one letter in all that time. I'm thinking, Jack, maybe you want to write to her now."

Jack looked at him. "Old man, you come up with the damned craziest ideas," he said, getting up and walking toward the truck.

"Where are you going?" Winston called after him.

"I'm going to buy some envelopes!"

He tried not to think about time. About how long it had been since he'd seen Meggie or how long it might still be. Or when Lillian might have something to tell her regarding the Pacers. Or how many weeks Meggie had left until the baby would be born. He worked at the shelter one day at a time. He worked at sprucing up the mission house, and making a cedar cradle board for the baby, and at whatever task Winston always seemed to have for him.

And he wrote the letters. He was careful not to burden Meggie with his misery over their separation, and he didn't speculate about their future or mention his impending court date. He wrote about when they were children instead. Or his adventures as a big tough marine—all those things he might have told her when he was away and didn't.

He asked her not to answer them, because he thought it might be too much of a chore for her and because he was afraid. He didn't want to open a letter from her, in what he knew would be joyful anticipation, only to find out that she had decided there was no hope for them after all. He supposed that his letters had been well received, that Meggie was glad to get them and wasn't upset by them. Lucas would have already come to the shelter to crack his head otherwise.

But he was hanging on by a thread and he knew it. He hated waiting. He hated not knowing. He hated having the Pacers still wandering around Window Rock doing who knew what. He had been advised by any number of people that the Pacers had been to the law-enforcement building several times recently, and the latest report had them going to see Meggie yesterday and today.

She shouldn't have to do this by herself, damn it!

He tried to talk to Lillian—with Winston in tow, of course—but it had been useless. Lillian only offered the same tired advice: Let Meggie do what she has to do. Stay out of the way.

But it was hard to keep busy—especially today. He had already talked to Sloan about Meggie—the blood pressure was within normal limits; there was no news from Lillian. The shelter was only at half-capacity. Eddie Nez was behaving. Will was still coming to do his community service, and he took care of many of the daily chores. Jack wasn't quite to the point of pacing the perimeter, but he was close.

He looked toward the nearest window at the sound of rain, a heavy "male" rain that had come in escort to the thunderheads he'd seen earlier. And the feeling of confinement and helplessness was suddenly unbearable.

He took a deep breath. Stood up. Sat down. Stood up again.

Winston was puttering in the kitchen, cleaning up the last of the debris from the evening meal. He could hear the old man chanting under his breath as he worked. He could hear the television in the dayroom. He could hear the roll of thunder and the rain.

He didn't sneak out exactly, but neither did he make any unnecessary noise. He just walked past the kitchen and out the back door, and he stood for a moment on the steps, exhilarated by the violence of the storm and by his impending rush to freedom. What he wouldn't give for that Norton motorcycle and a flat stretch of highway.

The battered pickup truck would have to do.

He drove with the window down—fast. He could smell the rain on the dusty earth, on the hot highway. He headed out of Window Rock toward Ganado with no thought of flash floods and no plan except to do something about his now overwhelming restlessness.

But there was nothing to be done except to drive. How far would he have to go to get rid of it? he wondered. He could see himself arriving on the West Coast and still feeling just as miserable as he did now.

I'm doing the best I can, Meggie!

He stopped at the Hubbell Trading Post, bought a soft drink and a bag of potato chips he didn't really want, and he hung around until the people inside the place began to wonder. Then he got back into the truck and drove again. It was nearly dark, and he decided to keep following the rough triangle of roads— Window Rock to Ganado to the interstate and then eastward toward Gallup.

From Gallup, he headed home, and he saw the flashing lights in his rearview mirror when he was less than a mile from the shelter—not a surprise to him because he was still speeding. He slowed down and pulled off the road at the first place that was wide enough, resigned to yet another encounter with the tribal police.

It was raining still, but it seemed the worst of the storm had passed. He sat with his hands on the steering wheel and watched the tribal policeman get out of his vehicle.

"Let's go, Jack," the officer said when he reached the open truck window, and Jack looked around sharply, recognizing the voice immediately.

Lucas Singer.

He swore under his breath.

"Get out of the truck," Lucas said, opening the door.

Jack stayed where he was. "Why?" he asked stubbornly. If this was something else with the Pacers, he was *not* going peacefully.

"Let's go, damn it!"

"No! I was driving too fast. You caught me. If you're going to give me a ticket, then do it. I'm not going anywhere."

"It's Meg, Jack," Lucas said. "Sloan sent me to find you. Leave the truck here and let's go."

"Meg? What's happened to Meg?" he said, scrambling to get out, because Lucas was walking away from him and not answering.

"Lucas!" he yelled, running after him.

"Get in," Lucas said over his shoulder.

Jack had no choice but to comply. "You tell me what's wrong!" he said as Lucas got in on the other side and slammed the car door.

"Her blood pressure went up again. The doctor sent her to the hospital in Gallup. He's going to do a C-section—he may have already done it. Where the hell have you been?"

"Nowhere," he answered, staring down Lucas's disapproving look. But he'd just come from Gallup. And Meg had been there.

"Well, you picked a hell of a time to make the trip," Lucas said, pulling sharply back onto the road. "You knew something like this could happen."

"All I know is what your wife tells me! When I talked to her his morning, she said Meggie's blood pressure was fine."

"That was then. This is now."

Jack gave a sharp exhalation of breath. "What did the doctors say?"

"Meggie's blood pressure is up, and they can't wait any onger."

"What about the baby?"

"I don't know. I've been busy hunting for you."

"You think I did this on purpose?"

"You didn't tell Winston where you were going. When I found you, I didn't see anybody holding a gun to your head. So, yeah. I think you disappeared on purpose."

"Lucas..." Jack said in exasperation. Yes, he had done exactly that, but he wouldn't have if he'd had any idea something was wrong with Meg. "Just drive, will you?"

Lucas drove with all the skill of a man long used to getting places in a hurry. When they arrived at the hospital, Sloan was waiting for them on the maternity floor. Jack watched her face carefully as he and Lucas approached. She was very good at seeming impassive, he realized.

"You got what you wanted, Jack," she said without prelude.

"What I wanted," he repeated, because he didn't understand.

She smiled then and took his arm. "A little red-haired baby girl."

Chapter Twenty-One

It was a long time before Meggie was returned to her room—or it seemed that way to Jack. The only thing he could do was wait—something he had always done so *well*. He did see the baby, from a distance—a tiny redhead, just like Sloan said. She'd been placed in one of those high-tech incubators, but she was fine. Everyone assured him of that. Standard procedure, they said, because she was early—but not dangerously so—and he'd been delivered by C-section.

He was in the corridor when they brought Meggie down, and he stood back until she and her medical equipment were situated. He waited silently until Lucas and Sloan had spoken to her.

What if she still didn't want to see him? he thought. Lucas would certainly tell her he'd gone on an improvised tour of the reservation and the interstate just when she needed him.

He hoped she needed him.

The door opened, and Lucas came out. "I told her you were here," he said. "Damned if I know why that made her happy."

They stared at each other until Jack abruptly smiled. "I don't know either," he said. "Thanks, man. Thanks for getting me here."

He didn't wait for a reply. Sloan was on her way out when he opened the door.

"Take care of my redheads," she whispered in passing.

And suddenly, he and Meggie were alone.

Her eyes were closed; she was so pale. After a moment, she looked at him and smiled.

"Meggie," he whispered, pulling a chair up close to the bed so he could see her face. He touched her soft cheek, smoothed her hair. "How are you feeling?"

She reached out to him, and he caught her hand. "I feel . . . sad, Jack."

"No, don't be sad. I've seen the baby—she's beautiful. And she's fine."

"Come lie down with me," she whispered, trying and failing to make room for him.

"I don't think I'd better—"

"Please," she said.

He hesitated a moment to weigh the consequences—none that mattered he realized—then sat on the side of the bed and unlaced his boots. He stretched out beside her and held her as close as he dared. He gently kissed her forehead and her eyes and he lay there, cramped but savoring the warmth and the feel of her body against his. He had missed her so much! The thought that the Pacers could still cause him to be sent away from her was nearly more than he could bear. He tightened his arms around her and pressed his face into her neck. He had a thousand questions, but he didn't ask any of them.

After a moment, she turned her head so that she could see his face. "What about us, Jack? Are *we* okay?"

"Yes!" he whispered, pressing her close again. "A little beat up around the edges maybe, but we're okay."

He could feel her smile. "Thank you for the letters," she said sleepily.

"You're welcome, Meg."

"I've been thinking about some things."

"What kind of things?"

"Things I should have told you and didn't."

"You don't have to do it now. You need to rest—"

"I want to tell you now, Jack."

He took a quiet breath. "Okay."

She took his hand and held it against her cheek for a moment. "When you left the rez, left me, it hurt so much I thought I couldn't stand it. But I always knew the reason you did it. Always."

"Meggie—"

"You thought you'd ruin my life—my education, my chance to *be* something—if you stayed."

He didn't say anything.

"Didn't you?" she asked.

"I still might," he said.

"No, Jack. If anything, it's the other way around. But I know how hard it must have been. I know how much you must have loved me then."

"I love you now, Meg," he said. "And, yeah, it was hard. But it's okay. We're okay."

She gave a wavering sigh. "I've done everything I know to do for the baby, for us. But you see, I could have done something a lot sooner. If I had, you wouldn't have been accused."

"I don't understand."

"John Thomas wrote me two letters. You found the first one in the motel room. The other one I left at school. It was in a box of things I stored with some friends. When I was still in the hospital in Albuquerque, I sent Patrick to North Carolina to get it. I had to have it if I was going to put an end to all this—"

She abruptly stopped, but he didn't press her to go on. He waited. He could hear noises in the corridor outside, but no one came in.

"He wrote it just before he died," Meg said after a moment. Her hand clutched the front of his shirt. "He said he was so tired, and he asked me to forgive him."

"For what?"

"For not being around, if I should happen to need him."

"If there was a baby, you mean," Jack said, immediately understanding what Meg didn't say and what must have been uppermost in John Thomas Pacer's mind.

"Yes," she answered, and he closed his eyes against the sudden pang of jealousy he felt.

"He said that he hoped I wasn't pregnant, that the worst thing he could ever do would be to give his mother a grandchild. He said he would never want a son or daughter of his to be forced to live up to her expectations the way he had. He said she was the only completely selfish human being he'd ever met, and that she should never have had a child or a husband. He thanked me for being his friend and he asked me not to forget him."

"Meg, are you saying his death wasn't an accident?"

"I don't think it was," she said, her voice barely audible. "I think he just couldn't stand it anymore. Maybe at first he only meant to go away for a while, but somewhere along that dark road, I think he decided nothing really mattered. I would never have shown anyone that letter, Jack. Never. He was dead, and, as bad as they were, I didn't see any point in hurting his family. I don't know how Carolyn found out I was pregnant. That first letter and some good guesswork, I suppose. Maybe somebody told her how often I'd been sick, how many classes I'd missed, and she put two and two together. I had to come back here because she was everything John Thomas said she was and worse. But she's not going to take my baby and she's not going to hurt you. Lillian has the second letter and she's made sure Carolyn knows exactly what's in it. I'll go to court if that's what she wants, if she wants everybody else to know, too. I'm so sorry, Jack. If I'd done this sooner, you wouldn't be—"

"Don't," he said, holding her tighter. "Don't even think about that. I mean it."

"When we were children, I was always afraid to let you see me cry."

"Meggie, why?" he asked, incredulous that she could have felt that way.

"Because I thought you'd hate it and you'd leave."

"Meggie . . ."

"But I'm going to cry now, I think." She took a deep breath, and he could feel her struggling for control. But then she abruptly pressed her face into his shoulder. "Oh, Jackie..."

He didn't try to make her stop. He simply held her close, and he understood that the sorrow she felt had nothing to do with him. Her tears were for John Thomas Pacer and his wasted life, and for the baby girl down the hall.

He felt no resentment toward the dead man, and he had no illusions that the worst was over. It didn't matter, because whatever happened, he and Meg had each other. She was his woman; he'd known that since he was twelve years old. She was the love of his life, and they would start again, be happy again. Later he would tell her so, and he would make her believe it.

I will be joyful forever, he thought, remembering some part of an ancient chant. *Nothing will hinder me... my words will be beautiful....*

Epilogue

It was nearly dark when Jack got home, but Meg didn't have to turn around to know that he'd arrived. She could tell by the baby's bouncing squeals of delight when the back door opened. To tell the truth, she was rather delighted herself, if considerably less vocal.

He had snow in his hair and he carried a big paper bag in his hands. He set the bag down on the floor, shrugging off his heavy coat and hanging it on a peg behind the kitchen door before he came to kiss them both soundly.

He lifted the baby out of her high chair. "Something smells good. It is *cold* outside," he said to their daughter, who immediately appreciated his weather report with a big grin. "So what are we having for supper?"

"Mutton stew, fry bread and company, if the roads don't get too bad," Meg said, feeding him a tidbit of the fry bread.

"No, they're clear. Who's coming?"

"Four of the Singers—Dolly, Lucas, Sloan and Will—Winston and Eddie Nez."

"Eddie Nez?"

"Yes, Eddie Nez."

"Meggie—"

"He needs a family, Jack."

"I don't see why when you've already adopted him into this one."

She gave him an arch look, and he laughed and shifted the baby into his other arm. The baby immediately laid her small head on his shoulder.

"Have you been good today, my daughter?" he asked her in English and in Navajo, stroking her red curls. "How's the tooth coming?"

She made a fretful sound, and he was immediately sympathetic. "Oh, I know it," he soothed her. "I wouldn't be a baby for *anything*. Ah-ha! Look what Mommy's got," he said, holding her so they both could peer over Meg's shoulder. "Totally delicious mashed-up carrot things! I'll feed her," he said, taking the Peter Rabbit bowl from Meg's hand. "You are going to *love* these, baby girl."

But the guests arrived in a gust of cold air and blown snow before he could even start—all of them, plus two of Will's school friends. Jack was immediately relieved of the baby and the carrots. Dolly cooed and held her, and Sloan cooed and fed.

And Meg worked happily in the midst of it all—Will and his friends' teenage-boy exuberance, Eddie Nez's shy pleasure at being included, Lucas's grudging acceptance of her choice of husbands, Winston's merry goodwill for them all.

And Jack Begaye's love.

This was what she had always wanted—to live happily with Jack and to have him truly become a part of her family.

The Pacers had gone. Ronald had accepted his dying son's letter, and without his support, Carolyn could do nothing. Eventually, she even stopped insisting that Jack had stolen their money.

But Meg would never take anything for granted again. She and Jack had come too close to never having their life together. They had come through a dark time, struggling with self-doubt and her illness and her fear that she would lose the baby. And looking around her now, she could hardly believe her good fortune.

Her eyes met Jack's across the room. He winked and pointed to the paper bag he'd left sitting on the floor, moving quickly to bring it to her.

"I have a question, Mrs. Begaye," he whispered, his eyes full of mischief.

"What is it?" she asked demurely, taking the bag.

"Is there any particular reason why I'm buying all these oranges?"

* * * * *

The first book in the exciting new
Fortune's Children series is
HIRED HUSBAND
by *New York Times* bestselling writer
Rebecca Brandewyne

Beginning in July 1996
Only from Silhouette Books

Here's an exciting sneak preview....

Minneapolis, Minnesota

As Caroline Fortune wheeled her dark blue Volvo into the underground parking lot of the towering, glass-and-steel structure that housed the global headquarters of Fortune Cosmetics, she glanced anxiously at her gold Piaget wristwatch. An accident on the snowy freeway had caused rush-hour traffic to be a nightmare this morning. As a result, she was running late for her 9:00 a.m. meeting—and if there was one thing her grandmother, Kate Winfield Fortune, simply couldn't abide, it was slack, unprofessional behavior on the job. And lateness was the sign of a sloppy, disorganized schedule.

Involuntarily, Caroline shuddered at the thought of her grandmother's infamous wrath being unleashed upon her. The stern rebuke would be precise, apropos, scathing and delivered with coolly raised, condemnatory eyebrows and in icy tones of haughty grandeur that had in the past reduced many an executive—even the male ones—at Fortune Cosmetics not only to obsequious apologies, but even to tears. Caroline had seen it happen on more than one occasion, although, much to her gratitude and relief, she herself was seldom a target of her grandmother's anger. And she wouldn't be this morning, either, not if she could help it. That would be a disastrous way to start out the new year.

Grabbing her Louis Vuitton tote bag and her black leather portfolio from the front passenger seat, Caroline stepped gracefully from the Volvo and slammed the door. The heels of her Maud Frizon pumps clicked briskly on the concrete floor as she hurried toward the bank of elevators that would take her up into the skyscraper owned by her family. As the elevator doors slid open, she rushed down the long, plushly carpeted corridors of one of the hushed upper floors toward the conference room.

By now Caroline had her portfolio open and was leafing through it as she hastened along, reviewing her notes she had prepared for her presentation. So she didn't see Dr. Nicolai Valkov until she literally ran right into him. Like her, he had his head bent over his own portfolio, not watching where he was going. As the two of them collided, both their portfolios and the papers inside went flying. At the unexpected impact, Caroline lost her balance, stumbled, and would have fallen had not Nick's strong, sure hands abruptly shot out, grabbing hold of her and pulling her to him to steady her. She gasped, startled and stricken, as she came up hard against his broad chest, lean hips and corded thighs, her face just inches from his own—as though they were lovers about to kiss.

Caroline had never been so close to Nick Valkov before, and, in that instant, she was acutely aware of him—not just as a fellow employee of Fortune Cosmetics but also as a man. Of how tall and ruggedly handsome he was, dressed in an elegant, pinstriped black suit cut in the European fashion, a crisp white shirt, a foulard tie and a pair of Cole Haan loafers. Of how dark his thick, glossy hair and his deep-set eyes framed by raven-wing brows were—so dark that they were almost black, despite the bright, fluorescent lights that blazed overhead. Of the whiteness of his straight teeth against his bronzed skin as a brazen, mocking grin slowly curved his wide, sensual mouth.

"Actually, I *was* hoping for a sweet roll this morning—but I daresay you would prove even tastier, Ms. Fortune," Nick drawled impertinently, his low, silky voice tinged with a faint accent born of the fact that Russian, not English, was his native language.

At his words, Caroline flushed painfully, embarrassed and annoyed. If there was one person she always attempted to avoid at Fortune Cosmetics, it was Nick Valkov. Following the breakup of the Soviet Union, he had emigrated to the United States, where her grandmother had hired him to direct the company's research and development department. Since that time, Nick had constantly demonstrated marked, traditional, Old World tendencies that had led Caroline to believe he not only had no use for equal rights but also would actually have been more than happy to turn back the clock several centuries where females were concerned. She thought his remark was typical of his attitude toward women: insolent, arrogant and domineering. Really, the man was simply insufferable!

Caroline couldn't imagine what had ever prompted her grandmother to hire him—and at a highly generous salary, too—except that Nick Valkov was considered one of the foremost chemists anywhere on the planet. Deep down inside Caroline knew that no matter how he behaved, Fortune Cosmetics was extremely lucky to have him. Still, that didn't give him the right to manhandle and insult her!

"I assure you that you would find me more bitter than a cup of the strongest black coffee, Dr. Valkov," she insisted, attempting without success to free her trembling body from his steely grip, while he continued to hold her so near that she could feel his heart beating steadily in his chest—and knew he must be equally able to feel the erratic hammering of her own.

"Oh, I'm willing to wager there's more sugar and cream to you than you let on, Ms. Fortune." To her utter mortification and outrage, she felt one of Nick's hands slide insidiously up her back and nape to her luxuriant mass of sable hair, done up in a stylish French twist.

"You know so much about fashion," he murmured, eyeing her assessingly, pointedly ignoring her indignation and efforts to escape from him. "So why do you always wear your hair like this . . . so tightly wrapped and severe? I've never seen it down. Still, that's the way it needs to be worn, you know. . . soft, loose, tangled about your face. As it is, your hair fairly cries out for a man to take the pins from it, so he can see how long it is. Does it fall past your shoulders?" He quirked one eyebrow inquisitively, a mocking half-smile still twisting his lips, letting her know he was enjoying her obvious discomfiture. "You aren't going to tell me, are you? What a pity. Because my guess is that it does—and I'd like to know if I'm right. And these glasses."

He indicated the large, square, tortoiseshell frames perched on her slender, classic nose. "I think you use them to hide behind more than you do to see. I'll bet you don't actually even need them at all."

Caroline felt the blush that had yet to leave her cheeks deepen, its heat seeming to spread throughout her entire quivering body. Damn the man! Why must he be so infuriatingly perceptive?

Because everything that Nick suspected was true.

* * * * *

To read more, don't miss
HIRED HUSBAND
by Rebecca Brandewyne,
Book One in the new
FORTUNE'S CHILDREN series,
beginning this month and available only from
Silhouette Books!

Dear Reader,

I was fortunate to have done a great deal of my traveling when I was still a fanciful child, completely unburdened by any responsibilities other than to truly enjoy the experience. The first book in this series, *One of Our Own,* came about primarily because I found an old sepia photograph of a smiling six-year-old standing in the Painted Desert—me. I knew the minute I saw it that I was ready to do a book with a Southwestern setting, but I was surprised to learn that when the book was finished, I wasn't ready to leave the people or the place behind. Hence this effort, *Meggie's Baby.* I hope you enjoyed it.

Best,

[signature]

There's nothing quite like a family

The new miniseries by
Pat Warren

Three siblings are about to be reunited.
And each finds love along the way....

HANNAH
Her life is about to change now that she's met
the irresistible Joel Merrick in HOME FOR HANNAH
(Special Edition #1048, August 1996).

MICHAEL
He's been on his own all his life. Now he's
going to take a risk on love...and
take part in the reunion he's been
waiting for in MICHAEL'S HOUSE
(Intimate Moments #737, September 1996).

KATE
A job as a nanny leads her to Aaron Carver,
his adorable baby daughter and the
fulfillment of her dreams in KEEPING KATE
(Special Edition #1060, October 1996).

Meet these three siblings from

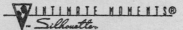

Silhouette SPECIAL EDITION®
and

INTIMATE MOMENTS®
™ *Silhouette*

Look us up on-line at: http://www.romance.net

MILLION DOLLAR SWEEPSTAKES

SWP-M06

FORTUNE'S Children™

New York Times Bestselling Author

REBECCA BRANDEWYNE

Launches a new twelve-book series—FORTUNE'S CHILDREN
beginning in July 1996 with Book One

Hired Husband

Caroline Fortune knew her marriage to Nick Valkov was in
name only. She would help save the family business, Nick
would get a green card, and a paper marriage would suit both
of them. Until Caroline could no longer deny the feelings Nick
stirred in her and the practical union turned passionate.

MEET THE FORTUNES— a family whose legacy is greater than
riches. Because where there's a will...there's a wedding!

Look for Book Two, *The Millionaire and the Cowgirl*,
by Lisa Jackson. Available in August 1996 wherever Silhouette
books are sold.

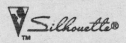

SILHOUETTE... Where Passion Lives

Add these Silhouette favorites to your collection today!
Now you can receive a discount by ordering two or more titles!

SD#05819	WILD MIDNIGHT by Ann Major	$2.99	☐
SD#05878	THE UNFORGIVING BRIDE	$2.99 U.S.	☐
	by Joan Johnston	$3.50 CAN.	☐
IM#07568	MIRANDA'S VIKING by Maggie Shayne	$3.50	☐
SSE#09896	SWEETBRIAR SUMMIT	$3.50 U.S.	☐
	by Christine Rimmer	$3.99 CAN.	☐
SSE#09944	A ROSE AND A WEDDING VOW	$3.75 U.S.	☐
	by Andrea Edwards	$4.25 CAN.	☐
SR#19002	A FATHER'S PROMISE	$2.75	☐
	by Helen R. Myers		

(limited quantities available on certain titles)

TOTAL AMOUNT	$_____
DEDUCT: **10% DISCOUNT FOR 2+ BOOKS**	$_____
POSTAGE & HANDLING	$_____
($1.00 for one book, 50¢ for each additional)	
APPLICABLE TAXES**	$_____
TOTAL PAYABLE	$_____
(check or money order—please do not send cash)	

To order, send the completed form with your name, address, zip or postal code, along with a check or money order for the total above, payable to Silhouette Books, to: **In the U.S.:** 3010 Walden Avenue, P.O. Box 9077, Buffalo, NY 14269-9077; **In Canada:** P.O. Box 636, Fort Erie, Ontario, L2A 5X3.

Name:_____

Address:_____City:_____

State/Prov.:_____ Zip/Postal Code:_____

**New York residents remit applicable sales taxes.
  Canadian residents remit applicable GST and provincial taxes.

Silhouette®
TM

SBACK-JA2

This exciting new cross-line continuity series unites
five of your favorite authors as they weave five
connected novels about love, marriage—and
Daddy's unexpected need for a baby carriage!

Get ready for

THE BABY NOTION by Dixie Browning (GD#1011, 7/96)
Single gal Priscilla Barrington would do anything for a
baby—even visit the local sperm bank. Until cowboy
Jake Spencer set out to convince her to have a family
the natural—and much more exciting—way!

And the romance in New Hope, Texas, continues with:

BABY IN A BASKET
by Helen R. Myers (SR#1169, 8/96)

MARRIED...WITH TWINS!
by Jennifer Mikels (SSE#1054, 9/96)

HOW TO HOOK A HUSBAND (AND A BABY)
by Carolyn Zane (YT#29, 10/96)

DISCOVERED: DADDY
by Marilyn Pappano (IM#746, 11/96)

DADDY KNOWS LAST arrives in July...only from

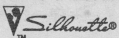

DKL-D

You're About to Become a

Privileged Woman

Reap the rewards of fabulous free gifts and benefits with proofs-of-purchase from Silhouette and Harlequin books

Pages & Privileges™

It's our way of thanking you for buying our books at your favorite retail stores.

PROOF OF PURCHASE
Offer expires October 31, 1996
SSE-PP159

Harlequin and Silhouette—
the most privileged readers in the world!

For more information about Harlequin and Silhouette's PAGES & PRIVILEGES program call the Pages & Privileges Benefits Desk: 1-503-794-2499

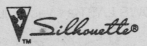

Silhouette®